More . . .

WAR PATH

Kerry Newcomb

St. Martin's Paperbacks

WAR PATH

ISBN: 0-312-97932-0

Printed in the United States of America

St. Martin's Paperbacks edition / May 2003

St. Martin's Paperbacks are published by St. Martin's Press, 175 Fifth Avenue, New York, NY 10010.

10 9 8 7 6 5 4 3 2 1

For Patty, Amy Rose, Paul Joseph, and Emily Anabel

Acknowledgments

I give glory to God.

I give thanks for the love and loyalty of family and friends.

A special candle must be lit for my agent, Aaron Priest, the best there is or ever was.

Much gratitude to my talented and patient editor, Marc Resnick, and to the righteous folks at St. Martin's Press for publishing my tales.

Lastly, to you, dear reader, I am truly obliged.

Author's Note

Before Davy Crockett or Daniel Boone, there was Johnny Stark, one of the first heroes of the American Colonies and a key figure during the early days of this young country. He was a bold, adventuresome man; rough-hewn, courageous, and determined to live free or die. *War Path* is a work of fiction based on both the man and the myth. In attempting to craft a story that captures the spirit of this remarkable individual, I've taken liberties when and where I wanted to, for the sake of the narrative or just because the spirit moved me.

I would be remiss if I failed to acknowledge Fred Anderson's *A People's Army* and *Crucible of War*, two brilliant works that provided wonderful insight into the period of time covered in my own writings. Also, I must further credit *The Journal of Major Robert Rogers* for some of the anecdotal references and local color, his standing orders for conduct, along with hearsay, recollections, personal narratives, and legend. Any departure from historical fact is strictly my own doing.

"Some climb to good,
  Some from good fortune fall . . .
For Destiny plays us all."

> —Abraham Cowley, "Destinie." *Metaphysical Lyrics and Poems of the 17th Century*, Herbert Grierson, ed.

"Let 'em have it!"

> —Standing Orders, Rogers's Rangers. *The Journal of Major Robert Rogers*, 1759 Dublin

Now sit you down.
Satahonhsatat! Listen!
For I shall speak of valiant men
and heroic deeds,
of battles fought
and garments rolled in blood.

The Sugar-Making Moon

1755

Prologue

"At the first dawn of day, awake your whole detachment; that being the time when the savages choose to fall upon their enemies . . ."

Johnny Stark was big, he was ugly, he had dignity, and he wasn't about to die. Not now. Not for a long time. So there he stood, blood seeping from his broken nose and staining the linen shirt he wore open to the waist. Stark's thick forearms folded across his barrel chest, his brown eyes, dark as pitchbark, flared with anger as he stared past his doomed companions; studied his Abenaki captors, weighed the odds which were none too good. If there was a way out of this mess, it would be hard going and it was going to hurt.

Two columns of warriors in war paint, twelve men to either side, faced one another along the banks of Otter Creek. The savages formed a gauntlet, a passage a couple of yards in width, and hardly inviting. They howled like wild beasts, waved their weapons aloft and exhorted their captives to bravely meet their fate for there was no honor in killing cowards.

"I wish I had stayed home in Derryfield," muttered one of the Green Mountain lads. By luck of the draw, bad luck too, Henry Walch had been chosen to be the first to try and reach the far end of the gauntlet and safety. None of his companions, not Abel Page nor Ford Fargo, chose to comment.

"Read 'em from the book, Henry," rumbled Stark, willing back the waves of pain.

"Chapter and verse," Walch replied in a thin voice. He could think of nothing else to add. He knew what he had to do, run like hell and ignore the punishment he was about to receive. Walch tucked his chin low, ducked and started down the slope toward the gauntlet. If he could reach the staff thrust into the ground at the end of the gauntlet . . . that's all he had to do. Stay alive. Stay alive and keep putting one foot before the other.

"You can make it, Henry," shouted Abel Page, the youngest of the four who clung to the fast fading hope that somehow they would all survive this terrible trial.

Despite Abel's encouragement and indeed to the younger man's horror, Walch didn't make more than a yard or two down the gauntlet before one of the warriors struck him a terrible blow with a war club. Walch's skull shattered like kindling beneath the impact of the smooth-carved, six-inch round knob of ironwood that capped the weapon. The hunter passed the pearly gates with his head split and his brains leaking down over his eyes like plum sauce.

Abel Page doubled over and retched.

"Damn," Stark muttered. A warrior standing close to him jabbed his musket into his broad back. Johnny's gaze hardened as he glanced over his shoulder at the man who had already clubbed him in the face and cracked his nose. "Bound or no, I'll wrap that musket 'round your scrawny neck," he warned.

"You tell him, Stark," said Ford Fargo, who like his brother, Cassius, had never been much more than a troublemaker in Cowslip, given to drink and a surly disposition. But the Fargo boys knew their way around the forest and could read deer sign and that made either of them welcome on a hunt. A twisted ankle had prevented Cassius from joining the hunters and sharing his brother's predicament. Ford ruefully taunted Stark. "Tell him how you wrassled that bear on the Mad River a'fore you were full growed. That'll skeer the murdering heathen right enough."

The Fargo brothers were short, stocky, farm-bred men who had envisioned a fortune to be made in the howling wilderness. On this fateful day, Ford wasn't thinking about wealth and privilege, but of his brother, Cassius, safe at home in Cowslip. Ford wished he were carousing with his elder sibling right this very moment. Oh to be with his kin back on the farm, downing flagons of rum, gorging on quail and pheasant and succulent pork . . . to see another morning rise up over newly planted fields of corn and squash and peas and hear the voices of his mates raised in loud song, to taste the hot sweet kisses of Tess McDonagel at the Kit Fox Tavern in Fort Edward across the mountains. Now brother Cassius would have to bed her for him, the lucky sod. . . .

The Abenaki warrior closest to them, a man who carried himself with an air of authority befitting a sachem, snapped orders to the other braves, then took his knife and sliced through the rawhide rope that had bound Fargo's wrists. His reverie shattered, and now free to take his chances, Fargo lumbered forward, then paused by young Abel Page and growled, "This is your doing. It was a poor watch you kept. You let 'em into our camp, damn your eyes!"

"Let him be, Ford," Stark warned.

Fargo snapped back, "I'll use my last breath how I choose. And mind you how I die, Johnny Stark; should you live to be giving an account to Cassius. Tell him blood for blood. I'll have blood for blood and nothing less." Then he turned and ducked low and lumbered off toward the warriors, his arms raised to protect his head, his fists clenched, his tattered shirt fluttering behind him like a beggar's cloak. In attempting to shield his skull, Fargo left his torso open and vulnerable.

As he entered the gauntlet, an Abenaki brave swung a mighty blow and caved in the yeoman's ribs. Ford howled as shards of bone pierced his lungs. Gagging, spitting blood, he stumbled forward in a zigzag motion that brought him from one side of the gauntlet to the other. A glancing blow left a lump over his eye the size of a goose egg. Like Walch before him, Fargo was no runner. Not that it would have mattered. The Abenaki didn't plan on any of their captives surviving the gauntlet. The moment he fell to his knees, the warriors closed in and finished him off. His cries faded beneath the crunch of flesh and bone.

The Abenaki, drawing back from Fargo's corpse, assumed their ranks again and proceeded to taunt the remaining two men. Was this the best these Yankees could do? Was there not one among them worthy of such sport?

Abel Page, tears streaking his youthful features, glanced aside at his towering companion. Johnny Stark, a head taller than the wide-eyed youth, cut an even more impressive figure when compared to the lithe, compact warriors who taunted and jabbed him with their muskets. Standing a shade over six feet in his moccasins, the raw-boned, twenty-seven-year-old long hunter from the Green Mountains was an imposing figure, despite the heavy rawhide cords that bound him.

Stark contemplated his captors This lot was well armed with fine muskets and steel blades given to them by the *voyageurs*. Years ago, Johnny Stark had decided he had no use for the French. He'd buried too many friends and neighbors, slaughtered by savages armed by the *voyageurs* headquartered north of Fort St. Frederick up on Lake Champlain. In this contested wilderness, the Abenaki had allied themselves with Montcalm's troops who appeared to have the upper hand and continued to press the British forces and their colonial allies. Not that Stark didn't bristle and chafe under English sovereignty whenever he had the chance, but at least the colonists and their mother country shared a common foe.

Abel Page chewed on his lower lip, his chest rose and fell as he struggled to breathe through the fear that gripped him like a vise. "We are done for, Johnny." His voice had a shrill quality, like the bleat of a frightened animal.

"Do not let them see your fear." Stark lifted his eyes to the hills. It was from this good land he took his strength, this untamed country where a man could roam and dream and . . . be free. From his earliest recollection, these forests, cliffs, and cold clear rivers had called him. The green fuse that burned in birch and maple and pine, that forced the rivers through the chutes, that fired the fierce gleam in the eyes of bear and lynx, fueled his proud soul.

"This bunch will have their way with all of us." Page scowled and tried to back away as a pair of warriors advanced on the youth and sliced through the cords that bound his wrists. "I would see my dear cousin again, bless her. If Molly were here she would shoot their lights out." He tried a game smile. His chin trembled, his eyebrows arched above his glistening eyes.

"That she would," said Stark. "And mine too for bringing you along on the hunt. I have much to answer for."

"It weren't your doing, Johnny. I'm the one who fell asleep and let these red devils into our camp."

But Stark could not free himself of the guilt. He had promised Molly he'd look out for her young cousin, promised Abel's parents, Ephraim and Charity that he would bring their son safely home. But the lad had never been cut out for the wooded places, for the forests and rivers that stretched from the Adirondacks into Canada and that the savages and warring French armies had turned into a killing ground.

The sachem shoved Abel and sent him stumbling toward the gauntlet. The warriors aligned along the bank began to wave their weapons in the air and exhort him to enter the deadly path stretching between them.

"No!" Abel said, freezing in his tracks. He turned toward the brave who had freed him. The warrior, distinguished by a blaze of jagged war paint adorning each shoulder and another band masking his eyes, threatened the frightened youth with a French dagger. The Abenaki gestured toward the gauntlet then addressed the youth in perfect English.

"Yankee . . . all you must do is reach the far side, do you see the Medicine Staff thrust into the ground? Reach it and live." His voice had an edge to it. Johnny took note of a jagged ridge of scar tissue that resembled a lightning bolt seared along the warrior's neck and upper shoulder.

"Please," Abel stammered. "We only came to hunt."

The frightened young man continued to hold his ground and held out his hands, imploring the warrior to show mercy, a quality the Abenaki had no word for when it came to driving the *Anglais* settlers from their hunting grounds. The sachem remained implacable. He knew if the white settlers were to be driven back into the sea, his people must be of firm resolve; their will, ruthless.

"Abel, give it a try. You were always fast. Keep your head low. You might make it. I'll warrant you will!" Stark shouted, knowing full well what his friend could expect if he failed to budge.

"We meant you no harm," Page muttered.

"Abel! Run!"

"You understand me. What is to be gained by shedding blood?"

"Go now, *Anglais*. It is the end of days for you."

"Abel!"

"No!" the youth replied, rooted in place. "He must understand. We are not enemies."

The Abenaki prodded his prisoner, jabbed the dagger into Page's belly. The younger man's eyes bulged with horror as he glanced down at the seeping blood. The first time had been a flesh wound. And still Page refused to budge.

"For the love of God . . . !" he cried out.

The warrior scowled, disgusted, and slashed the young man's throat. Abel Page sank backwards, clutching at the spurting wound; he sat with a muffled thud, made a series of short, garbled cries and rolled over on his side, convulsing. Then his eyes rolled up in his head and the tremors that consumed his body ceased.

Now it was Stark's turn. One of his captors struck him behind the knee with the stock of his musket. Stark's leg buckled and the big man went down. The warrior who had killed Page strode forward. Up close, the man appeared to be in his mid-forties, with the hooded gaze of a seasoned fighter.

"I am Atoan, Grand Sachem of the People of the White Pines. Run the gauntlet and you will go free. There is my son, Kasak, who guards the Medicine Staff. Four men has he killed in battle. But if you show courage he may stand aside. Reach the Staff and you will live. This is my word."

Stark's deep-brown eyes flashed with fire, his gaze seemed to bore a hole in Atoan, his mouth was an impassive slit, betraying nothing. A slight twitch along his right cheekbone belied the impression the big man's features had been chiseled from granite.

"*Kita!* Listen. Your friend said he came in peace and then died like a woman. Will you give us sport?"

"Cut me loose and find out." Stark held out his hands. Atoan grinned and approached. Behind him, the men with Atoan cocked their muskets. The Abenaki weren't taking any chances with their towering captive. So be it. Stark would give them a gesture to remember him by. *Whatever else happens, by all that's holy I swear they shall sing songs of this day, and weep for the lost.* But he needed to make some kind of unique gesture. Johnny glanced down at his fallen comrade, Molly's cousin. Abel Page had made a poor showing. So there was nothing to do but make these next few minutes count for them both. Johnny knelt by Page's corpse and dabbed his fingertips into the blood coagulating along the cruel wound. His hand came away sticky, moist and crimson.

Johnny held Atoan with his fierce gaze. "And just so you know . . ." Stark streaked his cheeks and forehead, donning his own horrid war mask with the blood of his friend, ". . . my name is Johnny Stark. And unlike young Abel here, *I do* mean every one of you murdering bastards *harm!*"

Atoan retreated a step as the man rose to his full height. He had not expected this much defiance and was taken aback by the long hunter's demeanor. Atoan had expected the man to beg for his life, he had never before encountered such a complete lack of fear among the Yankee colonists. Perhaps this *Johnny Stark* had the heart of a warrior after all.

In that instant he sensed a kind of kinship with the long hunter. *Have I found a worthwhile enemy?* Atoan wondered. And yet a man's worth was measured by more than just a name, but by deeds, so the sachem asked yet again, "Who are you, *Yankee?*"

And Johnny Stark growled in reply, "I'm the wrath of God."

Kasak, son of Atoan was young and brash and full of courage and determined that his brothers would sing songs of his valor, as they did for his father. The great Atoan had never been bested by an enemy; the Grand Sachem possessed the spirit of the wolverine. *Glory to Atoan who was quick and cunning and utterly ferocious in battle.*

Kasak, in his haste to escape his father's shadow, was ever the first to fight. He was a "young lion" springing pell-mell into danger, ever daring but too often foolhardy when stealth was called for. Kasak, like any young man who has all the time in the world, too often felt that time was wasting. He exhorted the warriors along the gauntlet to steel themselves. They responded in kind for they loved Kasak for his courage and his pride as they honored and feared his father and gave way whenever he passed.

The smell of blood was in the air, the gauntlet had claimed two of the Yankees and waited for the last. Kasak paced the ground before the Medicine Staff like a panther, his naked upper torso the color of hammered copper, lithe and sleek, he moved with feline grace and the knife in his hand was like a naked claw.

"Here comes the last of them. *Anglais*, give us sport. Or the next time we will send our women to make war against you!" Kasak shouted and the warriors along the gauntlet laughed and raised their war clubs and jeered at the last of their captives. But they fell silent when Stark knelt and painted his features with the blood of his friend. And when he turned and charged down the slope toward the gauntlet, the Abenaki braced themselves and began to exhort him to die bravely. Not for an instant did any of the braves doubt the outcome of this afternoon's sport. The long hunter's size only made him that much more of a target for their war clubs. He was like a great oak that they intended to fell.

"Come, *Anglais!*" Kasak shouted. "My knife is thirsty." His youthful features were streaked with charcoal and ochre, his head shaved but for a topknot of black hair braided with a raven feather. A necklace of shells and panther claws and pounded silver disks jangled against his hard chest as he paced and taunted.

Johnny Stark didn't need any more of an invitation than that. He barreled down the slope like a raging whirlwind, his long legs devouring the distance, pulse racing, his wild heart nearly bursting through his rib cage. The bold-eyed sun washed the clearing and the creek bank with a honeyed light that filtered through the entwined branches of the sheltering red oaks and glistened on the surface of the meandering waters.

It was a land of beauty.

It was a day of rage.

The warriors lining the gauntlet braced themselves for battle, each man eager to land a blow on the long hunter and send his spirit after those of his fallen comrades, Walch and Fargo, whose lifeless forms had been dragged off to the side to allow Stark an unimpeded entrance to the killing ground.

Fifteen yards . . . ten . . . five . . . Johnny Stark loosed a wild battle cry and veered to the side and charged the brave closest to him, a startled youth unprepared for this change of course. The young warrior retreated, his legs tangling, keeping him off balance.

This might be naught but a game to the Abenaki, but Stark had no intention playing by their rules and running the gauntlet. Damn if he'd be a mere target. It was time these red devils had a taste of their own medicine.

He ducked as the warrior swung at him. The long hunter drove his big shoulder into the brave and sent him reeling. He caught the brave by the wrist and twisted the war club from his grasp and before the other Abenaki could adjust to his tactics, Stark rushed the next lot, broke bones and bashed heads, spun and struck and powered his way along the length of the column.

Johnny blocked and battered, caught one man by the scruff of his buckskin shirt and spun him about and used him for a battering ram as a pair of warriors descended on him. Stark's human shield yelped as blows rained down upon him. Johnny forced his way forward, turned and blocked a second round of strikes that left the man in his grasp bloody and dazed.

The brave sagged forward. With a mighty effort Stark hoisted the smaller man aloft and hurled his limp, compact frame into the faces before him, knocking another pair of warriors to the ground.

"Come on, you cursed bastards, I'm for you!" Stark bellowed. His voice rang out above the chorus of war whoops like a trumpet's blare. "Here's for your songs. Is this sport enough for you? Come and take me!"

And they tried. Again and again the Abenaki braves closed in, only to be beaten back one by one. Oh, Stark was an easy target when it came to size, and they landed blows right enough, but nothing connected with enough force to cripple their intended victim. And he gave as good as he got, even better in most cases as he barrelled forward. And the force of his unexpected attack served him well and propelled him past many of Atoan's men before they could get in a good lick.

A gruff-looking warrior with a brooding brow and a deep hatred in his eyes rose up before the long hunter and swung his war club. Stark parried the man's attack, tore the war club from his grasp and now with a weapon gripped in each of his ham-sized fists, struck the Abenaki across the forearm, in the belly, then as the man doubled forward to retch, struck him between the shoulder blades. The red man dropped like a rock, landing face forward in the trampled grass.

Johnny Stark never broke stride but pressed on, he swung to right and left, whirling and battering and always moving toward the Medicine Staff. He had lost all sense of time and distance, he knew only the violence as he gulped in the pine-scented air, knew only the noise and sweat and the pain of glancing blows that failed to stop him, knew only his own iron will to survive.

And then he reached Kasak.

The younger man braced himself, brandished a war club and a French hunting dirk with a silver hilt and an eleven-inch blade of sharpened steel. Kasak lunged in low, expecting Stark to meet him head on. Kasak intended to rip open the long hunter's belly with a single thrust. But Stark danced aside with a quickness uncommon for a man of his size.

Kasak was fleet of foot and swifter by far than any of his peers and were this a footrace Stark would have been at his mercy. But this was a fight to the death. And it was in battle that Stark had the edge. He possessed an almost supernatural clarity of vision, the ability to read his opponent and *know* without understanding the how and why of it, what the man was about to do and in that instant begin to counter the move.

It was his strength as surely as his corded muscles and powerful physique.

Some men are born with a lot of *quit* in them, but not Johnny Stark. Early on in life he had learned there comes a time to run and a time to stand, and a time when nothing else will do but to suck up your courage, girdle your loins, and cry havoc. Committed to the struggle, Stark would continue to fight for as long as he drew breath.

As he had cut a swath through the Abenaki war party lining the gauntlet, so did he batter aside Kasak's defenses. The big man sensed the warriors gathering behind him and realized his time was running out unless he tried one last desperate gamble.

Kasak thrust forward with the hunting dirk. Stark dropped the war clubs and caught the smaller man's wrist and twisted until the brave's arm nearly broke. Kasak loosened his hold on his weapon and Stark wrenched it from his grasp, spun him around, and placed himself between Atoan's son and the advancing warriors. He grabbed Kasak by his topknot and yanked his head back and brought the French blade to the younger man's naked throat. The gesture stopped the Abenaki in their tracks.

The clearing fell silent.

Now there was only the moaning wounded, the babbling brook to his right, the gentle soughing breeze and rustling of branches, the faint buzzing insects, and the labored breathing of the young man whose throat Stark was about to slit.

The Abenaki drew back as Atoan walked though their ranks, past the injured and dying, down the slope and up the slight rise where his son had proudly paced and pranced like a young cougar. A trickle of blood seeped from the superficial wound left by the dirk's cruel bite and trickled down his son's coppery smooth chest. Kasak's eyes were wide with alarm though he tried to remain calm, but the proximity of his own demise left a hollow pit in his gut. Gone was his bravado. Now he just wanted to see another sunrise.

Johnny Stark faced them down, the lot of them, his gaze sweeping over the war party with their war clubs and tomahawks and leveled muskets. And silence reigned then, like the stillness after a storm. No bird called. Only the wind uttered a sigh as if nature had already become bored with the travails of men.

"There is no glory in fighting women. No songs live here," Stark called out, his voice echoing throughout the clearing. He contemptuously shoved Kasak aside, as if the young warrior's life was not worth taking. With an over-handed throw, the long hunter sent the French dirk spinning through the air. He buried the blade halfway to the hilt between Atoan's feet. A lesser man might have flinched. Not the sachem. There was only a subtle shift in his expression, relief that he still had a son, albeit a humiliated one.

Stark turned his back on the warriors arranged before him. He half expected a volley from their muskets to cut him down. He crossed to the Medicine Staff and tugged it from the ground, faced the Abenaki, and raising the Staff before him, broke it over his knee then tossed the shattered length of wood aside.

Still alive, Stark thought, and swallowed, dry mouthed, amazed they could not hear his hammering heart. He had begun to feel the bruises now, for he had not run the gauntlet unscathed. But he willed his body not to betray him, refused to limp or favor his left shoulder that felt as if it were fractured; pain shot through his right side with every breath.

The wall of warriors barring his path gave way at a word from Atoan. Stark walked from the river, retraced his steps, paused a moment as if in silent communion with the dead then continued past the bodies of his fallen companions, and ascended the grassy slope to where the Abenaki had left his belongings, intending to contest for them later after their prisoners had been dispatched.

He leaned down to gather up his leather shot pouch, powder horn and possibles bag, his knife and tomahawk, brass hunter's horn and Pennsylvania rifle. A shot rang out as he straightened. The report reverberated among the emerald hills. Stark froze, steeling himself against an impact that never came. He glanced over his shoulder and saw that Kasak had armed himself with a musket. But the gun had discharged into the air, through no fault of Kasak's. Atoan had apparently batted the barrel upward as his son had drawn aim on the long hunter. The sachem angrily wrenched the weapon from his son's hands and tossed it aside.

Johnny Stark deliberately took a moment to load and

prime his rifle then tucked the weapon in the crook of his arm. He brought the hunter's horn to his lips and blew a loud, clear blast of defiance that reverberated through the trees and to the hills beyond. Then without so much as a "by your leave," Stark vanished into the forest, heading southeast on a deer trail that would eventually bring him home.

"You should not have stopped me," Kasak snapped, his features flush with indignation.

"Johnny Stark . . ." Atoan said the name aloud. "This was a man," he added, determined to remember everything he had seen this morning. The sachem returned the French dirk to his son, the same weapon the Yankee had taken from the proud young warrior. The blade was stained from the superficial wound it had left across Kasak's throat.

"His blood was not yours to spill," said Atoan. "By taking his life you would have dishonored yourself. And you would have dishonored me."

"Then why didn't *you* stop him?" The younger man scowled.

"Johnny Stark returned your life to me. And I will not take his," Atoan matter-of-factly replied. And then he grimly added: "At least not today."

The Gathering Moon

1757

1

The pert young woman in hunter's garb knew Johnny Stark was miles away, leading a detachment of English troops to aid the beleaguered garrison of Fort William Henry. He had to be a good two-day's march from this clearing, yet Molly Page heard the long hunter's words of caution whisper in her mind.

Gently now, curl your finger around the trigger, breathe easy 'cause this white-tailed rascal will hear you sigh. Be like one of the trees around you, lass, be like the faintest breeze. Like the Injuns, let your spirit call out and hold that young buck in his place. See, hunting's a lot like praying, only something's gotta die when you "Amen."

Molly sighted along the barrel of her rifle, allowing for the wind, the angle of the shot, taking into account how the white-tailed buck grazed a moment on the sweetgrass then ambled forward, raised its head, senses searching the surrounding countryside for any threat.

Molly Page willed herself to merge with the shade of the tamaracks that surrounded her hiding place. The decayed remains of a lightning-blasted hemlock that had toppled last January concealed her in August, in the summer of her twenty-first year.

The barrel of her rifle nestled firmly in the crook of the fallen hemlock's forked branches, served to steady her aim. The Pennsylvania rifle with its 46-inch barrel took some handling for Ephraim Page's niece. The young woman was all of five feet two inches tall. The ladies of Fort Edward considered the skill of the hunt to be a man's domain. But Molly Page preferred the heft of a well-made rifle to the spinning wheel and reading trail sign to the chatter around a quilting circle.

It was whispered that the wilderness had bewitched her, for even at an early age she would abandon her chores and venture off into the woods, to learn the ways of places untamed by the farmer's plow. *Dear child*, Aunt Charity would say, hoping to talk some sense into her charge, *women are not supposed to be deerstalkers.*

Oh no? Molly inwardly replied. *Wait and see.*

She placed her cheek against the curly maple stock carved by Johnny's own hand, squeezed the front trigger to release the second. Now the slightest pressure would fire the weapon. Stark had carved the stock over the course of a winter month and tempered the gun barrel on her uncle's forge. He christened the rifle Isaac. It was one of a matched pair, the other, Old Abraham was with the relief column and in the hands of Johnny Stark. No pair of long guns ever shot as true, of that she was certain.

Ease your breath out, Molly, then let him have it.

The young woman did as she had been told, as she had practiced a hundred times before with Stark. But don't be thinking of his intense brown eyes and deep-hearted laugh. For heaven's sake, not now. She must concentrate on the task at hand or there would be naught but cowpeas and squash in the Page stew pot come the following week.

Molly exhaled, touched the trigger, a flash in the pan and the rifle roared, sending its .50-caliber ball hurling through space. The buck darted forward as the slug ripped through its vitals and lodged in its heart. The animal made a dash for a birch grove but only managed to cover a few paces before its legs buckled. As the last echo faded the wild creature collapsed.

Amen.

The young woman resisted the urge to immediately run to claim her kill. Molly didn't show herself until she had reloaded her rifle as Johnny Stark had taught her. Even this forest, south of the friendly, thriving environs of Fort Edward, was still a place of danger. The Abenaki had become emboldened with the encouragement of their French allies. From time to time, war parties had circled downriver, past the fortified settlement where the Hudson River nearly doubled back on itself and descended on small farms and isolated hunters, burning and looting before vanishing back into the forest, like will-o'-the-wisps.

A person couldn't be too careful. Well, anyone expecting to relieve Molly of her kill had better come loaded for bear. She would not surrender it lightly. She rammed home powder, ball and patch, primed the weapon and eased the flint onto the frizzen. She slung her scrimshawed powder horn over her shoulder, and quietly climbed out from the deadfall.

Sunlight filtered through the trees, illuminated the forest floor littered with decayed leaves, pine boughs, lichen spattered gray stone outcroppings; and where the sunbeams struck, wild sarsaparilla, scarlet wormroot and pink-petaled gaywings flourished. A pair of quarrelsome gray squirrels announced her passing as the woman rose from concealment and cradling her rifle in the crook of her arm, started across the clearing.

Her gaze continued to sweep the forest for any telltale sign of movement and halfway to her kill she heard a twig snap and froze in her tracks. Her grip tightened on the rifle as she tried to locate the source of the sound. Something moved among the birch thicket. Molly's heart began to quicken, her mouth turned dry. She brought the rifle up to her shoulder, holding it steady despite the weapon's considerable weight. But she knew how to adjust her stance to compensate for the rifle's heft.

"Don't you be shooting me, Miss Molly Page," a gruff voice called out. Cassius Fargo emerged from the thicket. His features were unmistakable; short of stature, blunt-featured, broad at the shoulders, his legs like twin tree trunks grounding his deep chest and wide thick waist. Like Molly, he wore a loose-fitting hunting shirt, earth-colored breeches and carried a Pennsylvania rifle. But Fargo preferred square-toed leather shoes to the buckskin moccasins that Johnny Stark had given Molly before marching off with the relief column. He removed his tricorn hat and waved it in the air. "I see you've found my buck. I shot it back yonder. My aim was poor and the beast gave me a run for it."

Molly scowled. It wasn't for nothing that Cassius was often referred to as "Bully" Fargo. But if he expected her to stand down, the man was in for a surprise. A wayward breeze tugged at her thick, curly hair, the dark red ringlets of which she had gathered at the nape of her neck with a leather string. Her eyes, like twin emeralds, aglow with a rare beauty, grew hard as granite. She quickened her pace and arrived at the downed whitetail a few seconds before Fargo and placed herself between the advancing farmer and the carcass.

Cassius was a difficult man to figure, quick tempered and dangerous when the black mood was upon him. Here was a man whose temperament, like the knife blade sheathed at his waist, had been honed to a cruel edge by frontier life. She glanced down at the buckskin pouch dangling from his belt, remembering the rumors that it contained a braided loop of hair woven from scalps, all of them Abenaki, the trophies of a private war Fargo had waged since his brother's death during the hunting trip that had also taken the life of Molly's cousin.

"I see only one kill here, Cassius Fargo, and it is mine." It troubled her, meeting him alone like this, as if it were more than mere coincidence they should have hunted the same hillside. Had he followed her from Fort Edward? The bustling settlement at the bend of the Hudson with its presence of English troops and Colonial Militia had attracted families from a variety of outlying communities, upriver and down. But where most of the local militia had marched off with the relief column on its way to lift the siege of Fort William Henry, "Bully" Fargo had remained behind.

"Now that's pretty meat," Cassius remarked, running a calloused hand across his stubbled chin as he studied the downed buck. The farmer's beard was as coarse as hog hair, shot with silver but black as pitch around his thick lips. He looked hungry, and not just for venison.

His gaze shifted from the carcass to the woman confronting him. She was small and supple-looking and he appreciated the curve of her hips, glimpsed every time the breeze ruffled the hem of her hunting shirt.

"Looks just like the one I've been tracking. My mistake I reckon."

"I hope you find your kill," Molly said. "Next time aim for the heart."

"I always do." Cassius scratched his chin. "You'll need help packing this over to the river."

"I'll manage."

"Uh huh, I 'spect you will." He grinned. Save for the wind in the branches of the tamaracks, their voices were the only sound right now.

Fargo made no attempt to conceal his lust. But there was more than just carnal desire at work here, there was curiosity and suspicion. Ephraim Page's niece was a peculiar young woman. It was rumored she had some kind of second sight, a way of sensing trouble that had nothing to do with reading trail sign. It was the kind of talent that had sent women to the stake in Salem years ago. Things were different now, and folks like Molly might be regarded with distrust but they were not openly persecuted. Then again, it was common knowledge John Stark had taken a special liking to the young woman, as if he had tried to fill the void left in her life by her deceased cousin.

And Stark was not a man to cross. He threw a long shadow in these parts. Not that Cassius Fargo was afraid of the big man. But he was wise enough to pick and choose the time and place to settle their differences. Of course, the long hunter was miles away from this secluded hollow and the more Fargo lingered, watching Molly and breathing in her woman smell, the weaker his will became and the more he fantasized how it would be with her . . .

"You know, I've always fancied you, Molly. No matter

if folks think you're a mite . . . er peculiar." He puffed out his chest. "A woman like you could do a lot worse. I'm strong and steady and own more land than most in these parts. And I warrant if'n you try me, you'll have none other. So come and give us a kiss."

"I'd sooner eat wormwood," Molly retorted.

"Harsh words. I've heard the talk, that when Molly looks to the horizon she can only see John Stark crossing the far hills. But it shouldn't be that way. We share the same wrong. Stark killed both our kin."

"The Abenaki killed Abel and your brother. You know Johnny had nothing to do with it."

"I only know that two years ago, Stark came home all on his lonesome from a hunt. Nary a one of the lads he took with him survived and I find that mighty peculiar. I warrant he sold them out to save his own topknot."

Molly's eyes flashed with anger. Her cheeks flushed. "You're the only man who says that, and not to Johnny's face I charge."

"I am not afraid of John Stark."

"No?" Molly took a deep breath and allowed her ire to cool. "You should be."

"I'll speak no more on it," Fargo said with a shrug. "But to show I do not begrudge you, I'll stay at your side. These here woods are no fitting place for a woman alone," he said.

"I'm never alone," Molly replied. "Not when Isaac is with me." She hefted the rifle in her hands, and did what needed to be done for Cassius to see it was now half-cocked and primed.

"So be it," Fargo growled, shrugged, touched the pointed brim of his tricorn hat and started off down the trail. He strode boldly, as if daring the underbrush to impede his progress. Molly was happy to see him go.

Once she had the clearing to herself, Molly set her rifle aside and began making preparations to take the cuts of meat and the deer hide and transfer them to her pack whose sapling frame would help support the weight of all she intended to carry out. It was going to take the rest of the morning and be hard bloody work but better this than butter churning or indulging in the local gossip for which dear Aunt Charity was famous, bless her soul.

Molly knew she had been the subject of some of that gossip and rather than find offense, had even taken pride in the fact that folks saw her as marching to a different drummer. She was already considered a spinster by many standards. No matter. There was only one man for her and one of these days she was going to set a snare that Johnny Stark couldn't wriggle out of, God love him.

And that is when she saw his troubled features, like a vision unexpected, as she knelt by the deer carcass and leaned forward over the animal and glanced down and saw Stark's reflection in the dead beast's round black eye.

Molly gasped. The image only lasted a second or two, but long enough to send a chill through her veins. And she was filled with a dreadful premonition that took her breath away. There was fire and noise. The screams of the wounded and dying reverberated in her mind. And there he was, her own true love, surrounded on all sides by danger. All of this, an eternity in the fraction of a second, caught in death's glossy blank stare.

Then the moment passed and she sat back on her heels, exhausted from the experience, heartsick, and consumed with anxiety and a portent of disaster. All she could do was call out "Johnny!" which was both a cry of alarm . . . and a prayer.

2

"Send out small parties to scout . . . to see if there be any appearance or track of an enemy."

here's Stark?!" Colonel Farley shouted to his subordinates, just before some French snipers shot his lungs out. "Where's the bloody militia?" The diminutive colonel wiped the soot from his bulbous nose and fleshy jowls with a silk kerchief. He was clearly shaken by their predicament. "Damn these Provincials. They've led us into a trap." He gestured with his silver-hilted small sword; 32 inches of straight steel flicked to and fro in the haze of gunfire.

"They fled the field at the first volley," came the reply. Farley's second in command, Major Michael Ransom of the 1st Regiment of Foot had to shout to be heard above the din of battle. The pockmarked young officer tried not to wince as a flurry of hot lead whined about him like angry hornets. A slug found his tricorn hat and sent it sailing off along with his wig, revealing the thinning wisps of his once luxurious hair like stalks of trampled yellow grass plastered to the pale field of his scalp. Ransom scrambled over and retrieved the periwig, for it was a symbol of both his authority and station. The hat was a loss, however.

Ransom and the men of the royal regiment, in their scarlet coats accented with buff-colored lace, their white breeches and hose, provided a handsome target for Atoan's warriors. But to the six hundred men of the 1st Regiment of Foot, their bright uniforms were a matter of pride and had served them well on the battlefields of Europe. Nor would they permit themselves to break ranks and scatter for cover. The 1st stood its ground.

And died, singly and in pairs.

The field of battle was a long narrow meadow bordered on two sides by forest. A rutted road ran the length of the mile-long clearing. It had been worn into the rich sod by the continuous passage of supply wagons, cannons, and caissons and the columns of soldiers who had made the three-day trek from Fort Edward to the palisades of William Henry, on the southern tip of Lake George.

There was hardly a patch of ground stretching two hundred miles from the bend of the Hudson River all the way to the forts of New France, north of Lake Champlain, that hadn't been watered with a crimson rain, and contested over by the Colonials, the British or their implacable foes. Today was this meadow's baptism of blood, yet it was just another deadly afternoon in what seemed a forever war.

Ransom, slow panic flaring behind his pale blue eyes, sidestepped his commander's flagrant gestures, even parried once with his own short sword to keep from being accidentally impaled. He hauled out his horse pistol and fired in the direction of the French and their savage allies while Colonel Farley continued to rant about the Provincials and how Captain Stark in particular had brought them all to ruin.

In the few short weeks since Michael Ransom's posting at Fort Edward, he had seen little enough to respect in the Colonial Militia. A soldier should stand his ground. There was a proper way to fight a war. British discipline and tactics had carried the king's colors through many an engagement throughout Europe and Africa. But after all, what could one expect? The Provincials were farmers, woodsmen, tinkers, tinsmiths and common laborers, all of them volunteers, not professional soldiers like His Royal Majesty's troops.

Despite that, Ransom could not heap blame on Stark's men alone. He was tempted to remind the Colonel that John Stark had cautioned against proceeding farther along the

road until the open meadow had been given a good scout.
It was Farley who had ignored the frontiersman's words of
caution, stressing the need for haste. Fort William Henry
was in dire need of reinforcements, there was no sense in
wasting time. Farley had ordered the regiment to cross the
meadow at double time. And so they did, marching in all
haste, drummers beating a rapid cadence, straight into the
jaws of the French and Indian trap.

Halfway across the meadow the 1st Regiment had encountered a withering blast of musket fire along both flanks.
The combined force of *La Marines* and Abenaki savages
concealed among the trees, blazed away at will; while Farley split the column, formed four skirmish lines and ordered
his men to return fire. Three hundred redcoats, standing
back to back, responded with one volley after another. But
it was impossible to see if their rounds were having any
effect. And as men began to drop to the ground, wounded
and dying, a sense of foreboding permeated the smoke-
filled air.

"Virtutis fortuna comes!" Farley railed, his voice turning shrill as the regiment poured another volley into the
forest line. They were his last words. Half a dozen musket
balls punctured him from neck to navel. He twisted about,
dropped his sword, balanced a moment on one leg till it
buckled then fell over on his backside, a deep stain spreading over his riddled coat.

Ransom rushed up and knelt alongside the dying colonel. "Fortune is the companion of bravery!" he softly said.
Farley nodded, blinked, his eyes rolling about in his head
as he struggled against the dying light. The words seemed
to give him peace. Or maybe it was the shock of dying
when he least expected it that glazed his eyes and trans-
ported him to a happier place, a memory far from the stench
of death and the rattle of musketry.

There was not a single coward among the 1st. Although word of the colonel's demise swept the ranks, the
regiment remained in formation, four columns of men facing both flanks. First the two kneeling rows fired in volley,

then the standing ranks, while officers paced along the column, exhorting His Royal Majesty's troops to resist this ambush, hold firm and punish the enemy. But the officers themselves were pretty targets in their bright red coats and one by one they pitched forward or collapsed, strangling on their own juices.

And all the while the Abenaki and their French allies kept up a steady gunfire from the stands of hemlock, red oak, tamarack and birch that provided ample protection for the marksmen concealed in the shadows. This armed host was determined to rout the British relief column.

English bayonets gleamed in the streaming sunlight. Powder smoke billowed, momentarily obscuring the rows of men. The world was awash with the clash of arms, the roar of muskets, howling savages, the rapid percussion of the French drummers back beyond the trees signaling *La Marines* to fire at will.

Ransom glanced about him. It was his command now. His command. And it was being wiped out. Soldiers were toppling like so many lawn pins. There were fewer officers now to utter encouragement. He wasn't certain he could hold them by the force of his persona alone. The futility of the situation had begun to take its toll. Even as he belabored his decision, a gruff-looking sergeant abandoned his position on the line and hurried across to stand at the major's side.

"Begging your pardon, Major Ransom, but it don't appear we can advance, sir," the sergeant exclaimed. Tom Strode, a fisherman's son whose family had never ventured far from Mousehole on the channel coast, was a gruff, hard-looking man with bushy sideburns and thick brown eyebrows that accentuated his frown.

"Thank you for your concern, Sergeant Strode, but I am quite capable of assessing the situation."

"Meaning no disrespect, sir," Strode replied, eyeing the fallen. "We've lost all but one of the drummers, Corporal Felker. If you want to sound retreat, uh . . . or to carry the battle to the savages, you might need to hurry or some damn Frog rifleman will have him as well. I can't beat no tattoo, I warrant none other can neither."

Ransom glared at the sergeant. Strode had crossed the line by abandoning his post. But the man made a good point. A decision had to be reached, the column must advance or withdraw. To remain in the center of this meadow, assailed on both flanks, was a suicidal course.

The major's belly rumbled and began to cramp from the tension. He paced through the acrid black residue that streaked the air and burned his throat with every breath. Forcing himself to ignore the rifle balls that sounded as if they were personally searching him out, the major clenched one fist to conceal his trembling hand, and tightened his grip on his officer's sword. Every few yards he shouted encouragement, hoping to inspire his troops to hold fast.

Hold for love of king and country.

And yet, through the haze of battle he was able to clearly see for the first time the hopelessness of their cause. Farley had not died alone this day. He had already been joined by a third of the relief column. It was up to Michael Ransom to save what he could. The very notion of retreating was distasteful at best. He glanced over his shoulder at the way they had come. The line of trees behind him beckoned, promised in the least a marginal chance of safety. The bloody Provincials had already disappeared into the woods, no doubt the cowards were racing pell-mell through the forest.

"I swear if I survive this day and return to Fort Edward, Captain John Stark and his volunteers will answer for their cowardice at the flogging post." Ransom's voice was thick with emotion as he issued his next orders. "Sergeant Strode, we must withdraw," he said in a clipped, painful tone of voice. "Fort William Henry will not see our colors this week, I warrant. Have Corporal Felker sound retreat."

For the 1st Regiment of Foot, it was the beginning of the end.

3

"Where's Stark?" shouted Robert Rogers, his appeal muted by the dense stand of timber separating him from the pandemonium of killers who had come to claim the meadow. In all his thirty years the frontiersman had never seen the likes of the trap Colonel Farley had marched them into. Rogers wiped his forearm across his sweat-streaked brow. His five-foot-five-inch frame still seemed too big for this deadfall at the edge of the meadow and he cringed further, imagining the musket balls were searching him out, thirsting for his vitals. But he and most of his men were still alive, for now.

His sides heaved with every breath as he gulped the warm air. The stench of powder smoke had yet to follow the militia into the woods. There was no shame in taking flight. And besides, Rogers had not fled the clearing on his lonesome. The entire contingent of colonists had turned tail and run like hell at the first volley from the French and Indians. It had been the only sensible thing to do. He craned his neck and peered through a break in the rotting bark. The English troops were maintaining their columns, but at a terrible cost. Their tactics seemed sheer folly, arranged as they were in the center of the meadow, both flanks receiving fire from a concealed enemy.

Rogers edged upward, still somewhat hunched, to catch a glimpse of his homespun-clad militia as they emerged from the surrounding forest to his right and left. *By heaven, where is ol' Big Timber?* he thought as he searched the survivors, hoping to catch a glimpse of Johnny Stark. His friend would stand out in any company, being a good half-foot taller than his companions. There'd be no mistaking his big-boned, rangy build; his square-jawed countenance and hopelessly skewed nose, the legacy of an Abenaki blow that forever marred what might have passed for rugged good looks.

"Where's Stark?" Rogers snapped at the first colonist to scramble over to his side. He searched the stragglers, finding a host of welcome faces but not that of the comrade at arms who had commanded them.

Moses Shoemaker, an irascible old buckskinner spat in the dirt, shrugged, took a chance and peered over the embankment he had just cleared in a single bound. His gray hair was gathered at his neck and hung down clear to his shoulder blades. A wayward breeze tugged at the loose-fitting sleeves of his hunting shirt. The man's thin, bony arms made him appear rather frail and far older than his fifty-two years. But Shoemaker was durable as sinew, pliant and strong.

"Careful, you old jehu," said the youth at his side. Locksley Barlow, that brash and boastful young man, slender, fair-haired, and good-natured to a fault, nudged the old-timer's side with the butt of his long rifle. As far as Barlow was concerned, no man was his better no matter how much experience or how many lines might be etched in the war map of his face. Young Barlow was the son of Fort Edward's finest silversmith and had inherited his father's skill with the poured metal. It was common knowledge that the silversmith's son was fancied by many of the local girls.

Rogers, Shoemaker, Barlow and the rest of the Provincials were no strangers to Indian-fighting and recognized a dire predicament when they saw one. Johnny Stark hadn't needed to tell them to run for cover. Instinct honed along the Great War Path took over at the first ripple of powder-smoke.

Despite their quick withdrawal from the field, the colonists had lost a few good souls at the first volley. Half a dozen men were sprawled near the wheel-rutted road. But where was Big Timber? Had he also fallen? Braving the ongoing exchange of musketry, Rogers raised his head over the rotting tree trunk and peered through a twist of branches to see if Stark's long-legged frame was lying out there among the wildflowers. His brown hair and deeply tanned features helped him blend into the concealment.

"He can't be dead," growled Sam Oday, another of the militia. "Or we'd have heard the earth tremble for sure when he toppled." The farmer had lived among the outlying settlements all his life and had already survived one disaster, having lost his family and been scalped and left for dead. Being on the brink of another massacre made him a mite anxious. "And then we'd all have to answer to Molly Page for his fall. I'd sooner face Atoan with a tin cup in my hand then cross the likes of her," he added with grave humor. What little hair the Abenaki had left him, Sam Oday wanted to keep. He adjusted the black scarf that concealed his scarred scalp, perspiration beaded along his forehead and soaked into the silken covering. Oday reloaded his pistols and primed his blunderbuss. The fluted weapon could spray a lethal dose of lead shot at close range.

"He was a good five yards ahead of me," Barlow blurted out. "Then Moses cut across my furrow and tripped me up."

"I saved your young hide," Shoemaker retorted. "You'd've been drilled for sure if I hadn't made you eat dirt."

"Heed him, Mister Barlow," Rogers spoke up. "Stay by Moses and you might live to see your twentieth year."

"That is if Nell Dulin doesn't set her family agin' you for all your misdeeds," Oday grimly chuckled. Unlike Cassius Fargo, hatred had not rotted his soul. The sense of loss that lurked behind his every expression was held in check by an inner strength that refused to let him break beneath the weight of a shattered heart.

"Misdeeds? Ha, I did not 'miss' a one with pretty Nell," Barlow laughed. But his voice had a hollow ring to it. It was the youth who had his own doubts about seeing the next dawn.

What now? Should we fight? Should we run? The silversmith was loathe to appear weak in front of his companions. So he set aside those questions though they were on the tip of his tongue and chose instead to echo Robert Rogers's concern for the fate of the one man from whom they all seemed to draw courage. He can't be dead. It just was not possible. Not him.

"Where's S . . ."

The question died aborning as a single solitary defiant blast from a hunting horn rang out above the clamor of battle, summoning every man jack of them to gather. To take heart.

And to, by God . . . stand!

4

ook there, *mon ami*," Captain Lucien Barbarat exclaimed from his vantage point overlooking the meadow. "Do you see? The English are withdrawing." The French commander stood alongside Atoan on a granite outcropping halfway up a wooded rise on the eastern flank of the meadow.

The two men were an unusual pair, there in the shade of the white oaks. Atoan, the Grand Sachem, his naked torso hard as chiseled red stone; his head shaved smooth save for a topknot of black hair adorned with an eagle feather. His smooth-worn buckskin breeches were decorated with porcupine quills and trade beads. The Abenaki leaned upon a great war club, a massive two-handed weapon carved of ironwood. It was gnarled at the tip and fully a third of its length sported a row of jagged flint "teeth."

Barbarat cut a dashing figure in his grayish white *justacorps*, the collarless coat favored by the French Marines from Fort Saint Frederick. He dabbed perspiration from his upper lip then tucked the silk kerchief back into one of his blue lace cuffs. His woolen waistcoat and breeches matched his *justacorps* in color and cut. A passing breeze ruffled the silver lace trim on the Frenchman's tricorn.

Barbarat's features were aquiline, finely etched, with a girlish mouth and delicate nose. But there was nothing soft about his gaze. His eyes belied the man's foppish appearance: look close, a killer lurked behind that pale blue stare.

Lucien smiled with satisfaction as the British regiment broke ranks and started back the way they had come, leaving a trail of dead and dying in their wake. Below them, the Abenaki warriors and French Marines of the Regiment Le Reine held their positions but kept firing.

"As I said," the Frenchman sniffed, "the Provincials were of no consequence, mere cowards. And the English are commanded by fools. Now is your chance. Send your men after them." The Indians sorely outnumbered Barbarat's command and unless they pursued the departing British the redcoats would escape.

"Few of my people have fallen. I am pleased to have it so."

"This is war, my friend. People must die in war."

"Let your people die, Barbarat."

"Kasak may not see things your way."

Atoan frowned. He had cautioned his headstrong son into remaining on the wooded slope on the opposite side of the meadow. But he could sense the young warrior's reluctance to obey. Atoan glanced down at the line of warriors among the trees. Several of the braves were looking to him, awaiting his signal to carry the attack to the retreating column.

All Atoan had to do was raise the war club over his head and the warriors would charge the redcoats. The sachem knew what his men wanted, the lust of battle was upon them. It burned in his own spirit as well. But he resisted the urge. He studied the forest's edge and the timber and tall grass the English were struggling to reach. What was it? What spoke to him now and whispered caution?

"*Sacre bleu,*" Barbarat blurted out. "Do you see? The Abenaki have the stomach for a fight after all."

"*Gagwi-yo!*" Atoan muttered. "What is this?" The Abenaki were streaming out of the woods on the opposite flank. Their war cries filtered through the ragged gunfire. Kasak had unleashed the braves under his command. Tomahawks, war clubs, and scalping knives glimmered in the sunlight. At the sight of such a fierce horde hurling toward them, the English column broke ranks. The retreat became a rout as men ignored their orders and fled for the line of trees at the southern edge of the meadow, where forest obscured the wheel-rutted road.

"The day is ours," Barbarat shouted. He lifted his hat and waved it over his head. A French drummer began to play a rapid series of drumrolls. The French marines cheered and fixed bayonets and joined the attack. "Why do you delay?" Lucien protested. "Seize the moment. What are you waiting for?"

From above the din of battle, the roar of the guns and the savage war whoops sounded a single clear trumpet call, a hunter's horn, blaring its brash, clear unmistakable note of defiance. Atoan had heard it before. And remembered the day. But Captain Barbarat was already racing down the slope, his sword drawn, leading his men into the fray.

"Kasak," Atoan shook his head. But he could not allow his son to face what was to come and not be at his side. Kasak was all he had. Atoan's headstrong son was the sachem's pride and his passion for this war. When *Tabaldak*, the Great Mystery, called Atoan by name and took him to join their ancestors, it was Kasak who must be ready to lead the People of the White Pines.

A man could face death knowing he had a son to carry on, a son to live for him.

Again the hunter's horn pierced the clamor and carried to Atoan on the hot breeze. "It's him," said the sachem. *Stark!*

Atoan, sensing danger, loosed his own shrill war cry that transfixed the warriors below. Then he raised the great and terrible war club over his head. "Join me, my brothers. Let the grass run red with the blood of the *Anglais*."

The Abenaki echoed his cry and brandishing their weapons, charged headlong into the fray. The English were ripe for the slaughter. Who would save them now from Atoan and his army of warriors? Who was there to stand against the horde?

5

Johnny Stark stood in the center of the road, the brass horn to his lips. He blew a single reverberating note that pierced the shadowy woodlands and called the militia to gather at his side. And they came singly and in groups, like ghosts in linsey-woolsey hunting shirts, each individual garbed as it suited him, and every man armed to the teeth, and anxious to return some of the punishment they had received.

Stark gathered them like some errant buckskin-clad knight of a bygone age, the great horn pealing out its summons, even as the demoralized English column began to retreat, as those stalwart souls of the 1st Regiment of Foot broke formation, lost their will to suffer any more losses, and dashed back the way they had come toward the safety of the woods.

Johnny squinted, furrowing his deeply-tanned brow beneath the green wool Scottish bonnet that kept his unruly mane from interfering with his aim. His hair, the color of ground ginger, betrayed him with a scattering of silver despite the fact he was fast approaching his thirtieth summer. Some of them had been hard years; he'd seen his share of dying and had lost count of the war parties he'd intercepted and driven back toward the French-controlled territory of Lake Champlain.

He searched the grassy sward but failed to spy Colonel Farley among the English troops; he suspected the diminutive officer might well have fallen. But he recognized Michael Ransom and gave the major credit for courage, as he tried to restore the will to fight in his brave lads, as he tried to force them through the strength of his own character not to turn and run but leave the field as they entered, in formation, and with dignity. But these men of Lincolnshire and Northumberland, Bristol, Torquay, and the Chiltern Hills had gorged themselves on dignity this day and found it bitter to the taste. More than half the reinforcements Farley and Ransom had paraded into the trap now littered the meadow with their lifeless forms. The will to live superceded Ransom's appeal.

Corporal Artemus Felker, the last standing drummer, on orders from the major, followed The Retreat with The Call, a series of pronounced drumrolls to inspire the lads to close ranks and maintain the column. Midway through his *ratta-tap-tap*, a flurry of musket balls splintered the drum's wooden case, one lodged in Felker's thigh. The drummer howled, stumbled forward, then crumpled over his instrument, further shattering the case and rupturing the hide head. Sergeant Strode materialized out of the acrid haze, rushed to the fallen man's side, caught his comrade by the upper arm and dragged him to his feet.

"My drum," Felker said through clenched teeth. He was a man of average height, average build, sharp-nosed, with close-set eyes.

"Bloody hell, she's done for Artie," Strode gruffly admonished, supporting his friend's weight. "Here come the damn French and they'll be playing final reveille over our bones if we tarry."

"Wait," Felker retorted and leaning down, retrieved a scrap of casing emblazoned with the cross of St. George, a symbol of the regimental colors. "Now, get me out of here, you lovely bastard."

The French and their Abenaki allies broke from concealment and charged the remnants of the column. And there was nothing Ransom could do to stem the rout. The column buckled, broke apart and dissolved before his eyes. The soldiers nearly knocked him off his feet as they rushed past. The major took a look at the approaching horde and joined the footrace.

He heard the sound of the hunting horn peal above the clamor, saw the long-hunter's towering figure commanding the center of the wheel-rutted path, where the road cut through the forest and the white oaks parted to permit the passage of the regiment. Ransom scowled. So the wretch had not fled after all, or at least had halted his progress to amuse himself with the regiment's slaughter.

If it is the last thing I ever do, I shall confront the coward, the major promised himself. *And make him pay for his dishonor.* The men of his command were being cut to ribbons, but the way the woods were closer now, Stark was closer, there in the middle of the path framed by the forest's edge where the trees and underbrush became more pronounced.

Perhaps some of them would survive to warn Fort Edward, Ransom considered. That was preeminent, warn Fort Edward, regroup, reinforce the ranks, and return to relieve the English defenders of William Henry in due time. He was the last to flee and purposefully slowed so none of his troops would see him bound past like a frightened rabbit. Real or imagined he could sense his pursuers gaining on him. An English major was a prime target, sweet prey for both the Abenaki and the French.

Before the major's eyes, men stumbled and fell to the ground to right and left. With every hurried step Ransom expected to feel a lead ball rip through his vitals and leave him mortally wounded for Atoan and his bloodthirsty heathens to have their way with him. He'd heard dark and grisly tales of torture and death endured at the hands of the Abenaki, the Hurons, the Iroquois and did not relish such a fate.

His wig blew away, Ransom never even so much as slowed to glance over his shoulder, nor did he consider retrieving it this time. He could replace the periwig, but not the head it crowned. He gasped for breath, almost tripped over his own feet, vaulted a dying comrade at arms, and focused on the big man directly before him, not twenty yards away. He ran headlong toward the long-hunter, determined to confront Stark and charge him with cowardice and drag him back to Fort Edwards to answer for his misdeeds.

Drawing up a few yards from the big colonial, Ransom gulped air, then began to harangue Stark for his conduct and that of the Provincials. He had barely begun when to his astonishment Stark dropped the hunter's horn and let it dangle at his side while in the same motion he brought up Old Abraham and leveled the long rifle directly at the major. Ransom balked, his mouth dropped open, he stammered a protest that Johnny Stark cut short as he squeezed the trigger.

Major Michael Ransom dove forward as the Pennsylvania long rifle flashed fire in the pan then loosed an authoritative thunderclap, spewing powder smoke and flame. The lunatic had tried to kill him was Ransom's first thought, as he dove face down in the dirt. Then he heard a cry behind him and rolled over on his shoulder in time to see a French lieutenant, brandishing a pistol in either hand, stagger backwards, his aim hopelessly interrupted by the fifty-caliber rifle ball that shattered his sternum and lodged in his heart. The lieutenant had hoped to claim the English officer for his own glory but found that glory had its price, one that fate and Johnny Stark forced him to pay.

The lieutenant emptied his pistols into the air and toppled backwards. Ransom staggered to his feet, his ears still ringing from the proximity of the rifle and the flame that had nearly singed his eyebrows. Stark grabbed him by the sleeve of his coat and dragged him toward the woods as another hundred guns echoed Old Abraham.

The Colonial Militia had regrouped and followed Robert Rogers to the sound of the hunting horn. The men had quickly formed a skirmish line in the underbrush where they had prepared to receive the French and Indians.

Though outnumbered by the force sweeping toward them, the first volley from the Colonial Militia blunted the attack, for practically every rifleman found his mark. The Abenaki warriors and French marines recoiled from the ter-

rible effect of those rifles which shot truer than any Brown
Bess musket or Le Carabine. They fell back upon themselves as another volley rang out.

Stark hauled the officer into the shade of the white oaks
and flung him behind a stout trunk while he reloaded.

"The Regiment . . ." Ransom managed to say in a voice
that was almost shrill with desperation. His first command
and it had to be this debacle, one that was none of his
doing. But he would get the blame. Not Farley. History
would no doubt accord him heroic stature and in the same
entry describe the battle as Ransom's rout. The very notion
galled him to no end. But maybe he could yet salvage his
career and good name. "I must . . . the Regiment. . . ."

"Went that way," Stark replied with a nod in the direction of the road down which the 1st had fled. The stragglers were still visible. Indeed the entire force, all that
remained, had slowed at the sound of the Colonial rifles.
But they continued their trek southward down the road that
must eventually lead to Fort Edward.

"We can still salvage this day," Ransom blurted out.

"Major Ransom, *this* day was lost the moment Colonel
Farley refused to let me scout that meadow. I reckon Atoan
himself's out there and I can guaran-damn-tee you he'll
rally his men and have them after us in no time."

Rogers, Moses Shoemaker, Locksley Barlow, Sam
Oday and half a dozen others emerged from the thicket to
join Stark and the English officer by the oak tree. The Colonials were busily reloading their rifles and pistols as they
approached. And then all around them, Ransom sensed
movement as the militia withdrew, following the regiment
through the trees, each man choosing the course best suited
to him.

"The heathen has regrouped. But he ain't quite as anxious as before," Rogers grinned. "Fool thing, Big Timber,
standing out yonder in the middle of the wagon tracks, toot-
ing on that horn of yours."

"Figured on them seeing me would keep the Frogs

busy while you and the lads got into position to welcome them," Stark said.

Moses Shoemaker fingered the tears in the big man's buckskin shirt. Musket balls had passed close enough to tear the hide but leave the man unscathed. "I got to teach you the difference betwixt a 'welcome' and a 'sacrifice,' you overgrown rooster. Remember even the cock o' the walk can wind up in the stew pot."

"Now see here, I am ordering. . . ." Ransom tried to interject.

"Can't hear you, Major, my ears is all plugged up and I'm nigh deaf from all the shooting." Shoemaker shrugged.

"Mine too," said Barlow. The silversmith touched a knuckle to his forehead in deference to the officer's rank then scrambled off after his gray-haired comrade at arms.

"Reckon it will be fall back and fight until the heathens have their fill," Sam Oday suggested.

Rogers glanced in Stark's direction. Both men were the sort that inspired others to follow them. He saw that the man he called Big Timber concurred. It was the way of Indian fighting, a running battle, keeping to cover, making the pursuer pay for every yard of earth and keeping him cautious to a fault.

"Get them home, Robert. I'll be along shortly."

"Now, Johnny, there's nothing you can do for the lads at Fort William Henry," said Rogers. He didn't like this at all and made no attempt to hide his displeasure. Ransom stood off to the side, furious at being ignored but at a loss for words. What was Stark up to now? Coward, lacking respect for the major's authority; the list of his transgressions was lengthening.

"Atoan would like nothing better than to hang your hair from his war belt," Oday spoke up. His fingers fluttered to the black scarf covering his mutilated scalp. He knew whereof he spoke.

"I say, I shall gather the regiment and follow you, sir."

"You can't follow me, Major. You've some stalwart lads, who have no lack of backbone when they aren't being slaughtered for no reason but there's nary a one can walk the trail I'll be forced to take. If I'm to reach Fort William Henry alive, I'll have to walk and make no sound of my passing, leave no trace, not even a shadow to give me away."

Ransom glanced at Rogers and Oday and as if to check whether or not they were finding amusement in the long hunter's exaggeration. But both men appeared utterly serious. Ransom did not like being played for a clodpate.

"As commander of His Royal Majesty's..." He glanced about him. And for the second time this day he asked, "Where the devil is Stark?"

6

See the dead, adrift on the whims of a moonless night. They were soldiers once, British-born and brought to the New World by the lords of empire; they were colonists, frontiersmen bred free and determined to stay that way. See the dead? They were the women who followed their husbands and lovers into the wilderness, who struggled to make a home on the shores of Lake George. They were the children, the precious few who danced and frolicked on the banks of Bloody Pond, who skipped stones and played with carved wooden dolls and soldiers and never suspected their lives would be cut short by tomahawks and war clubs, and like their parents left to perish beyond the walls of Fort William Henry.

See? Ravens have eaten their eyes.

Screech owls for their funeral dirge, stone and mist and black shadows write an epitaph for the dead.

Who are they searching for? What do they want? Redemption? Too late for that. Revenge? Perhaps. Or maybe just to laugh again, to love, to live. Broken bodies, ghostly arms twist and wind like a snake, writhing across a fresh dug grave. But no grave for these. And so they come. And so they pass. And pause on their spectral journey as if sensing the one who sits with his back to the birch tree, long legs stretched before him, rifle across his lap, head lowered, chin to chest, slumbering, his right hand holding his long rifle, finger curled around the trigger.

This one rests. This one breathes. This one burns with the same force that fuels spring.

And so the specters begin to circle, like gossamer

moths attracted to a flame, round and round, ever closer, thirsting for all that has been stolen from them, the sweet smell of rain-washed pine, the cool kiss of autumn showers, the bracing winds of winter, the seeping warmth of a summer's day, how the sunlight seems to melt into the skin and heat the coursing blood.

See the silent stalkers descending on their prey. The one they seek is all they were and could have been and would never be again. Martyred children with holes for eyes, women with faces like blank pages, men who died in anguish, everyone wounded, maimed, everyone reaching out to the one who lives, to take the breath from his lungs, the beating of his indomitable heart, to claim all that he is or ever will be.

The dead must have their due.

Johnny Stark bolted awake, cried out despite himself, swung his rifle around and fired into the fading remnants of his nightmare. The tongue of fire lapping from the rifle barrel and the ensuing blast brought him fully awake. He staggered to his feet and brandished his rifle as if to crush the skull of his attackers, swung from left to right, staggered back against an oak.

Mist left a damp kiss on his stubbled features. His chest heaved and fell as he struggled to regain his composure. The nightmarish visions took their own sweet time about dissolving, but at last they returned to nature, reassumed into the haze of the suspended water droplets that spawned them.

"Bugger this," the long hunter muttered and quickly reloaded, then hurriedly gathered his possibles bag and slung it over his shoulder. No telling who could have heard that gunshot. It had been a fool thing to do. "I'm as clumsy as a bull calf in a gospel shop." He was in enemy country now despite the fact that Fort William Henry was only another few hours' walk from this stand of timber where he had chosen to take a moment's rest.

Stark had spent the previous day dodging war parties and patrols of French Marines as he made his way from the bloody meadow, skirting French and Indian patrols. He avoided the road entirely and kept to the hills, working a zigzag course that he hoped would bring him to Lake George and the ramparts of Fort William Henry. But an overcast night like this left him in danger of blundering into the same enemy patrols he had earlier evaded. At last he chose to wait out the remaining hours of darkness and hit the trail during the wee hours of dawn.

The long hunter had not meant to fall asleep, especially so deeply. Now the rifle shot placed him in a world of trouble. The sound would carry in these forested hills. But there was nothing to be done for it, except to put as much distance as possible between himself and his cold camp.

He tried to shake off the unsettling effects of the nightmare. The ghosts had seemed so real. What had they wanted from him? Or was this a warning? He was not a man given to superstition. And yet this was the wilderness, a place of mystery and the impossible, a place of beauty and death. Here on the frontier, nature and the supernatural were entwined. But that skein was unraveling as the world of the "savage" collided with the encroachments of civilization. But he had seen things . . . ghost lights fluttering like angel's wings down in the valleys, lightning that fell to earth like bundles and rolled sizzling across the land, the tracks of beasts unknown to him, left behind from an earlier time and etched in stone, the skeletal remains of that which seemed both beast and human.

This latest experience had marked him, filled him with a sense of foreboding. What awaited him on the shores of Lake George? What had befallen the garrison? The questions continued to plague him across the landscape of this moonless summer's night.

The answers waited on the other side of dawn.

• • •

Atoan knelt by a stand of white spruce and listened to the stillness, enjoying the absence of gunfire and the cries of the dying. A man born for battle, he longed for a time of peace, a time before the coming of the French and English to this land, when the Abenaki walked these proud hills and were the masters of all they surveyed. In those days the People of the White Pines hunted the vast forests, ranged the mountains, fished the rivers, and answered to no one.

Now the sacred places were crowded with white-eyed interlopers, these "civilized" men who did not hear the spirit of the wind nor fear the heart of the wolf. They blocked the game trails, cleared the forests, scarred the earth with forts and towns, brought their spotted sickness to destroy the tribes, made treaties and broke them whenever they chose. And if they weren't stopped, soon, all would be lost. The People of the White Pines would grow weak and die or be crushed beneath the tread of the French and English and the colonists who continued to encroach on the hunting grounds and sacred places.

Atoan glanced over his shoulder at the campfires of the twin encampments gleaming in the night, one for the French marines of Captain Lucien Barbarat and the other, for the Abenaki warriors who had pursued the remnants of the English troops from "bloody meadow" back down the road to Fort Edward. With the militia to bolster their numbers, the English rout had stiffened and become an orderly retreat; one long continuous running battle as Major Ransom's command withdrew in stages, always contesting the advancement of their pursuers.

Every time the Abenaki tried to flank the troops by moving through the woods, they encountered a number of ambuscades set by the Colonial Militia. These marksmen kept under cover, fired a few rounds then disappeared back into the forest like . . . well . . . like the Abenaki themselves. Atoan could sense the presence of the man called Stark in these tactics although no one had claimed to have seen the big frontiersman since the fight in the meadow.

Atoan heard his companions approaching. He knew it would be his son, Kasak, and no doubt some of the young braves keenly loyal to him. The Grand Sachem of the Abenaki stood quietly, framed by a pair of white ash trees on the crest of a low hill. The night was moonless, a faint wind soughed, he lifted his gaze to the clouds, adrift on the whispering breeze.

"Father . . . why have you called off the pursuit?" Kasak challenged, in a tone of voice neither of his two Abenaki companions would have ever dared to use. He gestured toward the two warriors who had followed him from the encampment. "Tabid and Lobal have returned from scouting the English. They are not so far ahead. Our people are prepared to attack them once again."

Lobal was a youthful looking fighter, built much like Kasak, slender and powerful, his naked torso like his youthful features, streaked with war paint, his head shaved but for a topknot. He carried a musket and powder horn and a lot of bravado.

Tabid was a few years older than either Kasak or Lobal, but was obviously as anxious to continue the running battle for as long as it took. He wore a red coat stripped from the body of a man whose skull he had crushed with his war club. His buckskin breeches were stained with the blood of his enemies.

Lobal leaned on his musket and stood off to the side, as if reluctant to incur the wrath of Atoan should the sachem take offense at their intrusion. Even in the deepening night the younger braves could not help but notice the jagged scar that trailed down the sachem's neck and split his shoulder. How could one not be in awe of a man who bore such a mark, as if the gods themselves had touched with him with "the fire that falls from the sky"?

"Let them go. It will do us no good to lose more of our warriors."

"But, father . . . ?"

"Listen to me, Kasak. We can kill them all. But more will come. Let the rest of them return to their own kind, to tell of all that they have seen, the tale of our great victory. Fear will spread among them. And the English will lose heart. In this way we will drive them from our land."

"Captain Barbarat has promised us many scalps, many guns if we do not let them escape," Tabid spoke up. He was anxious to prove himself in battle and return with the spoils of war that he might offer to the father of a young woman he fancied.

"The Frenchman does not care how many of his warriors he loses. The great father in France will send him more, always more. They are like the English, as numerous as the stars." Atoan glanced toward the three young men. "I know my people by name. My heart is wounded at the loss of any of my people. It ends here. We shall return to our village to sing of our victory and mourn our dead."

"Atoan should join us at the ceremonial fire," said Lobal, puffing out his chest. "None can stand before you in battle. The English fled from you like so many rabbits."

"There was one who did not run." The warrior folded his arms across his powerful chest, an image in his mind of the man with the hunting horn, rooted like a great oak in the center of the road, standing his ground while others rushed past, eyes ablaze, his rifle blazing, arms like thick limbs.

"I saw him," said Lobal.

"I *remember* him," Kasak added. "Stark."

Atoan studied the distant fires. The French drummers were beating a call to stack rifles and take their evening meal. He thought of Barbarat. The alliance with the French was a necessary evil for now. It served its purpose. But when the Abenaki no longer needed them, Monsieur Barbarat and his kind too would suffer the same fate as the English troops and the colonial settlers. *Drive them all into the Great Water.*

"My father is wise," Kasak remarked, obediently. But

there was a sense of resignation, a tone to the compliment that suggested "wise" was synonymous with "old."

The Grand Sachem of the Abenaki watched his head-strong son lead his companions back the way they had come, following the deer trail to the clearing in the valley below. In the distance, the road to Fort Edward beckoned. Even a small band of defenders, if determined, could make a stand behind the fort's massive, earthen battlements. But no matter how formidable, if the English lost heart, then it too would fall.

He lost all track of time, there on the wooded slope, listening to the sounds of the warm night, mind racing through the events of the past few months. Kasak continued to worry him. The young man had too much courage. It caused him to forge ahead when he should pause to read the trail. He lived for today's victory and lacked the insight it took to make such a victory count for more than songs of glory. But that was the way of youth. So it had been with Atoan, before he learned to hear beyond hearing.

A flutter of wings, the rustle of branches, caught the warrior's attention. He looked up among the dark twist of branches, recognized the distinctive head and ashen gray plumage of a great horned owl. The bird began to call out in a high-pitched screech that softened to a low chortle Atoan had learned to mimic as a boy. The owl was a night stalker, cunning and quick, with talons to rend and a razor-sharp beak. And it was more than an owl, if one only had eyes to "see."

"Atoan, son of Az the Hunter, I am here."

"Welcome, Mahom, my Grandfather. So you come to me again."

"Because your spirit walked in mine. So I have come to you."

The sachem crouched on his haunches and, with a twig, traced in the dirt for a few moments as he collected his thoughts. The sound of his people, chanting, singing songs of conquest and brave deeds carried to him from the valley.

"*It is good, Grandfather. I speak the words that are in my heart. Tell me. What will become of my people?*"

"*They will live, they will die, it is the way of things.*"

"*Today we have defeated the English. They flee before us like rabbits.*"

"*But there will be other days.*" The owl stretched its neck and craned its head from left to right. It dipped its head and preened yet it was always watchful, always hunting. *Beware of Kiwaskwek, the beast. For tomorrow he is born.*"

"*Should I fear an infant?*"

"*A storm is born. It rages. And the people tremble. How old is the first flood? Yet it washes you away.*"

Atoan did not like the sound of this. There were hidden caves and lonely hilltops where superstition prevented the People of the White Pines from ever venturing. It was never a good thing to walk in the footsteps of the gods. "*How will I know this Kiwaskwek?*"

"*You have seen him, though he is not yet born. But he will be. And then you will know. For his father is fury, and his mother, blood.*"

"*Man or monster, how shall I find him?*"

The owl shot from the branches and disappeared into the night, dropping out of sight into the depths of the forest where it sank onto its prey. A small animal uttered a pitiful cry as the night stalker made its kill. And in the distant dying echo, Atoan thought he heard the spirit creature reply.

"*He will find you.*"

7

Fort William Henry, a once seemingly impregnable outpost, had been reduced to a shapeless pile of charred blockhouses, crumbled redoubts and cabins, collapsed walls, and shoveled-in trenches on the grassy banks of a startling blue lake. If it hadn't been for the shambles of the fort and the grisly discovery Stark made outside the fortifications, the site might have seemed pristine, with the morning sun climbing above the hills to his right and the cloud-swept sky and forested shoreline mirrored on the surface of the waters.

Yes, idyllic, Stark thought, a veritable Eden, but for the hellish scenes of destruction among the swaying oaks and sturdy pines, and the stench from the butchered remains of the garrison's former defenders who littered a field more than a hundred yards from where the fort once stood.

Johnny Stark had no formal military training but what had befallen the defenders was plain to see. One only had to read the sign, like tracking a deer, to find the truth as to what had happened here.

The troops and the families who made the garrison their home were arrayed along and to either side of the road leading out from the soot-blackened remains of the front gate that opened toward the lake. The corpses in the lead, like all the rest of the soldiers in tattered red uniforms and torn breeches, were unarmed. There was not a single musket or pistol to be found. He might have surmised the troops were looted but there was not even a cartridge case to indicate the men had left the battered walls carrying their weapons. And several of the lead soldiers still clung to makeshift flags of truce, the white banners blood-spattered and affixed to axe handles and lance shafts most of which were strewn about, shattered in most cases but still clutched by those grimed fingers now frozen in death.

The garrison must have surrendered and was probably paroled to Fort Edward, for that was where this road would take them. The English defenders would never have marched out from their beleaguered bastion and through the French redoubts unless they had been assured of safe passage. Their trust was obviously ill-placed.

Apparently, once the column of soldiers and civilians were well clear of the fortifications and the siege redoubts of the French lines, something had gone terribly wrong. Stark recognized the subsequent mutilations as the handiwork of Abenaki war clubs and tomahawks. Perhaps the French had been unable to control the bloodlust of their allies; or maybe they had been active participants and joined in the wholesale slaughter. Either way they must share in the blame.

And in the retribution.

Johnny Stark steeled himself as he removed a spyglass from his belt and surveyed the dead for any signs of life. There were more ravens here than he could count. The carrion birds were feasting on the remains of soldiers, Colonial Militia men, their wives and children. Stark gasped and averted his gaze for a moment, overcome by the enormity of the massacre. There looked to be more than a thousand casualties left to rot along the road.

He knew many of these homesteaders. Like his friends and neighbors around Fort Edward they too had moved close to Fort William Henry, assuming there was safety being so near the proximity of the British troops stationed within. It had proved to be a reckless gamble.

Stark continued to survey the crumpled, twisted forms, speaking their names beneath his breath as he recognized one then another, frozen in death, families with whom he had broken bread, children he had bounced upon his lap, older siblings he had taught the ways of the wilderness. *Oh,*

God, so many. Even the infants, their skulls shattered. He wiped the moisture from his eyes on the sleeve of his fringed hunting shirt.

It was the children, their innocent remains discarded like so many rag dolls that brought Stark close to the breaking point. The horror of it all was more than any man should have to bear. Again he raised the glass to his eye and forced himself to continue the search. He owed the fallen this much. Eventually he altered his stance and began to study what little remained of the fortifications, but again found nothing salvageable. The English artillery had evidently been captured and carried off on French boats for *La Marines* of Fort Saint Frederick.

Stark grudgingly admired the thoroughness with which the French had completed the destruction of this English bastion. What their cannonades and axes had not accomplished was finished off by buried kegs of gunpowder under the direction of French engineers.

He heard a sound, a moan that seemed to drift toward him from out in the meadow, apart from the congregation of corpses. A pair of hungry ravens dropped out of the sky, intent on dining on the remains of someone or something out among the tall grass. An enormous paw batted them away. Stark heard a halfhearted howl, a protest of pain, then a weak but defiant growl. The ravens, startled and caught off guard by this new attack, decided they had business elsewhere and rose, protesting, into the sky.

Stark tucked his spyglass away and trekked across the field, gingerly stepping around the grisly forms, shot and hacked and scalped and now pecked at and partly devoured. The ravens lifted away from their feast as he passed, then alighted once more in his wake. As he drew close to the depression in the tall grass, a massive head rose up and gave him a warning growl.

The long hunter recognized the black mask and seamed jowls of an enormous mastiff and remembered the beast had not only been the property of the commanding officer but had served as a kind of mascot for the entire garrison.

It was a huge and powerful bitch, weighing a little over two hundred pounds and standing nearly a yard tall at the shoulders and fully seven feet in length, from its black nose to the tip of its brindle tail.

The animal lay on its side, its flesh streaked with blood from half a dozen tomahawk wounds and a puckered bullet hole along its ribs. Perhaps the mastiff had been left to die of its wounds because those who had caused the death of its master were loathe to approach such a terrible beast and risk a maiming. Could the animal have feigned its own death?

As Stark approached, the beast tried to stand but its effort only increased the flow of blood seeping from the bullet wound. The mastiff sank back on its haunches. But its ears pricked up as Johnny spoke gentle words of encouragement.

"Easy, girl. You're a fine one, you are. If the heathen hasn't done you in by now then I'll warrant it was meant you should live." He knelt by the animal, allowed the mastiff to catch his scent, then he stroked its neck. He fished in his possibles bag and found a strip of jerked venison and gave it to the animal and continued to talk while he drew his knife to probe the wound. While the mastiff devoured the venison, Stark dislodged the musket ball that had lodged beneath the puckered flesh. The mastiff's brindle coat was caked with dried blood, but his probing had opened the wound injury once more.

Stark dug in a pouch Molly had given him as he marched out from Fort Edward and found a poultice wrapped in sailcloth. Molly had concocted the poultice from a mixture of strong black tea and boiled, softened root of balsam fur that she had pounded into a paste. Stark unwrapped the concoction and smeared the paste over the animal's wounds and bound the worst with a torn piece of cloth and a length of leather string. The poultice would staunch the flow of blood and promote healing.

The dog watched him work with a curious expression as if the mastiff were weighing whether or not to chomp off Stark's arm clear up to the elbow. Eventually the animal decided the long hunter meant no harm and lay its head back upon the cool grass.

"Well then, I've done all that I can for you," Stark softly said, sitting back on his heels. What was the animal's name? There was no telling. But a dog this big deserved no less than a title. "Now then, Duchess, will you stand?" The mastiff whined and protested. For the next few minutes Duchess made quite a show of attempting to stand then falling back. "Rise up. Come on. We dare not tarry in these parts. The Abenaki and their French allies will return. And woe to us both if those Stiff-rumps find us here. Come along." He stood and started to cross toward the forest's edge. A glance over his shoulder told him the dog had the will to follow but had simply lost too much blood. Duchess rose up on all fours, managed a couple of steps, then collapsed, whining.

Stark cursed and returned to the animal's side. The masitff stared at him with its large, sad eyes. The long hunter set his rifle aside, glanced around for any sign of movement among the trees. The breeze shifted and carried the stench to his nostrils. Stark had to keep from gagging. He listened to the wind, the chatter of the ravens like mad monks dining on the dead, the rattle of tree limbs, like clicking bones, as they rubbed against each other with every errant breeze.

The long hunter knew what he had to do. There was one survivor of this massacre and by all that was holy, John Stark was going to bring him home. "So what must I do? Carry you?"

The mastiff placed a paw on the man's foot. Stark shook his head in disbelief. Was the great beast truly that far gone or playing the long hunter for a dupe? "Bloody hell, Duchess indeed. I reckon rank has its privileges or so I am told." Johnny muttered and setting his rifle aside, knelt by the dog and gathering the animal by its brindle coat, hoisted Duchess upon his shoulders. "Damn if I will leave you behind," he grimaced as the animal's great weight settled on his shoulders. "I swear on my mother's grave, God rest her soul, but I regret that venison I gave you, for I fear it has only added to your bulk."

Duchess barked. The sound set his ears ringing.

Stark groaned and steadied himself, bearing the weight of the mastiff like another heavy pack. The seventeen miles to Fort Edward just doubled in length with the added burden. So be it. He lifted his gaze to the hills he would have to cross and almost second-guessed himself. He grimaced as he squatted down and took up his rifle. Then he headed for the trees, leaving the dead to the cruel efficiency of nature.

When Stark at last gained the forest's edge and the shade fell around him like a cool cloak, he took a moment to turn and face the scene of slaughter, taking in from a distance the morbid chatter of the ravens, the dead beyond active protest who somehow managed to speak the words he heard with his heart.

"Remember us. Remember. . . ."

He allowed the scene to become etched in his heart. These same ghosts had called him by name, charged him with retribution the night before, to free them from the clutches of an endless night.

Avenge us. Have pity. Weep for us.

"No," said Stark. "Weep for the Abenaki . . . weep for the French . . . from this day forth."

Up until the last couple of days, Atoan and his French allies, *La Marines* had confined themselves with raids, brief forays to discourage the colonial settlers and drive them back to the coast. But this was wholesale slaughter; men, women, and children. It turned his stomach even as it lit a fire of resolve in his heart.

"There will come another day!" he shouted. His words echoed off the emerald hills, carried down to where the sunlight danced upon the shimmering waters. The French and Indians wanted a war, he'd give it to them. But he would fight it *his* way. From this day forth vengeance would have a name.

Johnny Stark.

8

To the weary eyes of a hunted man, the moonlit battlements of Fort Edward were just about the prettiest sight
imaginable. The great earthen breastworks rose twelve-feet
high and were at least half that thick. Blockhouses at each
of the five corners of the irregularly-shaped structure assured that whoever tried to storm the walls would be caught
in a crossfire of grapeshot from the nine-pounder cannons
nestled behind the sheltering ramparts. The main gate was
further protected from frontal assault by the swiftly flowing
waters of the Hudson River. From this point on, taking a
boat any further upriver was hardly worth the effort.

Outside the fort proper, the meadows and rolling riverbank were ablaze with log cabins and stone farmhouses
and carefully tended fields. The settlers had surged in from
the east coast, lured by the rich farmlands, open countryside
and the proximity of the English troops stationed at the fort
for the protection of the colonies and to guard against
French incursions. Over the year the number of inhabitants
had swelled to a sizeable community of several hundred
families. And this did not include the regiment stationed
inside the fort. But there were less of them now, Stark
mused, wondering how many of his own comrades and
neighbors had survived the retreat from Bloody Meadow.

From this bend of the river, a steady parade of British
troops, Indians, and colonial adventurers had carried their
canoes and bateau the seventeen miles overland to Lake
George, the gateway to Lake Champlain which in turn
flowed north and emptied into the St. Lawrence River, the
great artery to the Canadian coast. A man alone could make

the journey in a long hard day, climbing hills, and abandoning the twists and turns of the wheel-rutted road connecting Fort William Henry to the settlement of Fort Edward. It took a good deal longer for a man alone, having to dodge war parties, elude French patrols, a man encumbered with a dog the size of a small horse! ·

The wilderness was one long seemingly endless invitation, a string of shining hillocks and jewel-flecked lakes linked by glittering rivers that made a man ache to explore them all, follow each to its source. But standing on the night-shrouded hillside, in the aftermath of a warm summer rain that had soaked him to the bone, Stark was less concerned about exploring the Adirondacks and keener on finding a warm fire and dry clothes, not to mention ridding himself of the burden he had labored under for the last three days.

Oh sweet sight of home. Like the promise of paradise to a grieving sinner, the smell of freshly-roasting venison drifted to him on the moistened breeze. The mastiff stirred where it lay draped across the big man's shoulders and growled, catching the scent.

Stark knelt and gently slid the animal off his benumbed frame. The long hunter sighed with relief and stood, stretched the stiffness out of his back and arms. Duchess whined as if each breath might be her last. But she gamely raised her head and continued to sniff the air. The animal smelled the wood smoke and the pronounced aroma of sizzling meat roasting over open fires, caught the mouthwatering scent from cast-iron cauldrons of hearty stew hung above the crackling flames, warm slabs of crusty bread to sop up the meat juices in the stoneware bowls. Johnny's stomach began to growl.

He pictured the comfortable confines of the Page farmhouse, a sturdy two-story structure of logs and gray stone set on the edge of the settlement. A cheerful fire in the hearth. Another ablaze in the summer kitchen out back. Ephraim and Charity set a fine table. There'd be venison roast and sweet corn and perhaps a chokecherry pie.

And in the aftermath of an evening meal, Molly would bring out the clay pipes for Ephraim and Johnny. The two men would enjoy their tobacco and debate the necessary presence of the British in the colonies while Molly sat nearby, watching the big man relax, her smile full of mysteries, that disturbing expression on her face, the look of a woman who knew some special secret a man like Stark could not hope to fathom. In his mind's eye, he imagined, even now, how the tobacco smoke must be drifting through the open shutters as it followed the trail of the roasting venison up the slope to man and beast on the rise overlooking the settlement.

Suddenly the mastiff abandoned its pitiful pretense and rose up on its legs and barked. Then to Stark's amazement Duchess seemed to experience a miracle healing as she trotted forward a few feet, glanced back to see what was keeping the big man. The mastiff's tail began to wag with furious abandonment. The dog started down the hill toward the settlement then paused again, sensing Johnny was holding back.

"*Blood and 'ounds*, you black-faced Dasher. You've gone and played me for a fool," Stark blurted out. "And here I have carried you all the way from Fort William Henry, more'n seventeen miles what with trying to keep off the road and make my own trail! Saved your life, by heaven and damn near broke my back when you could walk all along!"

The mastiff barked and shook its massive head, flinging droplets of spittle and milky-white saliva over everything within a few yards of the dog's jowls. Stark grumbled and wiped the residue from his hands. Again Duchess barked and this time ran up and nearly knocked the big man over when she placed her ham-sized paws on his chest.

Grumbling, the long hunter checked the animal's bandaged side while struggling to remain upright. The animal barked, fanning his face with its hot breath, loosed its deep, guttural bark that nearly rendered Stark deaf, then dropped down on all fours and began to pant and pace before him.

"Wait up, Duchess. Folks down yonder are apt to be a might skittish after all that's happened. Best we let them come to us."

To that end Stark gathered enough deadwood to make a fire large enough to be seen by the sentries manning the earthen and timber ramparts of Fort Edward. Once the limbs were stacked, Stark added some kindling, then dusted that feathery pile of dried leaves and twigs with char cloth. He struck his knife blade on a length of flint and showered the tinder with sparks. Before long he had a robust blaze lighting the hilltop.

Taking up Old Abraham, Johnny Stark shouldered the weapon and pointed it at the sky. "This will announce us," he said and fired into the air. The rifle shot echoed down the long hills. While the flames continued to devour the wood behind him, Johnny reloaded and fired again, then discharged his pistol. He unslung his hunting horn and blew several times on the brass instrument, sounding out his familiar call.

Minutes later the moonlit settlement began to teem with activity. First came the answering gunfire, tongues of flame lapped the night air as men hurried from their houses and cabins and fired into the air. He could hear the excited voices, a chorus of happy shouts, as if a celebration had just begun. Then joining in with the Colonials, a series of drumrolls floated over the walls of the fort to mingle with the blaring discordant "halloos" from other hunting horns as the entire settlement joined in to welcome one who was feared lost after the rest of the relief column straggled in.

Johnny Stark had come home!

9

Johnny Stark made his way through the ranks of his countrymen and climbed atop the boxes stacked in the center of the Council House, a longhouse erected in the center of the settlement where the colonists were wont to gather, to air their grievances and settle their disputes before one and all. Lanterns were hung from every post supporting the timber and mud-chinked roof overhead, and the glare from all those sallow lights painted the log walls with dancing shadows that belied the serious nature of this gathering.

Molly was there escorted by her kindly uncle, Ephraim Page, who had insisted Charity remain at home with the other womenfolk, until after Stark gave his report. Ephraim, with his flowing white beard, unruly white hair and somber black frock coat more closely resembled some biblical prophet or a fire-and-brimstone Bible-thumper than a gunsmith. However much he thought this was a man's affair, he knew his sage advice would be wasted on his headstrong niece. Much like her Irish mother, Molly Page had a mind of her own and she was going to be with Johnny Stark and did not care to listen to any word to the contrary.

Stark glanced in her direction. Whatever emotion the sight of her instilled remained hidden beneath his stony expression. His gaze swept across a row of familiar faces. There was Sam Oday, black scarf concealing his mangled scalp, blunderbuss in the crook of his arm. Moses Shoemaker, wrinkled and wise, a bandage around one bony calf where a musket ball had carved through his leathery muscle, and Locksley Barlow, leaning on his Pennsylvania long rifle, his youthful eyes grown serious now, since the events of the last few days. Barlow had helped carry Shoemaker throughout the retreat and was not going to let the wounded old jehu forget it, not for a while anyway. Robert Rogers worked his way to the fore and held up his hand to bring some order to the congregation.

"Quiet down now, good lads," he said, then noticing Molly (they weren't all lads here) attempted to correct himself, then decided the hell with it, he was already down the trail and beyond turning back. Anyway, in her hunting shirt and breeches she could almost pass for one of the young men if she tucked her hair back and stood so as not to emphasize her rounded figure. "Quiet, and we will hear what Johnny has to say."

"Better wait for the column I seen marching down from the fort," Cassius Fargo called out from the doorway. "I reckon Ransom has sent one of his aides to give a listen." The dour-looking frontiersman glanced sharply in Stark's direction where the big man commanded the attention of his comrades at arms by the sheer force of his character and towering build. Cassius frowned, his brow knotted like a length of coarse rope someone had glued to his forehead. Fargo abstained from further comment, but cleared the doorway as the tramp, tramp, tramp of a dozen soldiers marching in close order drifted through the opening, followed soon after by a youthful-looking lieutenant, a foppish young dandy dressed in the uniform of the 1st regiment. Allan Penmerry had missed accompanying the relief column due to a stomach disorder although there was some discussion among the militiamen that the disorder was that he had no "stomach for a fight." Penmerry's escort dutifully waited outside, allowing the lieutenant to venture alone into the Council House. He made no attempt to hide his disdain for these provincials and longed for the day when he might walk the hallowed hills of Cornwall again.

Penmerry's pale green eyes swept across the crowd and alighted on the man of the hour. It was obvious the officer in his red coat and white periwig, his silver-hilted sword dangling from his belt, felt decidedly uncomfortable in the midst of this rough lot. Even the townsmen seemed only one step removed from the savages who plagued the frontier, although storekeepers and craftsmen like Ephraim gave him hope that some semblance of civilization might eventually prevail on the frontier.

"Mister Stark!" Penmerry spoke the name in a precise clipped tone. "It is proper to report to one's commanding officer on returning from a patrol."

The lieutenant heard a growl, deep and guttural, from off to his left and allowing a quick look, caught sight of the mastiff which in the glare of the lanterns looked even more formidable. The Cornishman gulped and his eyes widened. He retreated a few steps, placing half a dozen of this rough lot between him and the dog. Penmerry seemed to recall that the mastiff had been the property of the commander of Fort William Henry. Evidently the animal had switched its allegiances and cast its lot with this rough bunch.

"You are welcome here, Lieutenant, come and go as you please, but from this day forth, I answer to none but God and these good friends," Stark replied and received a chorus of "Here-here's" from the gathering.

"Tell us then," Ephraim called out. "What word from Fort William Henry? How do our countrymen fare?"

"Yes," said Rogers, "and were you able to approach through the French lines and give them hope?"

"I should hope you assured them that Major Ransom has assumed command and will prepare another relief attempt?" Penmerry interjected, maneuvering through the crowd. Stark's earlier remarks bordered on treason to his way of thinking. The youthful officer wrongfully assumed the presence of his uniform would curb such sentiment and keep it from spreading.

Moses Shoemaker nudged a bony elbow into the side of fair-haired Locksley Barlow. Shoemaker wrinkled his nose, indicating the perfumed scent that suddenly assailed their nostrils as Penmerry drew abreast of them.

"Blood and 'ounds," said Shoemaker. "If you ain't the

prettiest smellin' man." A few of the men within earshot began to chuckle.

"Not to worry, Moses," said Barlow, unable to restrain his wit. "No one will ever mistake you for a nosegay." His remark elicited an even greater response, but the laughter soon died as Stark began his tale of what he had seen and the horrible fate that had befallen their comrades up on Lake George.

"The defenders of Fort William Henry are beyond hope," said the long hunter. The silence that followed could have been carved with a tomahawk.

Molly's hand fluttered to her mouth; she gasped, sensing his meaning before any of the rest. Then the gravity of his pronouncement swept through the Council House.

"Speak plain, Johnny. Tell us what you saw," she added. Her gentle voice spoke what was in all of their hearts.

"William Henry has fallen. And all its defenders murdered. Every man, woman, and child."

Molly wasn't the only person to utter a cry of horror. Grown men, hardened frontiersman like Sam Oday who had seen death and endured torture, looked visibly shaken, some were forced to sit on whatever barrel or crate happened to be close at hand. Others began to shake their heads as if denying Stark's report would undo what he had seen.

"The garrison apparently surrendered. From the look of things, I imagine Lieutenant Colonel Monro marched them out under a flag of truce, right to their deaths." Stark glanced around, seeing the effect and struggling to contain his own emotions once again as the image of the massacre returned to mind. "I don't know if the French had a hand in it or just stood by and watched the Abenaki set upon the column but it was plain to me that Monro and his soldiers and colonial families under his protection had no way to defend themselves. The French would not have allowed them to depart bearing their 'smoke poles,' powder and shot."

"Damn . . ." Rogers muttered.

"Yeah," Stark added, glancing in the direction of his ambitious friend. "I don't know about you lads but this child has had all the English *protection* he can stomach." He scrutinized his companions and then settled on the officer in the red coat. His aside was repeated through the crowd and there generally followed a consensus of agreement. Johnny focused on Penmerry. Ransom's aide shifted uncomfortably beneath that harsh scrutiny. The long hunter's stare held an edge keen as a skinning knife. "You've got your report, Lieutenant. Best you run on back to the fort and present it to Major Ransom, with my compliments."

Penmerry looked stunned. The enormity of the disaster was just sinking in. If Fort William Henry had fallen then where would the French and Indians strike next? The answer was frighteningly apparent.

Here!

Ignoring Stark's belligerent attitude, the periwigged lieutenant straightened, turned on his heels and marched from the Council House, ignoring as best he could the glares that followed him as he retraced his route to the broad, open doorway. A minute later he had snapped an order to his escort and the men closed ranks behind him and followed the officer back toward the gloomy battlements of Fort Edward. With the English officer safely departed, Stark shifted his attention back toward his companions.

"Now we may not have been the first folks out here," said Stark. "But we've watered this land with our own blood, buried good friends and loved ones, and earned the right to stay. No one, not General Montcalm, not Atoan and the whole Abenaki nation is gonna drive us out."

Rogers nodded and gestured to the people gathered in the Council House. "We all feel the same way, is that a fact?"

The crowd voiced their agreement in a ragged but enthusiastic chorus of accord. "But what'll we do, Johnny?"

a burly young farmer's son called out. Half a dozen other men chimed in.

Stark waved the crowd to silence. "I'm glad you asked that, Danny Dulin, because me and Rogers have a plan. We've talked on it before. And it involves every man...." (He felt her eyes bore into him like a pair of hot pokers.)

"And every woman . . . here."

10

Ow, that hurts, Molly" said Stark rubbing his shoulder after she punched him in the arm.

Molly planted her hands on her hips and glared at him in the front room of the cabin he had built on a knoll overlooking the star-strewn surface of the Hudson River. It was a humble yet comfortable place, nestled between two pastures, one belonging to Uncle Ephraim Page, the other to scarred, kindly Sam Oday, who was a good neighbor and eager to offer a helping hand to any man who approached his door. Over these many months, Molly had worn a footpath across the field from her uncle's farmhouse. Her behavior might have caused some to speculate about the pair, but Aunt Charity loudly defended the girl she had raised since childhood. Molly was both an innocent flower yet wise enough to pick proper company for herself. And Johnny Stark was a man of principle. No lass need fear his intentions—of that she was certain. The "innocent flower" punched him again.

"Blood and 'ounds, lass, what's come over you?"

"That's for running off on your lonesome and scaring me half to death thinking your scalp was dangling from some Abenaki's war belt."

"Blast it all, but you're a fractious woman," Stark bemoaned.

"And this is for returning safe and whole, alive and in one piece," she added, drawing close. She stood on tiptoes and her arms went around his thick neck and she brought her lips to his. And after she kissed him once, she kissed him again, then eased back a few inches to study his noble, if slightly crooked, features that she found so appealing.

Molly glanced down for a second; she could see the kiss had the desired effect. Stark's cheeks flushed. He looked speechless and a bit mooneyed. Good, that was perfect. After all, they were alone in the cabin and anything could happen and no one the wiser, well almost no one, if you didn't count the couple of hundred townsfolk who probably spied her crossing the field by lantern light, carrying a basket of food for the one she cared about more than any other.

"Bless my soul, Miss Molly, I must remember not to get myself killed more often." He ruefully rubbed his biceps deciding that a bruised shoulder was a small price to pay for the sweet wine of her kisses.

"You do that, Johnny Stark," she replied.

He grinned and glanced around at the simply furnished interior of the place. It was a fitting home for a man who spent most of his time outdoors, sporting only a hand-hewn table, a pair of ladder-backed chairs and a stout bed with a chest at the foot. A smaller table served as a night-stand and supported a porcelain pitcher and bowl for washing. Molly had added some niceties in his absence, calico curtains framed the windows, a quilt draped across the foot of the feather mattress on his overlarge bed.

He filled the washbasin from the china pitcher and dunked his face to wash the residue of powder smoke from his features, splashed the back of his neck and straightened. Droplets of water glistened in his shaggy brown mane. His gaze was drawn to the moonlit river and the steep bank of the opposite shore. After the gathering in the Council House, after he had spoken his piece and left the debate for others to hammer out the details of his plan, Stark had slipped off into the night and headed for his cabin. Half an hour later Molly arrived with food and drink. He didn't hesitate to wolf down a chunk of bread soaked in meat drippings and folded around a slab of smoked ham.

"The hour is late. But I reckon half the settlement knows you're in here. Wonder what folks will be saying?"

"They'll say that Johnny Stark can track like a wild Indian and knows the forest better than the critters that call it home," she replied ". . . but the man's nothing but a fool if he doesn't marry Molly Stark." She was not a woman to mince words. But damn if he didn't look pale all of a sudden. "Courage, Johnny, courage. You swoon and Robert Rogers will never let you live it down." Molly knew that would get to him. Rogers liked to think he was the better man, that he could outrun, outfight, and best any wild Indian at his own game. Molly knew better.

Rogers was brave enough, but he was an ambitious man, unlike Stark, who cared little for the trappings of authority. Rank had only recently begun to matter, when he'd seen lesser men lead so poorly. Playing second fiddle to some English martinet had nearly cost the lives of too many neighbors and friends.

"Robert Rogers has a lean and hungry look alright," Stark chuckled. "But let him play his game out and take what glory he can. He does not lack for courage and will stand his ground when the musket balls fly. And we shall need fighting men in the days ahead." He looked down and all but lost himself in the twin pools of her eyes.

"There you go again. *Fighting men.* This is my war, too. And I won't help win it sitting around with Aunt Charity, making quilts or spinning yarn."

"I wanted to talk to you about that," Stark began. He was bone tired and not sure he was up to the coming confrontation. And when her expression became tight-lipped and her eyes narrowed into slits, he was certain.

"Don't even think it." She crossed to her rifle leaning against the hearth. His rifle, *Abraham*, had been hung above the rough-hewn mantle. She picked up *Isaac* and cradled the finely-balanced weapon in her hands. "This is my country. And I will fight for it."

"And the devil take the one who tries to stop you."

She nodded. "Bet on it." Molly walked across the room toward the front door and took up her lantern. She tossed her head like a colt, gave her red curls an enticing flick.

"You never know how useful someone like me can be."
The saucy young woman stepped across the threshold and
vanished into the night.

"Heaven help the poor bloke who finds out," said
Stark.

He walked to the door and stepped outside to watch
the lantern bob to and fro as Molly made her away across
the meadow toward Ephraim's house, a two-story, ramshackle farmhouse with a barn twice as large as Stark's
cabin. He could still taste her kiss. It helped. He had seen
things these past few days that had marked him. But being
with her made it all bearable and gave him hope.

Stark would have asked for her hand if he only had
something to offer but a tiny cabin on a windswept knoll
overlooking the Hudson. Molly deserved better. Indeed, she
deserved the best.

A great black shape bestirred itself and climbed out
from underneath the cabin steps. Duchess padded around
the steps and quickly approached her new master for a
scratch behind the ears, her broad, deeply-seamed brindle
head wore a forlorn look.

"It's your war, too," he added.

The beast seemed satisfied.

11

Charity and Ephraim Page were sound asleep in the front room of the two-story farmhouse Ephraim had built with the help of John Stark, Robert Rogers, and many of the townsmen and Green Mountain lads. The pair were incorrigible, forsaking their warm beds to wait up for Molly, and dozing on either side of the stone hearth. The glare of a whale-oil lamp washed across Ephraim's bearded features where he sat slumped in his wing-backed chair, a worn leather-covered Bible in his firmly clasped hands. His white beard fluttered as he snored, it rippled like drifting snow across the field of his bony chest.

Aunt Charity, eyes closed and her head lolling to one side, a shawl about her shoulders, had never known anything but the lot of a pioneer's life, and that was all she wanted out of life. She was the kind of person born to set down roots in the wilderness, keep a home together, and endure. The rustic life suited her, but once settled she had no desire to see what lay beyond the hills or seek some river's source. Charity Page was rooted in the soil of this land now and nothing would bestir her. She intended to keep this house and their farmland safe, make this wilderness into a home, and neither the French nor some implacable savage like the Great Atoan, was going to drive her out. It was this woman's quiet strength that her niece found so endearing.

Molly set her rifle against the wall next to the door and stepped quietly into the room, taking care not to disturb the woman in the ladder-backed rocking chair. She quickly assessed the situation; her aunt and uncle had no doubt chosen to await her arrival back home from Johnny Stark's. No doubt the news of the calamity that had befallen their kinsmen on the shores of Lake George had caused many a family to burn the late-night oil. Indeed, she had noticed a telltale glow seeping between the shuttered windows of houses and cabins throughout the settlement and had witnessed patrols march from the fort to take up watchful positions on the outskirts of the settlement. They would at least provide some warning should hostiles approach.

Charity and her husband were by no means wealthy compared to merchant folk who made their homes in places such as Boston and New York, but they lived tolerably well, earning their comforts with their farmland and Ephraim's gunsmith shop, a stout-looking little cabin he'd situated near the Kit Fox Tavern, close to the proper center of the settlement. A good gunsmith was always in demand, and with Locksley Barlow and his cousins to till the fields and bring in the crops, the older couple wanted for little, save the return of their son, dead these long months.

Molly was no stranger to loss. Her own parents had succumbed to smallpox when she was but a child. But she had come to terms with her loss and lived for the future. The red-haired young woman smiled wanly, the dead being beyond her grasp, and gingerly approached her aunt.

Charity and her good husband of many years were a study in contrasts. The farm woman was pleasingly plump, with rosy round cheeks and an upturned nose. Her wealth of silvery locks were tucked beneath a lace cap. Her brushed woolen sleeping gown collected in tucks and wrinkles about her ample bosom and expansive hips. Her features, in slumber, were free of worry lines and pretty in a homespun way, the look of a durable woman whose inner strength is centered in faith and a sense of good humor.

Ephraim was reed thin, with the air of a prophet about him, and a nose as long and crooked as a beak and features wrinkled from staring into the sky's white glare. He'd been plagued with bouts of melancholia since the death of his son. But Molly's presence had been their saving grace. The couple doted on their niece and took great comfort in her.

Molly moved aside a small table on which her aunt had placed a porcelain teapot, cup, and saucer, and hooking a small, padded footrest with her toe, pulled it over and placed it alongside the rocking chair. She sat and placed her hand on her aunt's. Charity stirred, her eyes opened, she blinked.

"Land's sake," she exclaimed, momentarily disoriented. Ephraim coughed and rubbed his eyes and tried to focus on the dimly-lit interior. One of the lamps was in need of a fresh supply of whale oil.

"Who is it? Hold the line, lads . . . for what we are about to receive. . . . uh . . . Molly?"

"Back safe and sound. You need not have waited for me. I am perfectly safe with Johnny Stark."

"Yes," Charity sighed. "More's the pity."

"Wife," Ephraim sternly admonished while Molly grinned.

"Husband!" Charity retorted right back at him. "Johnny Stark needs to be thinking about something more than just fighting the French and Indians. He is not getting any younger and neither is Molly. All of her friends are properly wed and bearing sons and daughters." She patted her niece's hand. "Or grandsons and granddaughters."

"Still it decries the good book that you should encourage one of our own to wantonness." Ephraim pressed the Bible to his chest as if saluting the wisdom to be found within those pages.

"I encourage nothing of the kind," Charity scoffed and shook her head, then cast a knowing look in the younger woman's direction. She failed to stifle her yawn. "I am only attempting to guide Molly here upon a most precipitous path." She nodded and smiled at Molly. "But Ephraim is correct. With all this terrible trouble that has befallen us, it might be best if you do not keep such late hours beyond the safety of these walls." Charity checked her teacup and drank the last of what she found.

"Isaac is always at hand," Molly gently reminded them

with a glance toward her rifle. "I am not afraid of anything." She stood and kissed her aunt on the cheek, did the same to her uncle and then climbed the stairs to the bedrooms upstairs.

Charity glanced in Ephraim's direction. "Now, that's what worries me," she said.

"Amen," her husband replied.

12

Stark glanced over his shoulder through the open doorway of his cabin and considered returning to his chair inside. But the night beckoned, the sound of the river rushing over sheets of submerged shale; foaming and bubbling in backwater breaks was a siren call the long hunter could not deny. He knelt and scratched the mastiff behind her ears, then left the steps and meandered down toward the riverbank, a shore strewn with lichen-covered rocks. Further downriver he could make out the expanse of an island in midstream.

His friend, Robert Rogers, had laid claim to that stretch of woods and sand in the center of the Hudson, set midstream between the two riverbanks and in the shadow of the English fort. He proclaimed it Rogers Island. Stark grinned, thinking of his comrade at arms. Robert Rogers was hungry for rank and glory, aspired to have his name written on the pages of history whereas Johnny Stark had other goals. He valued freedom above any rank; good land and independence was worth far more than gold. Then he thought of Molly Page and his blood warmed. Yes, good land, independence, and a good woman.

Upriver, wrapped in darkness, a final tier of rapids limited travel, although Johnny Stark had taken Molly up to the headwaters, a couple of years back. They had explored the mountains to the north and found a chain of ice-cold lakes that the Abenaki called the "Tears of the Mountains."

No colonist would ever come up with a better name for the place. He admired much about the Abenaki, not that it would deter him from fighting them. That was the tragedy of this war, that red man and white man could not find a way to live in peace. Maybe one day, Stark thought. But he doubted in his lifetime. He thought of the butchered remains beyond the walls of William Henry. There had been too much cruelty, too much dying on both sides. And for what? Some days it seemed as if he and Atoan were just pawns in this struggle between the age's two great powers, France and England.

That too needs to change, he thought. "But not now," he sighed. First the settlement had to survive the coming months.

Duchess, who had followed him down the path from the cabin, bristled and uttered a deep-voiced, guttural growl. Someone was approaching. For an instant, an image flashed through Stark's mind, that of his trusty rifle back where he left it, on the spruce wood rack above the mantle in his cabin.

A man venturing anywhere these days without his smoke pole was a fool. The wilderness could be a harsh teacher and unforgiving of the careless. Stark slipped a knife from the sheath at his side. The blade was hand-forged, tempered true and sharpened to a fare-thee-well. He tensed. The hackles rose on the mastiff's back, increasing her size. She could have passed for a bear in the darkness.

"Stark," said Major Ransom. "I will thank you to call off the dog. I believe someone mentioned to me that was Colonel Monro's mastiff?"

"Maybe, but she's orphaned now, and going it alone." Stark returned the knife to his belt. He checked the shadows for some sign of the officer's escort and realized, much to his surprise, that Ransom had come alone. "Well now, Major, I never thought you officers went anywhere without a company of *lobsterbacks* to watch your arse."

Lieutenant Penmerry's report must have been alarming, if it had driven the fort's commanding officer into committing such a rash act. Stark had to raise his estimation of the man. Maybe the officer had more gumption than Stark gave him credit for. He made a mental note to never again underestimate a British officer. It appeared Ransom was likewise confronting his own personal dilemma. That he chose to exorcize his demons beyond the scrutiny of the men who would have to follow his orders made a kind of sense.

"John Stark." Major Ransom muttered the name like he would a curse. "Do I place you under arrest and have you flogged for fleeing the field of battle or thank you for saving my life?"

"I would not try the former," cautioned Stark. "And the latter is unnecessary." He waited for the officer to approach and then the two men continued abreast of one another along the riverbank. "Flogging," he added with contempt. "You officers are mighty free with the lash."

"Flogging teaches discipline, Mister Stark. Without discipline, an army cannot hope to succeed." Ransom tugged on the hem of his coat. He had exchanged his disheveled uniform for one proper and fitting and not stained with blood and powder burns. Moonlight glinted off the white embroidered facing on his tunic and the silver hilt of his sword.

"The only thing a lash ever taught a man is how to turn his back," Stark replied. He was not impressed. "The 1st Regiment of Foot had discipline at Bloody Meadow, and you lost half your lads. And the poor bastards at Fort William Henry looked like they had plenty of discipline as they marched out to be massacred!"

Stark knew it was highly unusual for a colonial of his station to address an officer of Ransom's rank and stature with such familiarity. But Ransom had left that privilege behind at the gate. The two men had survived the disastrous relief attempt, battle, and the rout toward Fort Edward. It was quite evident John Stark really did not give a damn if the Englishman took offense.

Ransom bristled at the big man's tone of voice. Only within the walls of Fort Edward had the major begun to experience a sense of safety. And even that was suspect. He imagined the possibility of an armed host of French and

Indians massing just beyond the hills, preparing for an all-out·assault on the ramparts. And the command had fallen to him. Indeed, for the moment the future of the English presence in the Adirondacks rested upon his inexperienced shoulders.

Ransom swallowed his pride, breathed deep and folded his hands behind his back. He had not slipped through the side entrance of the fort only to become embroiled in a conflict with this uncouth frontiersman. "Rogers paid me a visit."

"Robert is not a man to waste time."

"He told me of your plan. . . ."

"It is both of ours. We have talked on it some."

"He mentioned you both seek a separate command of the Colonial Militia and that it should be considered apart from the King's troops."

"Not militia," Stark said, eyes glinting in the moonlight as he faced the power of the mighty Hudson. "Rangers." He turned and faced the English officer. "Do you want to win this war?"

"Of course I do," Ransom answered.

"Then let us fight to win. We shall raise a force of Rangers who can outmarch, outsail, outrun and outfight any Abenaki or Frenchman in the New World. I will handpick the force. Each man will have to be a crack shot and skilled with the hawk and knife. And they will have to know the woods." Stark folded his powerful arms across his broad chest.

"It is most irregular. I will no doubt have to answer for it," Ransom mused, stroking his pointed chin. "That is, when General Amherst arrives to assume command. And he most assuredly will do just that, when my dispatches reach him."

"Avenging what happened this week ought to buy his good graces."

"I don't know," Ransom said, stroking his chin. Up-river to the north, the enemy waited; at least he hoped they were waiting and not advancing for the final battle.

Stark knelt, drew his knife and began to draw in the soft moist earth of the riverbank. A crude map took form, clearly visible in the moonlight. Indeed, the two men had no problem seeing one another's facial expressions. Both looked worn and troubled by the events of the past few days.

"Look here," Stark began, drawing an elongated circle in the dirt. "This is Lake Champlain." He drew a long appendage to its southern reaches. "And this is *Tisinondrosa*. That's the Abenaki word. It means 'the tail of the lake.' The great lake narrows here and becomes more like a river, about twenty five miles long and a quarter of a mile wide. It ends in *La Chute*, I'd say that's about four miles of rapids which connect Lake Champlain to the northern tip of Lake George. And all of it is under French control. Fort Carillon at the mouth of *La Chute* and Fort Saint Frederick to the north where the lake broadens."

"It is their own private waterway," Ransom drily observed. "But there is nothing I can do. I'd need an army of several thousand men to drive out the French and push them back north across Lake Champlain. And at the moment, I fear what the French command has in store for Fort Edward. That is my immediate concern."

"And mine," Stark said. "Maybe we need to get those French marines worried about something other than Fort Edward."

"Oh . . . what?"

Stark placed his foot across the tail of the lake, leaving an imprint upon the French territory. "The French and their Abenaki allies want a war, let's give it to them, Major," said John Stark, his voice seductively soft. But he was speaking words of death not love. He drew his foot across "the tail of the lake" and obliterated both forts in the process.

"Rangers, eh? A separate company, answering to you and Rogers." Ransom pursed his lips a moment and absentmindedly chewed on the inside of his mouth as he considered the proposal. It was a gamble all right. But things could not possibly get any worse, could they? "Tell me then, once more. In detail. Exactly what sort of command do you have in mind?"

"Trust me," said Stark. "It will be like nothing you've ever seen."

The Leaf-Falling Moon

1757

"If you find the enemy encamped near the banks of a river or lake, which you imagine they will attempt to cross for their security upon being attacked, leave a detachment of your party on the opposite shore to receive them, while, with the remainder, you surprise them, having them between you and the lake or river."

Benoit Turcotte wanted a woman. And he had wanted a woman ever since leaving the settlement of Fort Saint Frederick, when he and his crew of stouthearted rivermen had been ordered by Captain Lucien Barbarat to proceed on to Fort Carillon and refrain from indulging themselves in the taverns and crib dens standing cheek to jowl in an estuary south of the waterfront.

The local citizens were glad for the constant comings and goings of the freighters, the steady stream of trappers and Indians, and for the presence of the French marines stationed in the fort. Such traffic filled the purses of the merchants with gold and provided a livelihood for the farmers and craftsmen, all of whom turned a blind eye when it came to the vice-ridden establishments spawned by the brisk commerce.

"On to Fort Carillon," said Turcotte, mimicking the effeminate French officer with the cold blue eyes. Standing at the stern of the bateau, a shallow draft boat manned by nine rivermen who propelled the craft against the current with oar and pole, Benoit Turcotte kept a firm grip on the steering oar, his coarse hands the color of the weathered oak. *"Mais oui,* our brothers and sisters to the south cannot go another day without salt pork and dried apples and flint!" The freighter spat on the floor of the bateau. He could sense his crew watching him and did not doubt they agreed with him. He was certain Captain Barbarat and his aides would find time for a taste of wine and a lady's caress. Officers never went without. But there was not a man in uniform that could have endure the rugged life of a *voyageur.* Of that Turcotte was certain.

Yes, he wanted a woman. He quietly appraised the eight men that made up his crew. Ha, they all did. And five miles from Fort Carillon, fortune provided. Here along the rocky lakeshore, where the tail of the lake angled off toward Lake George, the forests of pine, oak, maple and birch grew down to the water's edge. Back beyond the trees a network of shallow caves and overhanging shale ledges had provided shelter for Abenaki hunting parties since time immemorial. But a new resident had taken over one of the natural caverns and hung a wide wooden sign down by the shore for all the rivermen to see.

Corette's La Chute.

It was a natural landing, a perfect site. And as Benoit Turcotte and the *voyageurs* perused the cavern in the trees, three lovely *femmes* strolled from the shadowy recesses and hurried down the shaded path to the water's edge where they called out to the men in the bateau and urged them to come ashore and pass the time in song and drink and perhaps a dalliance or two or ten.

"Sacre bleu, will you look at that?" another of the men spoke up, leaning forward on his oar. He gestured with his stocking cap and then waved at the woman who had just lifted the hem of her skirt to permit them a glimpse of her ankles. She wore no cotton stockings and was a comely lass with long, thick, fiery red tresses and oval features like fine rare china. She must be new at her trade, he decided, because there was a freshness about her, a virginal spring

to her step as she waved to the river men and invited them
to join her and her sisters.

"*Bonne journee, mes chers. Que les jeunes hommes
êtes beaux.*" The woman's voice carried to them across the
sun-dappled surface of the lake. It was a sweet sound, like
the wind in the hemlocks or dewdrops on lady slippers, lo,
the pale pastel sky captured in a water bead. "Good day,
dear ones. What handsome lads you are. *Jouez avec mes
amies et moi.* Come play with my friends and me."

Turcotte glanced over his shoulder. "*Que dites-vous,
des hommes?* What do you say, men? Captain Barbarat is
twenty miles behind downriver. His orders cannot reach
us." That settled the matter. The rivermen cheered and began to pull in earnest for the landing. Fort Carillon could
wait, as long as they reached the settlement by sunset,
where was the harm?

As Turcotte looked on, eyes aglow with excitement,
the other two ladies, both of them taller than the first who
had called to them, waved their kerchiefs and beckoned the
freighters who took lustful note of how tightly the women's
bodices were laced about their abundant bosoms and how
they flaunted their charms, these wantons in their drawstring skirts.

"Pull, my brothers. Bring us quickly to shore," said the
man at the stern. The oarsmen did not need to be told what
to do, they could hear music now. Someone was playing a
fife within the cavern. And a couple of men who appeared
to be the proprietors emerged to see what all the commotion
was about and on seeing the bateau, quickly set a pair of
oaken kegs on the wooden tables in the shade beneath the
ledge. Turcotte imagined the interior of the cave provided
entertainment of a more intimate nature. M'lady would
have her boudoir set to the rear.

"Pull on those oars, lads, pull I say for I have a powerful thirst."

"Drink can wait," said the man closest to Turcotte.
Claude Lanyon at the first oar lock had his eyes on the
ladies. He looked as if he were ready to charge across the

water. The man all but vaulted over the three-foot side of the boat.

"Careful, M'sieur Lanyon. Will you walk upon the water? I say do not. After all, you are a Frenchman, not God," Turcotte merrily exclaimed as he guided the thirty-foot-long craft up on to the riverbank. As the oarsmen clambered out of the boat, the harlots retreated up the slope, laughing and carrying on like the flirts they were. Depending on their age and disposition, Benoit Turcotte was of a mind to try them all.

The brisk October air was pungent with the smell of wood smoke, spilled rum, tobacco, and the mouthwatering aroma of frying fish. He wrinkled his nostrils and caught the scent of lilac and rosewater. Turcotte vaulted over the side of the bateau and helped his crew drag the boat farther up onto the muddy embankment. Then with a whoop and a holler the *voyageurs* charged up the slope, heading right for the cavern and the three women.

Turcotte was squat and thick-skinned, slightly bowlegged, weathered as an old oar, with a marked fondness for rum and whores, the taller the better and he headed straight for the longest-limbed lass who coyly avoided his crude approach. Benoit frowned, struggled to keep his temper under control, swallowed his pride and continued to pursue the harlot who had caught his fancy. "*Bon matin,* my cherub. Do not seek to protect that maidenhood we both know you no longer possess. Come here, my little cauliflower, do not be shy. I'll wager you have a pretty mouth and could suck *La Chute* dry." He began to unbutton his breeches. "See what I have for you, my sweet." And still she turned away. "See the gift I have brought you?" He searched inside his coarse spun cotton shirt and produced a five sol silver coin from a small leather pouch dangling against his chest.

"Five sol piece just for you, my temptress," Turcotte said in a husky voice. "My but you are a tall one, come and drink with me and afterwards perhaps we shall go alone, you and I, and enjoy one another's company." By heaven, she had a stride, this one. He envisioned her long legs wrapped about his waist. The fantasy spurred the freighter's efforts and he hurried to catch up to her. The effort left him out of breath. But determination and lust fueled his final steps. She was waiting, her back to him, standing abreast of the kegs. Good, at least he did not have to walk far to get drunk.

"Let me see you, my sweet, give us a look at what I am paying for." He caught up with her and placed a hand on her shoulder and felt a surprisingly well-muscled torso beneath the chemise she wore.

"How's this?" the harlot replied in a deep voice and spun about.

Turcotte gasped and staggered back on his heels. "She" sported a dark growth of chin whiskers, sideburns, a thick, low brow and muscled chest. Sergeant Tom Strode, on loan to the Rangers by order of Major Ransom and assigned to learn the ways of these Indian fighters, hauled out a large-bore flintlock pistol from under the folds of his skirt, cocked the weapon and sighted down the barrel.

In an instant, the party of *voyageurs* was surrounded by Rangers in dyed green buckskins who materialized out of the undergrowth with their rifles leveled at Turcotte and his crew. A veritable mountain of a man strode forward and bowed, sweeping his Scottish bonnet across his powerful chest. A massive-looking dog trotted out and took up a position alongside the Ranger. The mastiff growled, the sound came from deep in the animal's chest, primal and menacing.

Turcotte gulped. He had heard of a man like this, from when he last traded among the Abenaki. A name leaped to mind. Johnny Stark? Yes, it had to be, look at the size of him. There were rumors Stark and his Rangers had intercepted war parties and struck at French patrols along Lake George, but he had never come up this far north. Lake Champlain with its chain of forts and Abenaki villages was considered well beyond his reach and uncontested territory.

Not anymore.

Turcotte shrank back from Stark and glanced about at the three "women," only one of whom was *la femme*. Molly Page, who had called to the *voyageurs* from the shore, brandished a brace of small-bore yet lethal-looking pistols and even now held Claude Lanyon, her would-be paramour, at bay.

Poor Locksley Barlow appeared mortified to be dressed as a harlot. However, the bearded English sergeant who had caught Turcotte's fancy seemed somewhat resigned to his fate. Benoit Turcotte's shoulders sagged, and he was filled with genuine disgust at the way he had fallen for the trap. With a sigh and a shake of his head, the man swung about and searched Stark's icy gaze for a trace of mercy.

The towering figure softly uttered a command and the other Rangers immediately fell upon their captives and disarmed them. The mastiff continued to snarl as if the beast was daring the *voyageurs* to make a break for the lake.

"Welcome to *Corrette's La Chute, mes amis*," Stark said, his voice cutting through the sweet cool air.

He did not say "friends" as if he meant it.

Stark hadn't been able to find a dress that fit him, for which he silently gave thanks. Or else his comrades at arms might have forced him to share in their embarrassment. He kept to the trees, in a grove off to the side of the growing collection of bateaux drawn up on the shore and watched in bemused silence as his men had their fun at the expense of Barlow and the British sergeant.

"By heaven, you lads is pretty as a paddock of newborn calves," Moses Shoemaker cackled as he bowed courteously and doffed his tricorn. Locksley Barlow scowled as he tugged on the laces of his French bodice.

Molly Page arrived from hurrying down the footpath that led from the shadowy interior of the cave. "More boats are coming, m'ladies," she exclaimed. The red-haired young woman stepped up to her recalcitrant "sisters," Barlow and Strode, and helped them with their disguises, quickly adjusting their bonnets and tightening the laces on their bodices once more, being sure to emphasize the swell of the knotted cotton padding that gave the illusion that each man was a well-endowed woman.

"Blast it, Molly," Locksley complained. "I cannot take a proper breath."

"But can you dance?" she quipped and pinched his cheek. Molly glanced back toward the grove of red maple and caught Johnny Stark admiring her from afar. Realizing he had been discovered, Stark shifted his attention to the lake and pretended to study the distant flotilla of half a dozen bateaux approaching from the north, obviously another shipment bound for Fort Carillon. She curtsied and waved a kerchief that she kept tucked in her bodice between her breasts. Johnny sheepishly acknowledged by touching his Scottish bonnet and then disappeared through the afternoon shadows, up the slope toward the cave where better than thirty French crewmen and freighters had been bound and left to their own devices under the watchful glare of a single well-armed Ranger.

Locksley Barlow and Tom Strode continued to complain about their ordeal. They looked enviously at their friends, this company of Rangers all of whom wore garb similar to Johnny Stark's; a Scottish bonnet, buckskin shirt, deerskin moccasins, and breeches dyed a forest green, carrying their rifles and hatchets, powder and shot.

"God help me," said Sergeant Tom Strode. The Englishman had been grudgingly accepted by the rest, after being posted to the Rangers. He would have preferred to be back at Fort Edward. But what was a soldier to do? Major Ransom had ordered him to observe the colonials and learn their skills in the event the major established the Regiment's own company of king's Rangers.

"If there's trouble and one of these bloody Frenchmen sends me under," Strode said aloud for his companions to hear and take note, "I charge every man here to strip me naked and not plant me in these geegaws."

"I dare say you would scare the angels into perdition

dressed as you are," Sam Oday drily commented, perched upon a log, wooden fife in hand. Oday, along with Robert Rogers and four other men, had donned some of the clothes they had taken off their captives. With a half-dozen shallow draft boats drawn up on the shore, the scene might look suspicious without some of the *voyageurs* milling about. Sam Oday and another of the company, a broad-beamed, corn-fed youth named Danny Dulin began to play a merry little tune upon their wooden flutes.

"I dare say, Mister Strode, if you want to gambol with me you might have plucked your chin whiskers," Moses cackled. The old graybeard hopped about and danced a jig and tried to catch Strode by the arm but the sergeant pulled away. "Don't be shy, love, or you'll not receive a single ha'penny from this child."

"Lay hand on me again, you old sot, and I'll gut you like a codfish," Strode growled, slipping a hand to the hilt of a knife he kept within his lace-trimmed sleeve.

"Quit complaining and start tempting," Robert Rogers hissed beneath his breath. He motioned for Shoemaker, Oday, and the rest of the disguised Rangers to join him around the campfire they'd built on the lakeshore. He called for them to sing and laugh and carry on as if they were drunk on rum and good fortune. "Come on, lads, we've just delivered our goods to Fort Carillon and come away with money in our pouches. And here's the ladies who will lighten us of our cares and our purses." At a glance, they'd appear to be counterparts of the Frenchmen in the flotilla of boats slowly ascending the lake.

Sam Oday and Danny Dulin continued to play. Some of the men began to kick up their heels, leap about and swill from their clay jugs. From all appearances, they had drawn their boats ashore and planned to bide a few well spent hours in the company of these strumpets. Molly took Robert Rogers and dragged him off to one side and forced him to dance. Moses grabbed Locksley Barlow and pulled him aside. Barlow grimaced, but having resigned himself to this ruse hours ago, tried to play the part to the best of his ability. However, every time Shoemaker tried to whirl him about, the younger man would trip over the lace-trimmed hem of his skirt.

Johnny Stark raised a spyglass and inspected the shore camp. Everything looked as it should, the bateaux were drawn up on the muddy shore. He had to grin as Rogers's men, the pretend *voyageurs*, dragged the reluctant "harlots" out toward the fire and forced them to dance as they played their fifes and clapped their hands.

"You'll have to sleep with one eye open after this, Johnny Stark," one of the company muttered from behind him. It was Cassius Fargo, a dangerous man in a time when such were needed. Stark had been surprised when Fargo offered to don the green buckskins, for the man made no attempt to conceal his animosity. But a common enemy often made for unlikely allies.

"I always do," Stark replied. He was keenly aware Cassius still blamed him in part for the death of his brother. The Fargos were an odd bunch, bred by a cruel, Bible-toting old seadog who had driven his wife to an early grave and instilled in his offspring a deep sense of kinship and blind loyalty to family.

Stark remembered some years back how Old Man Fargo died when a well collapsed in on him. His sons had left their father entombed and simply started a new well on the other side of their farmhouse and moved on. They were a peculiar bunch indeed. Stark could feel the eyes of the man, boring into his back.

"Best you Green Mountain boys fan out through the trees," he called out. "We will take them by surprise and leave them with their companions in the cave." He took care to add, "But if there's trouble, hold your fire till Molly's out of harm's way."

"She joined as one of us, she ought to take the same chances," Cassius muttered, easing back into the shadows.

Stark swung about and faced the man. "And she does. But someone cuts down on the *voyageurs* and brings her to harm, they will have to answer to me."

"I have been told she can take care of herself," Cassius remarked.

"So I hear," Stark noted, his tone of voice adding import to the response. And Cassius wondered if Molly had spoken to anyone of that time back in August when Fargo had followed the woman into the woods. He met Stark's cool gaze, but the big man was as hard to read as a bloody heathen. Fargo smiled.

"Do not worry about me, Major Stark." He licked his thumb and then moistened the sight on his rifle barrel. "I always hit what I aim at."

He eased behind the trunk of a sugar maple, its leaves a scarlet canopy overhead. Stark felt a prickle up and down his spine as he turned his back on the man. He checked the rest of his company. The Rangers were concealed in the emerald shadows of a forest awash with the brilliant colors of fall, leaf-laden branches of gold, scarlet, rust red, Lincoln green, dark browns, a tapestry of trees gloriously arrayed across the hills and along the path leading up from the water's edge. Stark crouched alongside the mastiff among some tall green fronds that somehow found enough sunlight to thrive in the forest. The mastiff growled and glanced over its shoulder at Cassius Fargo. Stark scratched Duchess behind her ears.

"Yeah, I don't like him either," he told the dog. To their right and farther up the slope was the cave itself, that deep low-roofed depression in the cliff, a gaping hollow where the low, wide shelf of granite jutted from the earth to create a natural chamber.

Here came Rogers and his disguised companions trailing up the path toward the barrels of rum and ale they had set in full view upon a pair of wooden trestles below a second makeshift sign across which they had scrawled the name *La Chute*.

The ruse had worked for the better part of the day. They had captured six crews, taken six bateaux loaded with supplies for the French forts. Lake Champlain, the rivers, and the surrounding hills and mountains were home to the

Abenaki, the Iroquois, and to French settlers from every walk of life. Much like the English, some came to put down roots and build, others to take what they could and move on.

Stark studied the approaching boats. The ruse had worked again. But he felt a twinge of misgiving. There were four boats, two large craft, two smaller; he made a rough estimate of another twenty-five *voyageurs*. That many could mean trouble all at once. And they were almost to the shore.

He shifted his stance, rose up from the fronds, and maneuvered the looking glass until Molly filled the eyepiece. She wore a white drawstring skirt over a calico chemise. Her bodice was French cut, sleeveless, pink-and-white striped, and clung to her shapely form. By heaven, the red-haired lass was a fair sight. A man would have to be made of stone not to appreciate the rounded contours of her lithe figure. He'd grown accustomed to seeing her in buckskins as they had been on the trail for almost three weeks. He had to grin and then glanced aside at the mastiff.

"That is some woman," he muttered. "To look that good and still be able to shoot the eye out of a horsefly at twenty paces." Duchess lifted her sad, seamed face and stared balefully at Stark, then snorted and crouched down on her belly.

The four bateaux pulled up on the shore, their crew spilled over the side and hauled their boats safely up onto shore then came charging up the slope, through sunlight and shifting shadows, as if each man were running a race to see who would have the first draft of ale, who the first romp "in bushy park." Everything was going according to plan. And then it all fell apart.

"Alarme!"

"Damn," Stark muttered, looking in the direction of the cave. "Shut those Frenchmen up," he muttered.

"Alarme! Alarme!"

A chorus of warning shouts continued to reverberate

from the recesses of the cave. The prisoners within were willing to risk being shot to warn their companions. Several of the *voyageurs* on the path drew up sharply, caught off guard. Their hands dropped to their pistols while the rest of the boatmen slowed to a walk, then stopped and exchanged glances, undecided. A few paces away were the women and the kegs of rum and the promise of a dalliance. But the cries issuing from the cave could not be ignored.

Stark stepped into view.

The *voyageurs* looked somewhat stunned at the sight of him. He leveled Old Abraham and ordered the lot of them to surrender. Locksley, Strode, Molly Page, and the men disguised as *voyageurs* produced their weapons and took cover behind the tables. The rest of the Ranger company rose from hiding and spread out behind Stark, their rifles cocked and primed.

"Drop your knives and pistols, no one will come to harm," Stark shouted, his voice cutting through the stillness that permeated the clearing in front of the cave. One of the *voyageurs* shrugged and tossed his pistol aside on the path. Unfortunately the pistol discharged, gouging a hole in the trampled earth.

Stark never knew if the mastiff had been startled by the gunshot or acted out of some subtle instinct, but the beast lurched against his leg, nudging the big man aside just as a shot rang out from behind Stark and a lead ball fanned the air and clipped his ear as it whirred past. Stark winced, ducked instinctively, saw one of the *voyageurs* directly in front of him twist on his heels, fire into the air, and topple over backwards.

"No!" Stark shouted. But it was too late. His voice was lost in the roar of gunfire.

14

"Burn the boats. Set them ablaze. We must quit this place. No telling who heard all the noise," Stark ordered. A black pall of gunsmoke shrouded the path. The melee had lasted but a few minutes, long enough for men to die and for those who didn't, to toss aside their pistols and surrender. Molly emerged from a cluster of birch trees that had screened her while she discarded the dress and donned her buckskins. She looked relieved but not nearly as much as Barlow and Strode who swore oaths that hell itself would freeze over before they ever suffered the indignities of a bodice again.

The bodies of the freighters who had been killed in the brief but murderous exchange of gunfire had been dragged off to the side of the path. The survivors, a little more than half the number of men who had come ashore, had been bound and left in the cave along with those who had risked their lives to warn them of the danger, men like Benoit Turcotte and his companions who were the first crew to be taken in by the ruse.

The path and clearing reeked of powder smoke and drying blood. The stillness that followed was broken by the hurried exchanges among the Rangers as they gathered what supplies they needed and loaded their canoes. Robert Rogers approached from the lake that he and several of the men were preparing to set out upon. He cradled his rifle in the crook of his arms as he drew abreast of Molly Page and Big John Stark.

"Best we portage around Fort Carillon and head into

Lake George. With any luck we can make it before night-fall; if not, by moonlight then."

"Luck," Stark grumbled. "Poor luck that pistol discharging." Molly leaned in to Stark and standing on her tiptoes, reached up to dab the blood from Stark's ear where the rifle ball had notched his flesh. "Ow!"

"You've been wounded."

"I knew that before you began to torment me," he grumbled. "But no matter, I have another ear."

"Well you don't have another head. What a silly thing, to step out like that."

"I thought if I showed myself they might surrender."

"Better listen to Molly," Rogers said. The three watched as flames sprang up from the bateaux. Moses Shoemaker and half a dozen men had set them ablaze. "Shame to waste such good boats. But we don't have the men to carry them across country. But what of the men in the cave?"

Before Stark could reply, Cassius Fargo joined in the discussion. He looked as if he regretted the French surrender. "I say the French spared none of ours at William Henry," Cassius Fargo exclaimed. "And no one spared my brother. You remember that I warrant, John Stark." He busily rammed powder and shot down his rifle barrel. "Let them suffer the same fate." Fargo gestured toward the cave. "I can set a charge off and bring the ceiling down and even bury them for you, all Christian-like."

"We will leave them. Someone will be along," Stark said. He leaned on Old Abraham, his gaze sweeping over the path, the clearing, and finally the mouth of the cave.

"Leave them! The devil you say," Cassius scowled. "What say the rest of the company?"

"I did not ask them," Stark replied. His gaze hardened. "There has been enough killing today." He reached out and caught Fargo by the arm. "Robert Rogers and I lead this company or we end it right here and you make your own way back to Fort Edward."

Fargo searched the faces of the two men, and could

clearly see they meant exactly what they said. He had no wish to leave the company, especially not in French and Indian territory. He turned on his heels and almost tripped over the mastiff that had wandered up behind him.

"Tell your dog to get out of my way," Fargo snapped.

"She has her own mind and does what she wants to. I'd step around her, but you do what you want."

Cassius's face grew flush with anger. He aimed a kick at the mastiff. Duchess leaped to her feet, bared her teeth and loosed a savage series of barks that forced Cassius to jump out of harm's way. The animal's slobber spattered his breeches as the man made a wide arc around the mastiff. Fargo lost no time in retreating down the path to the canoes.

Duchess settled herself directly in the middle of the path again. "Get out of the way," Stark said, grinning, and slapped the beast across the rump with his Scottish bonnet. The animal jumped, startled, and then cleared the trail. Stark turned to Molly and Rogers. "I'll be along in a minute," he told them. They nodded and started back to the lake while Stark continued on alone into the shelter of the cave. The air was cooler here and the light dim as he ambled toward the back wall where the *voyageurs* were arranged against the face of the cliff, their arms bound behind them.

"I have burned your boats," he said. A chorus of groans and curses rose up at this announcement. "Your friends in Fort Carillon or some Abenaki war party will probably spot the smoke and come to investigate. If not, then you must free yourselves as best you can. With some effort you can loosen your bonds." He felt their eyes on him. The Rangers had suffered only a few minor wounds. The *voyageurs* had lost several of their own. He knew the feeling. *Let them hate me. But let them fear me as well.*

"Captain Barbarat will have his marines after you, *monsieur*," Benoit Turcotte spoke up. "He conquered Fort William Henry, and he will hunt you down for this."

"He won't have far to look." His expression hardened. "You have not seen the last of John Stark."

He lingered for a moment, to let the gravity of his words sink in. The war had come to them. Then he turned and left them alone, with their thoughts and his warning. So the Frenchmen's commander's name was Barbarat.

I'll remember.

Out of the gloom and into the fierce light of day, Stark paused, taking in the sight of the swaying branches, the sentinel trees, the glories of autumn above the blood-patched sod. His left ear began to throb. He winced as he touched the raw flesh where the tip had been shot away. He could still feel the heat of the rifle ball that had clipped him as it whirred past on its way to a *voyageur's* heart. Someone directly behind Stark, one of his own company, had possibly saved his life. He noticed Cassius Fargo, standing by the water's edge, framed against a backdrop of leaping flames and coiling black smoke.

Or tried to kill him.

15

Above the treetops, broad formations of Canadian geese and smaller speedier little clusters of emerald-winged teals raced southward across an azure sky, following some secret invisible trail among the clouds, a course etched in their untamed hearts by the whims of nature and the unfathomable call of the great beyond. But the workings of creation and the miracle of southern migrations were for another day, when men like Stark might have the time to ponder his own connection to the world of the hart and the hawk.

Johnny Stark and Robert Rogers had pushed the Rangers unmercifully. Rogers, although tentatively in command, often drifted back to the rear of the column to check for any sign of pursuit. Both men were equally determined to put as much distance as possible between the Ranger company and the site of their latest raid. Keeping to the opposite bank where they concealed their canoes for a return foray, the buckskin-clad raiders passed the looming walls of Fort Carillon under cover of night. Mid-morning found them a half-day's march from *La Chute*. It was the kind of forced march a Ranger must make or be left behind.

Press on . . . and on.

A couple of miles from the wooded landing where they had concealed four bateaux among the reeds and rushes fringing Lake George, the mastiff, trotting ahead of the column, began to whine and paw the earth, turning up clods of dirt, and decayed leaves and gray rocks.

John Stark hurried forward to investigate. Duchess had cut across some recent *Injun* sign, mocassin tracks along a deer path. Now the homeward trek took a different turn. Stark and Rogers drifted off to confer apart from Molly and the company of Rangers.

The column waited. Moses Shoemaker found an outcropping of granite and stretched out against it, luxuriating in a patch of sunlight like an old hound. Tom Strode, the fisherman's son, studied the lake. "Wonder if a man could feed his family on the catch from yonder pond?" he mused aloud.

"The only way to find out is to shuck that red coat of yours and clear you a home site," said Sam Oday.

The British sergeant glanced over at his scarred companion. The man had lost family, suffered torture, and still he remained. Why? Because the frontier was his home. "Tell me, mate, were your dreams worth the sacrifice?"

"Better to suffer and dream than sleep without hope. My wife and dear daughters died free. And when my time comes, so will I. There's not many in this world who can claim that."

Molly walked up alongside Oday and placed her hand on his shoulder. "Well said. You speak for all of us. Bless you, Sam."

"Be careful now, Molly, or your apt to see Judgment Day a spinster," Shoemaker spoke up, lightening the moment. "Best you quit trailing that big rooster yonder and share my blanket," Moses added with a mischievous grin.

"Or mine," said Locksley Barlow, gnawing a strip of jerked venison he'd retrieved from his possibles bag.

"Or mine," another of the company called out. And laughter rippled through the ranks as the reply was echoed by each of the men in turn.

Molly scowled and shook her head and turned away lest they catch her smile. She casually observed the two men standing apart from the column. Johnny Stark and Robert Rogers were locked in a heated debate with the latter becoming more agitated. But at the last they seemed to reach an accord, tempers cooled and a short while later the two men rejoined the patrol.

Rogers announced he would take half the contingent and continue on to the boats, for it was important to reach Fort Edward as soon as possible and give a report as to the success of the raid and the increased French activity around Fort Carillon. He called for volunteers to accompany Stark who intended to follow this recent trail that wound like a brown ribbon through the trees and across a hilltop.

Molly Page and thirteen of the Rangers cast their lot with Stark. Sam Oday, Shoemaker, Barlow, Strode, each man in turn stepping across to side with John Stark. The last man to volunteer was Cassius Fargo, which surprised everyone. However, Molly frowned and took note. Johnny had already been wounded once. It was not going to happen again if she had any say in the matter. Stark though, accepted one and all without question and with a wave and a "Good luck" to Major Rogers, trotted off down the trail with Duchess in the lead. Stark had a mighty stride and Molly and the rest had to hury to keep up.

Press on....

By late afternoon, with thunderheads gathering on the southern horizon, the company trudged wearily up a steep, heavily-wooded bluff and through a stand of curly maple that overlooked the deep blue waters of the lake.

Nearing the crest, Stark called a halt and crept to the edge of the promontory and waited. The great mastiff stretched out at his side, tail wagging and striking the ground with a thump ... thump ... thump. Molly knelt by Stark and the mastiff and scratched the dog behind the ears. The woman was thankful for the breather although she refused to let on how spongy her legs were becoming.

"I am grateful Robert took another route," she said.

"Oh?" Stark replied, searching the distance. The rest of the company held back, stretching out upon the sward, relaxing in sunlight and shadow. "Rogers is a good man."

"I know that," she continued. "Just of late he seems a mite quarrelsome. I swear the man has traded in his good Christian name for 'Major.' "

Stark chuckled. "When we were a provincial militia it

didn't mean so much. Now that the Regiment has made it official and put him in command, Robert does set quite a store by the title."

"And you'd think he had gone and hugged a porcupine the way he carries on when you don't give him his due." She had become aware of a growing tension between the two friends, especially whenever Johnny questioned Rogers's lead. He looked across at her and grinned. Duchess snorted and rumbled. Molly and John reached out together to stroke the dog's ears, their hands met and lingered. Johnny turned a bit red and became flustered and returned his attention to the trail ahead.

Oh, but that was Johnny Stark, he marched to a different drummer. From the moment she laid eyes on the big rascal better than half a dozen years ago, she had loved him. He wasn't handsome like Locksley Barlow or a wealthy landowner like Robert Rogers or even Uncle Ephraim, but there was something special, something unique about Johnny that appealed to her.

"Men like Robert place a great value in the trappings of rank and breeding," she drily observed.

"Yes, and more's the pity. When it comes to staying alive out here, lineage is about as useless as teats on a bull. Gold lace and brass buttons never helped a man keep his topknot."

And Stark was a survivor. Like the Abenaki who first trod these thousand hills and traversed their maze of streams and rivers, John Stark had learned the language of the untamed places; his soul soared among the trees and on the wings of the wind.

This was the kind of man Molly Page chose to love and the Rangers would follow, through hell or high water. *So farewell, Robert Rogers, hurry on to Fort Edward, let this man be*, thought Molly, crouching so close as to be in his shadow. *Let him go his own way and search the hills.*

Stark tried to concentrate on the hills and the forest but he could feel Molly's heart reaching out to him. Bless her, but the lass was proving to be a distraction. Perhaps they ought to head on out then and take their chances among the trees. Just as he was prepared to wave the company forward, three crows exploded from the treetops and swooped upward, their great black wings pummeling the air. Something . . . or someone had startled them from their roost. Duchess growled.

"Easy," Johnny muttered as he scanned the forest floor. Seconds later he caught a glimpse of an advancing war party on the march toward the lakeshore. He glanced over his shoulder at the remainder of his command, raised his right arm, opened and closed his hand three times and then made a fist. The signal was unmistakable. The Rangers scrambled to take cover and prepare an ambush.

Molly, Moses Shoemaker, Locksley Barlow, and the rest of the men quickly scattered about the fringes of the little glade, where the trail cut through the small clearing. Molly moved through the underbrush as effortlessly as a shadow. At first she had considered fighting alongside the man she loved. Then another thought came to mind. Back at the Tail of the Lake, during the skirmish with the *voyageurs*, a rifle ball had nicked Stark's ear and come close to taking off his head. Had one of their own tried to kill him?

Possibly. And they might try again. But who? Well, Johnny Stark wasn't the only one who had a premonition about such things. Molly Page knew just the spot for her and it wasn't alongside her man.

16

*Y*ou're a piss-poor marksman," Ford Fargo whispered in his brother's ear. At least that's what Cassius heard, like the merest rustle of a passing breeze. Ghosts are like that, easily mistaken for the cry of a loon, the wind in the branches of the tamarack, a leaf scratching across a shuttered window, a laugh heard in the dark or worse, at brightest noon . . . when there's no one there. "*But then you was never my equal, Cassius, not with a smoke pole, and not with the women.*"

Cassius closed his eyes and shook his head but the voice remained. The dead continued to harangue the living. He wasn't surprised. After all, they'd both heard their father call to them on stormy nights, his tortured cry rising from the spot where the well collapsed on him. "*I would have made that high and mighty bastard John Stark pay in blood had it been you he got killed. Made him pay long before now, brother, but you always needed time to work up to things.*"

Cassius Fargo stood beneath the shading branches of a maple tree. Like all the others dotting the heavily wooded hillsides above Lake George, the tree was gloriously bedecked in its autumn raiments. Leaves of scarlet and gold littered the good earth, gave the impression that some royal procession of nobles had passed this way and left fragments of their royal robes in its wake.

"Hold your fire till we see the whites of their eyes," Stark whispered as he made his way around the clearing. Fargo's features wrinkled into a scowl. Damn if the big bastard didn't make a proper target.

"I'll hold alright," Cassius Fargo thought, determined to bide his time. He waited until Stark darted behind an outcropping of lichen-covered gray stone large enough to conceal his great size. Then Cassius made his way through the maples until he found a spot that offered a direct line of sight. The long hunter would have to show himself to shoot, he'd have to rise up and reveal at least his upper torso, and this time Fargo wouldn't miss.

Fargo was confident and in his mind's eye could even envision the attempt in its entirety. He could picture the Rangers as they open fire, the Abenaki drop, scatter, driven back, reeling; for a moment all is confusion, cries and gunshots and no one notices when Cassius Fargo takes his shot. Stark claws at his chest, drops to his knees, his mouth framed in a silent scream. . . .

Suddenly the would-be assassin detected someone moving up behind him, glanced around in alarm half expecting to encounter his brother's ghostly form joining him beneath the sheltering trees. His thick features paled and a gasp escaped his lips. Then he recognized Molly Page as she made her way through the trees, keeping in the shadows until she crouched within a yard of Fargo. Her weathered buckskins were a close fit. The brute hungrily eyed the curve of her hips and the creamy whiteness of her throat.

"I hadn't expected you to fight at my side, Molly Page," he said, keeping his voice low.

"I'll make my stand where I'm needed."

"Maybe you are worried for me after all, eh?"

"I'd hate to see you have trouble with your aim," Molly warned, barely above a whisper.

"Lay beneath me and I'll prove my *smoke pole* can find its target, every time."

Molly shrugged and slid over to him. Fargo checked the perimeter, found they were adequately concealed from view. He could not believe his good fortune. He reached for the redheaded woman as her right hand shot out and placed a knife against his throat.

"See here, Cassius Fargo. Do not talk to me as you

would some tavern wench or I'll carve out your tongue for
its offense." Fargo made it clear he was not about to argue
with the point of her knife. She nodded and returned the
blade to its sheath then took up her rifle. "And mind your
aim," she once more cautioned, "for Isaac will be watching
you." She patted the rifle barrel for added effect.

Fargo scowled and turned his attention toward the trail.
He could still feel the kiss of her steel against his jugular.
His thoughts began to simmer over like boiled milk and
left him troubled and seething with anger. No woman had
the right to speak to him in such a tone. Someone needed
to teach Molly Page her place. Someone. . . .

The Abenaki war party appeared on the trail about fifty
yards downhill. Stark estimated about twenty warriors, perhaps a few more; he did not bother to make an accurate
count and chance revealing his position. Let the warriors
approach undisturbed. Stark crouched and rested against the
speckled gray rock that provided concealment and protection.

Duchess began to growl, sensing the war party. The
mastiff raised her jowly head and sniffed, her black face
becoming even more wrinkled as she tested the air. Stark
placed a hand on the animal's back and she stilled at his
touch. He glanced over at the British sergeant, Tom Strode,
and Moses Shoemaker with whom he shared the outcropping. Both men checked to see if their rifles were primed
and the flints properly set.

"Leastways you've not dressed me up like a tart,"
Strode softly grumbled, scratching his bushy sideburns.

Stark had to grin. He glanced past his companions and
checked what he could see of the company. Blast it all,
where had she taken off to?

"Molly's across the way," Moses whispered, grinning
at the big man, reading his thoughts. The old Indian fighter
would never reveal that Molly had charged him with watching over the long hunter. If Stark ever found out, Moses

figured he'd be hung out to dry by the big lout. So he feigned innocence and prepared himself for battle, placing a brace of pistols on the ground underfoot. "I saw her plop down by Cassius Fargo."

Stark shook his head. What was she up to? He touched his bandaged left ear. The wound had already coagulated. "Fargo . . ." he muttered beneath his breath. "Now there's a bad seed."

"You'll have to settle with him one of these days younker. Better sooner than later," Shoemaker added in a low voice.

Stark nodded and eased around the edge of the outcropping and was rewarded with a rare sight, a column of Atoan's men, carrying the spoils of a recent raid, slaughtered hens and hogs, bolts of cloth, silver trinkets and blankets. Nary a one of the braves suspected the trap that Stark was about to spring just . . .

about . . .

now!

Big John Stark set his worries aside, rose up so that all his men could see him along with the column of Abenaki warriors fresh from their depredations. The buckskin-clad braves appeared stunned at the sight of the towering figure who seemed to have materialized out of the emerald shadows. Tabid, distinguished from the rest of the Abenaki by the red woolen soldier's coat he favored, reacted on instinct and raised his musket.

"Let 'em have it!" Stark roared. He fired "Old Abraham" from the hip while at the same instant he raised his hunting horn to his lips. Flame blossomed from the muzzle as the charge sent a .50-caliber lead ball spinning through the air to shatter Tabid's breastbone and tear through his vitals. Duchess sprang from concealment. The mastiff charged through the rippling gunfire and dragged another of the warriors to the ground.

Tabid, flung backwards on impact, fired his musket skyward, half twisted in midair, then collapsed, mortally wounded. He slammed his shoulders against the hard ground, heard the thunder of battle erupt, heard the war horn's blare, watched through a darkening red haze as his companions fell before a volley of rifle fire that erupted from all sides. Dying, he recognized his killer.

And somehow . . . it helped.

Lobal crouched well back from the clearing, rooted in place as surely as the white pines that concealed him. He was ashamed, knowing that his friend Kasak would have flung himself into battle, despite the fact that it was already lost. But Kasak's father, the Grand Sachem, Atoan would not have blundered into the white-eyes' trap to begin with. Lobal, who was young and often courageous to a fault when he was surrounded by his peers, suddenly went weak at the knees in the face of his own demise. If he had not left the war party to gather some blackberries there would be one more Abenaki among the dead and dying on the hillside.

Tabid was the first to fall but several more quickly joined him in death. The Rangers charged from the trees, firing their weapons and howling like demons and the worst was *Kiwaskwek*, the beast of the Green Mountains, John Stark. The towering figure was unmistakable as he fell upon his enemies and cut them down with rifle and tomahawk. The struggle lasted but a few minutes. Then the gunfire faded into echoes and Lobal was alone.

He placed his back against the tree trunk, sick of heart, conscience-stricken he had survived, yet guilt was not so strong as to encourage him to throw his life away. After all, Atoan must be told what had befallen the war party. The Grand Sachem would not expect Lobal to suicidally join the fray. But this knowledge did not make it any easier when Lobal chose to give the killing ground a wide berth and skulked off through the woods, hounded by the memory of the moans and death cries that had reverberated down the long hills.

Beneath a lingering black haze of powder smoke, Fargo
knelt by one of the dead warriors. He did not know this
was Tabid; the man was just another grisly trophy for
Fargo's war bag. Tabid's war against the white eyes had
come to an end.

Fargo was a bitter man. He had missed another opportunity at Stark, but a clearing littered with dead redskins
soothed his disappointment. The moment the firing stopped
the swarthy killer charged out through the tendrils of black
smoke, brushed past Molly Page and hurried across the
clearing to kneel by Tabid's corpse. Fargo grinned and
hauled out his scalping knife. *This was going to be a pretty
one.*

He placed the steel edge to the warrior's forehead, ignoring the distaste of his companions. Suddenly a shadow
fell across him. And the heated muzzle of a long rifle
shoved the blade aside.

"None of that, Cassius Fargo," said John Stark.

"You ain't never complained about my scalp bag before."

"They weren't taken in my company."

Fargo glared up at the figure towering over him. "I'll
have this scalp and any others I choose."

"Not while you wear those buckskins and march with
this company. We are Rangers. I'll carry the war to the
Abenaki and French and give as good as I get or better but
on my word I draw the line at butcher's work."

"They killed my brother and two other men."

"We've all lost friends and family. Look at Sam Oday,
no one's suffered a more grievous harm, but you don't see
him dishonoring the dead."

"Back away from me, Stark. Or you'll be the one answering for my brother as well you ought." Fargo wrenched
the dead man's head to one side and started to carve away
his scalp. Stark reached down and hauled the man to his
feet and shoved him back. Fargo stumbled, hit the ground

rolling, scrambled to his feet and lunged for Stark.

"Johnny!" Molly called out, seeing the sunlight glint off the blade. Stark saw it too and turned aside, caught Fargo by the wrist, pulled the man forward and stuck out a leg. Cassius went flying head over heels. The knife skittered across the ground. He jumped to his feet and darted in toward Stark who caught the smaller man on the tip of the chin with a left hook, then kicked the man's leg out from under him. Fargo yelped and fell to one knee. Johnny clubbed him with his right forearm across the side of the man's neck. He groaned and dropped forward, caught himself on his hands and stayed that way for several moments while the earth whirled.

Duchess started forward growling, hackles raised and full of menace. Johnny called her off. The mastiff grudgingly retreated. Fargo straightened and sat back on his haunches. His opponent waited, fists clenched. Cassius shook his head indicating he was finished.

For now.

"There will be another day, John Stark," he said.

"Yes and a bad one for you, on my oath," Johnny replied. "Now take up your rifle and leave us for I will not march with a man I cannot trust."

Fargo scowled and crawled to his feet and gathered his weapons and cap. The rest of the company watched him in silence. But searching their faces he found no sympathy in the likes of Strode or Oday or Barlow. As for Moses Shoemaker, the irascible old bastard was even grinning!

Cassius' own eyes hardened. He noticed Molly watching him from behind the others and in that moment Fargo began to formulate a plan. There was a way to make Stark answer for humiliating him. Cassius Fargo had only to bide his time, to watch and wait. And as for the others. . . .

"You follow this man and he will bury you all, every mother's son of you. Mark my words."

The Rangers seemed unmoved. Their features were etched with powder smoke, the fire of battle still burned in their eyes. But there was no cruelty here, only a willingness to risk their lives for kin and country. A war had been thrust upon them and they were determined to carry the fight to the enemy. But it was clear they had no use for Cassius Fargo's brand of cruelty.

"You are fools. Bloody fools."

"Best you run along now, Cassius," said Moses Shoemaker leaning on his long rifle. "Go on back to your farm. We'll do what needs to be done."

"Fools," Fargo repeated beneath his breath, taking in the entire column of men with a sweeping glance. He shouldered his rifle and stalked off through the woods.

"Prime your rifles, lads, and gather up the war bags these heathens are carrying. Perhaps we can return them to their owners or their families." Stark gestured toward the dead Abenaki. He could feel Molly staring at him and turned as she approached. "What?"

She pursed her lips. "I was wishing it had ended here."

"Fargo?"

"Yes."

"He cannot hurt me."

"Don't be to certain." Molly looked toward the trees, the trembling shadows that suddenly seemed malevolent. "Men like him can find a way."

17

"Bring me the head of John Stark!" Colonel Lucien Barbarat exclaimed, his shrill voice ringing out across the glassy surface of the lake, to the opposite shore less than a quarter of a mile across the sluggish current. "Who will rid me of this meddlesome colonial?!" His words reverberated throughout the blackened cove, where he stood amid the cold-charred ruins of the bateaux and supplies that had been bound for Fort Carillon.

Lucien Barbarat could already envision General Montcalm recanting his words of praise and removing the rank he had so recently bestowed upon the officer who had orchestrated the downfall of Fort William Henry and the defeat of the British reinforcements sent to its aid. But those achievements were in the past.

And Lucien was confronted with the fact that he had not been able to fulfill General Montcalm's orders and move against Fort Edward. Instead, his marines had been dispatched all along the length and breadth of Lake George and the tail of Lake Champlain, in an effort to curb the frequent raids that had begun to undermine French control of the territory. His gaze swept over Benoit Turcotte and the half a dozen other boatmen, all of whom longed to be elsewhere then cringing in their shackles on the shore where Stark's Rangers had lured them to disaster. The rivermen had a benefactor in the person of Father Jean Isaac, a rail thin Jesuit priest who had been traveling to Fort Carillon in the company of Barbarat.

"*Mon Colonel*, these men fell victim to their vices. But no man is beyond forgiveness."

"Please, sir, we made a terrible mistake, a weakness of spirit that will not happen again. They tricked us," Turcotte exclaimed.

Barbarat nodded. "There was a woman I am told."

"A lovely woman, with a well-turned ankle, a slender neck, and the face of a goddess." The other boatmen nodded, they mightily concurred. Turcotte held up his calloused hands in prayer and supplication. "She bewitched us, *Père Jean*, as sure as I am standing here."

The black robe placed himself between the officer and Turcotte. Despite his slight frame and small stature, Father Jean Isaac was endowed with the commitment of his calling. His deep blue eyes blazed with the strength befitting a man of profound faith. His scarred hands bore mute testimony to the torture he had endured bringing the "Christian" God to the tribes of the northeast.

"A witch? I have heard of such things," Barbarat mused. He turned his back on the priest and the prisoners where they stood flanked by a company of marines in white and blue tunics. Barbarat continued down to the water's edge where Atoan and his son had just returned from the opposite shore. The two were similarly garbed in buckskin breeches and fringed hunting shirts. Lobal was with them, so young, like Kasak but far more nervous.

The Grand Sachem wore a grim expression beneath his mask of ocher war paint. A passing breeze fluttered the raven feathers that adorned his topknot. His dark eyes were pools of wisdom and foxlike cunning. Beneath that implacable demeanor beat the heart of a man whose very soul was etched by war and survival.

This savage is far more clever than he lets on, Barbarat thought, *the Grand Sachem could be trouble sometime in the future.* Now Kasak was another story. Atoan's son was a bold and headstrong youth. Lucien Barbarat knew how to exploit such qualities to his own advantage.

Kasak entered the circle of ruins, black dust rising from each footfall as he strode across the blackened earth. Atoan skirted the debris, reluctant to leave his tracks upon the shore. He cradled a Pennsylvania long rifle in the crook of his arm and moved with sure and silent steps.

All that announced his arrival was the faint rattle of the shell and bear-claw necklace that dangled from around his throat and rested against his powerful chest. The Grand Sachem gestured the way they had come. "The canoes were drawn up on the shore and covered over with the long grass and branches."

"My father and I have found the tracks," Kasak proudly interrupted, puffing out his chest as if credit for the discovery was his alone. "The *Anglais* used eight canoes."

"Perhaps thirty men," Barbarat muttered, assessing the enemy. "Or less. But where are they now?"

"The *Anglais* left their boats, made their way over the hills opposite Fort Carillon, past *La Chute* and down to Lake George," Atoan replied. "Some left by bateaux, others followed another path.

Lucien nodded. "*Mon ami,* I am confused. Then how did they escape? You sent raiding parties on both sides of the lake to watch for *Anglais* raiders."

"Lobal has brought word that Tabid's war party was ambushed. The Rangers fell on them from both sides of the trail and killed many of our warriors. Only Lobal escaped."

"Was it Stark?" Barbarat glanced past the war chief's shoulder and glared at Lobal who remained a few paces back, his head lowered, the look of a man not wishing to call attention to himself.

"It was the beast," said Atoan. But he did not speak of the warning he had received from *Mahom*, the spirit who took the form of a Great Horned Owl. *Beware Kiwaskwek, the monster. He will find you.* The French officer would not have understood. Few of the white men could hear beyond hearing, few walked with the spirits of the wild places. But some did, perhaps this John Stark, maybe, and that troubled the Grand Sachem. He would have to find out for himself. Soon. . . .

It was an unsettling thought. The massacre of Fort William Henry's garrison, instead of sending the Yankees reeling in terror from Abenaki lands might have had the opposite effect and only hardened their resolve. *The beast will be born of blood.*

Well, there had been plenty spilled. And ever since the fall of the *Anglais* fort, Abenaki raiding parties had been ambushed, French patrols attacked, and now these bateaux, looted and burned. Atoan glanced at the ashes on the shore, he scrutinized the trampled earth, caught the telltale signs of the skirmish that had been both brief but savage.

And he remembered all that Lobal had told them, all he had seen. Stark and his Rangers struck hard and fast. Tabid never saw them until it was too late. It was a slaughter. And then these Rangers disappeared into the forest like the morning mist, like so many shadows. . . .

Like the Abenaki.

"Rangers," Lucien sneered, one hand cupping his chin, his cold blue eyes looked as if they had been chipped off some distant horizon and set in his aquiline features. "But they are only men. And Englishmen at that."

"Mais oui, mon Colonel," said Atoan, trouble in his voice. "But they fight like us."

Ambush. Trickery. Subterfuge. These were not the tactics of a gentleman. But then, the colonials were anything but men of breeding. "I will yet teach this 'beast' a lesson and cage him proper, on my oath," said Colonel Lucien Barbarat. "It is only a matter of time." He had seen all he could stomach of this site and started toward the canoes that had carried him south from Fort Saint Frederick.

"Colonel Barbarat!" one of the marines called out. It was Sergeant Moquin, a seasoned campaigner from the old country and other wars. He was in command of the detail that had escorted Turcotte and the other *voyageurs* who had been placed under arrest and singled out for punishment. "What of these prisoners?"

The Jesuit priest stepped forward, by his expression, appealing to the officer's better nature.

Lucien glanced at the men, almost as an afterthought, then he shrugged, and smiled. For a fleeting second, Father

Jean Isaac thought Benoit Turcotte and his unfortunate companions might see another sunrise. But before the priest's words of thanks and praise could gush forth, the newly commissioned officer barked out his orders.

"Accrochez-les haute!" Barbarat exclaimed. "Hang them high!"

The Winter Moon

1758

18

"Which one is Stark?" Sir Peter Drennan inquired. The personal aide-de-camp to General Jeffrey Amherst scrutinized the shore of Rogers' Island, set like a teardrop in the middle of the Hudson River. The bow of the johnny boat dipped beneath his weight. Grayish white slabs of ice bumped against the oak hull, reminding all aboard that another month from now they might make the crossing on foot.

Behind Drennan, Major Michael Ransom stoically bore the crossing in silence. He wondered if they would make it safely to Rogers' Island without being unceremoniously dumped into the frigid gray waters where Sir Peter's bloated form might float or better still, sink like a rock, nay a boulder, beneath the ice-cracked river.

Of course, the unfortunate demise of nobility while in Ransom's charge ought to make for a bleak Christmas and it could only further threaten the major's already precarious career. So if the boat capsized, Ransom might have to try and drag the amazingly obese officer to the riverbank. Failing that, he'd better sink along with him.

Although they shared the same privileged birth, it was clear each man had his place. Sir Peter, a colonel at the tender age of thirty and only a few years older than Ransom, had become the knighted head of his family's estate. It was a title Michael Ransom aspired to, but for the moment it exceeded his grasp. Justified or not, his reputation had been tarnished by the disastrous defeat at Bloody Meadow. Only the fact that the major had conducted an orderly withdrawal and saved the colors kept him from being returned to England in disgrace.

Ransom dug his hands into his great coat and exhaled slowly, his breath hanging on the cold still air like a cloud searching for a home sky. The two oarsmen put their backs into it and managed to pull the unsteady craft safely to the shore. Drennan stepped over the gunwale and slipped in the mud, cursed, regained his balance and wiped his hands clean on a kerchief he produced from a secreted pocket nestled in the folds of his black cloak.

"Blast and hell this God forsaken wilderness. Give me the Chilterns any day, what?"

"Indeed, Sir Peter," Ransom obligingly agreed. He checked the somber gray sky overhead. He'd already seen a few flakes of snow this morning. "And a baked goose stuffed with sweetbreads, plum pudding, and mulled wine."

"Here, here," Drennan chuckled and politely applauded. "You are a man of taste, sir, and obvious refinement." He noticed a group of buckskin-clad Rangers gathered out in front of the longhouses. Several of the Indian fighters smoked their pipes as they warmed their hands by a cheerful campfire. Black smoke curled from the chimneys signaling that more of the Rangers had sought shelter from the brisk wind behind stout log walls chinked with clay. Another half a dozen of the Rangers congregated before an overturned tree stump that had been trimmed, turned base upwards, and set upon a small scaffold about chest high. The woodsmen took turns throwing their tomahawks at a card one of the Rangers had pinned to the stump. The one who succeeded in cutting the card from a distance of about eighteen feet would win a jug of rum to ward off December's chill.

After several attempts, one of the Rangers succeeded in landing his tomahawk dead center, much to the chagrin of the men who had hoped to win the jug for themselves. Drennan took note of the man's success and postured that this indeed must be Stark.

"No, your grace, that is Robert Rogers," Ransom replied.

"Ah, the commander of the company."

"He has assumed this rank, yes," said Ransom as he joined Sir Peter on the shore. There could only be one commanding officer and Robert Rogers had quietly laid claim to the title. "But the men follow Stark," the major added.

As the English officers looked on, Rogers returned the jug to his companions who cheered his generosity, then taking leave of his men, walked across the trampled earth toward the English officers who met him halfway, drawn to the cheerful warmth of the well-tended campfire. Sam Oday sat hunched forward by the flames; water bubbled in a black pot into which he had thrown a fistful of loose tea leaves. As the English officers in their great coats drew close, Oday chose to drift off toward the men with the jug of rum, leaving the blaze he had tended for those in command.

Ransom was grateful for the warmth. Drennan, despite the rolls of fat that should have kept him warm, stretched out his pudgy fingers to the dancing flames, and all but purred. He looked up at the tough-looking man in the buckskin hunting shirt. When Rogers did not doff his Scottish bonnet but only raised a knuckle to his forehead in salute, Drennan cast a quick glance aside at Ransom, in obvious disapproval.

"Major Robert Rogers of the Colonial Militia," Ransom pronounced, "may I present his lordship, Colonel Peter Drennan."

Drennan looked the Ranger straight in the eye, and frowned, his round red jowls stung by a sudden gust of wind. The sudden discomfort reminded him that this island was the last place he wanted to be. Somewhere within the walls of Fort Edward, a high-backed chair, a flagon of spiced ale, and a platter of roasted pork awaited his pleasure.

"At your service, gentlemen," Rogers grinned. "Welcome to my island. Major Ransom tells me you have expressed an interest in what we are doing here." He waved them forward and then indicated the collection of long-houses, firing stands, a powder magazine, racks of tanned hides and the like. The site could have passed for an Aben-aki village.

"Sir Peter is visiting us on behalf of General Jeffrey Amherst," Ransom explained.

"Major Ransom has extolled the virtues of your pe-culiar command," Sir Peter said. His thick fleshy features were red from the cold. "It is most irregular." The officer spoke in a gravelly voice, the legacy of a monthlong bout with fever and congestion that made drawing a breath through his nose nigh on impossible. "However as we pre-pare to mount an offensive against the Marquis de Mont-calm, your forays have proved an effective distraction for the French, the general must admit."

An outcry arose from the perimeter of the encampment and Drennan caught a glimpse of a towering individual in buckskins leading a column of similarly dressed young men at a dead run through a grove of fir and maple trees. Ap-parently the company had just ferried themselves across the river and disembarked on the tip of the island. From the looks of their red cheeks and labored breathing they had been running for some time.

The formidable figure in the lead did not call a halt until the men stumbling along behind him were within ear-shot of the English officers. The column maintained its for-mation as the men came to a halt, although several of them had to double over and support themselves, hands on knees, while they regained their wind. Only the man in the lead, and another boyish-faced "lad," seemed oblivious to their recent exertions.

The big man stood tall and straight, his long rifle clasped in his right hand, the thumb of his left hooked in the broad leather belt circling his waist. He paused there, in repose, an aura of power and self-restrained violence seemed to emanate from him. The man's great chest rose and fell, breath streaming from his nostrils upon the clouded air. One could imagine some mythic beast snorting steam before unleashing a fiery blast of brimstone and death.

"Now that is Stark," Major Ransom told the general's aide.

"Ah . . . the great beast of the Adirondacks who has carried the war to the French."

"The French have put quite a price on him we have learned. Fifty Spanish reals for the man who brings in the head of John Stark," Ransom added. He was still amazed at how quickly news of any sort traveled through the wilderness, despite the distances.

"A tempting payment," Drennan mused. "I dare say I wouldn't sleep well myself were I the man."

"John takes pride in it," Robert Rogers frowned and shifted his stance, resenting the way his friend seemed to dominate the interest of his peers, both Rangers and British officers alike. "See here, Colonel, Stark is a worthy soldier, and certainly casts a long shadow. But like many of these mountain folk, he lacks vision."

Ransom detected a note of jealousy in Rogers's voice. But there was a degree of truth to his observation. The English officer respected Stark, as any soldier would, because the man could fight and was unafraid to seek out the enemy. But as for lacking vision? Now there was the conundrum. Ransom suspected John Stark could see clearer than any of them. In some ways that made him not only necessary but dangerous.

"Dear heavens," Sir Peter blurted out, catching a glimpse of several scarlet waistcoats beneath the green-fringed hunting shirts. "Those are men of the Regiment." On closer inspection it appeared these regulars had been in a scrape or two for some were favoring an assortment of wounds and most had features blackened by gunpowder.

"But, of course, your grace. These Rangers have been so successful at carrying the war to the French I felt it behooved us to establish a company of king's Rangers to work in conjunction with the Provincials," Ransom explained. "See Sergeant Strode there. He has performed admirably on patrol with the Colonials and recently played no small part in a successful excursion to the north."

The major took care to avoid giving an in-depth account of the raid and the ruse that saw the sergeant dressed as a tavern wench. Ransom had heard the report directly from Strode, back in the fall. At the time he had been tempted to voice his objections. But it was hard to "object" to the destruction of French property. However, Ransom made certain Strode's account went no further than the walls of Fort Edward. He felt no call to elaborate in his dispatches all that had transpired. Besides, he doubted Amherst or the colonel or any of the other officers safely removed from the frontier could handle the truth.

Stark's voice rang out upon the cold crisp air.

"Remember, lads, mind you the Abenaki, for they have few peers when it comes to wilderness fighting."

"The savages will retreat if they must and live to fight another day," the youth acting as his second in command called out. This man's voice was softer than Stark's but carried a similar note of authority. The lad had obviously proved his worth somewhere down the War Path.

"Remember how we handled those French marines, take heed the next time you cross paths with them or Atoan's redsticks," Stark continued. "As you withdraw, if the rear comes under attack, then let the main body and the flankers turn about to right and left and confront the enemy. The same if the enemy strikes upon your flank. That way the enemy will always be opposed by the entire command. Drive them back and then continue to withdraw."

"Stark, if we may have a word with you!" Robert Rogers called out. The long hunter glanced in their direction, handed over the command to Sergeant Strode who took charge of the King's Rangers and ordered them to the longhouse that had been built for them near the sleeping quarters of Rogers' Rangers. Stark muttered an aside to the youth standing close at hand then the two of them sauntered over toward Rogers and the Englishmen. Stark acknowledged the officers with a nod of the head. His chiseled countenance looked weathered and dark from a week-old growth of beard the color of his dark ginger mane. He halted a few paces from Major Ransom.

"John, you know Major Ransom, of course," Robert Rogers began, "and this is Sir Peter Drennan, the personal aide to General Amherst. I believe he has come to see what we are about."

Stark studied the officers in their scarlet coats and polished buttons, their periwigs and silver swords. Colonel Drennan waited. But he received even less of a salute than Rogers had accorded. In fact, Stark accorded the two Englishman none whatsoever. Rogers's eyes flashed his friend a warning. Stark shrugged it off. They had just returned from a morning's run through the woods on the opposite shore from Fort Edward. Standing here in the cold, his limbs were beginning to tighten up. He longed for a hot cup of strong black and perhaps a wedge of Christian cheese and a slab of Aunt Charity's fresh-baked bread.

"John Stark," Sir Peter said, as if by saying the long hunter's name, he intended to remember it for future reference. "It is customary to remove your bonnet and salute those officers under whose command you have the honor to serve. I am sure you expect no less from the men who follow your lead."

"Your pardon, Colonel, but the only thing I expect from my men is to bring the war to the French and the Abenaki. I expect them to kill the enemy before he can do the same to us."

Ransom inwardly groaned at what the officer considered outrageous behavior. He'd receive an earful once he and Sir Peter Drennan had returned to their quarters within the fort. Stark could be brusque and damnably insubordinate. But the major had given up trying to break the man of it.

Instead, Ransom had chosen to put up with such conduct because he knew Stark and these Rangers had forced the French to worry about protecting their own settlements.

These magnificent woodsmen and trackers were buying the major precious time, allowing him to remain within the ramparts and prepare for an eventual assault. He continued to seek reinforcements from General Amherst who was marshaling his forces to the east. Alas, thus far, the general had not chosen to comply with Ransom's requests. The major had hoped a man like Sir Peter might rectify the situation.

"See here," Drennan began, staring up at the long hunter, incensed by his familiarity. "As long as you are in service to the crown. . . ." The heavyset officer's admonishment died aborning when the "youth" alongside Stark removed her bonnet and allowed her striking red hair to form a glorious cascade of thick curls and ringlets about her features and over her shoulders. Her eyes were as green as the dyed buckskins that covered her lithe frame.

"I . . . I . . . oh my . . . what is this? A woman? In colonial uniform and . . . commanding the king's troops?" Drennan's mouth dropped open as he searched for the proper words but failed. He could only turn once more to confront Michael Ransom, who sighed and shook his head, sensing his career was unraveling right before his very eyes.

Molly grinned, wiped a smudge of powder smoke from the tip of her nose, inadvertently smearing some across her cheek. She leaned on her long rifle and held out her hand. "Welcome to Fort Edward, Colonel!"

19

I am marked by the beast. I have heard his spirit, along the Great War Path. I can mark his passing where the widows moan for their dead husbands, fathers for their slaughtered sons. But I am Atoan, and I have left my own mark upon the land. We stalk each other, following a trail of fire and blood.

I shoulder my war club, I gather my knife and musket. If it is to be, then let it be now. I am the Grand Sachem, the first in battle, the last to leave the bone fields of the dead. Spirits above me, shadows under my feet. But I am not afraid. The voice of the wind sings in my heart and I am filled with courage. Hear me, Kiwaskwek, one of us must die, before long.

But which of us? And yet . . . who are you? And why does Mahom whisper your name? A man should know his enemy.

The dream faded as the man awoke.

Atoan knew what he had to do. He rose from his blankets and moved silently about the crudely constructed longhouse where many of his warriors were sprawled in sleep. He carefully picked his way among the sleeping forms, moving with the grace and agility of a hunting cat; the war chief gathered his weapons, his shot pouch, and powder flask, and stole through the woven-rush door.

The gray light of predawn gripped him with invisible talons of ice. He sucked in his breath at the first caress, continued past the smoldering embers of yesterday's cook-

fire and crossed unannounced through the camp until he
reached the fringes of the Abenaki encampment where he
paused, a man facing east, and began to chant softly to
himself the welcoming prayer before the first light.

> *Mother earth, listen to my heart's song.*
> *Release the golden one that the earth*
> *might be healed.*
> *My eyes, healed.*
> *All that was broken*
> *by the dark of night,*
> *made whole.*

As the winter sun edged above the wooded crest of
distant mountains, Kasak emerged from the longhouse to
find his father, standing on the shore of a frozen creek
where the ice-crusted waters flowed out of a forested hillside a quarter of a mile from Fort Carillon and well out of
sight of their French allies.

Back in the compound, the Abenaki had begun to bestir
themselves. Smoke began to curl from the tops of the huts
and lodges where the cookfires within were vented through
the roof. One look at Atoan's rigid features and his stiffened gesture of welcome and Kasak could tell his father
had been up for at least an hour, keeping vigil in the bitter
chill of the fast approaching daylight.

"Father . . ." The younger man rubbed the sleep from
his eyes and yawned, then reminded himself the next time
he ventured outside he needed to bring the great coat Barbarat had presented him with only a few weeks earlier.
Atoan was too suspicious of the French. And too proud,
Kasak thought, to fully realize the profits to be gained from
their alliance with Barbarat.

Atoan shook his head, motioned for him to be quiet.
He gestured for his son to stand at his side. Winter lay upon
the land, draped the white pines and the spruce and fir with
a mantle of freshly fallen snow. The air was still and in-
tensely quiet and each and every sound from camp rode

the stillness unfettered, undistorted by distance and the terrain. Colonel Lucien Barbarat had ordered the Abenaki to make their camp in the shadow of the great walls of Fort Carillon but Atoan's will was iron.

Kasak could not see any wisdom in refusing the French officer and that dissatisfaction underscored his words. "We ought to be warming ourselves by the cookfires of our French brothers. The long guns that guard their soldiers can protect us as well. And *La Marines* have plenty of food to eat. Barbarat has offered to feed us inside the fort."

"*Gagwi gedidam!* What is that you say?" Atoan hissed. "Have the Abenaki become like children and the French our mothers, that we must suck at their teats?" The Grand Sachem shook his head and sighed. It was as if his very spirit clouded the air before his lips, billowed and disappeared into the crisp cold light of morning. "When the Abenaki can no longer feed themselves, when the Abenaki must crouch beneath French guns for safety, on that day I will have lived too long."

"My father twists my words," Kasak exclaimed. "No white man runs me."

"We shall see," Atoan replied. "Remember, my son. We walk the French road because it suits us. The guns they give us shoot straight . . ." He reached out and tapped the hilt of the dirk Kasak kept sheathed at his side. ". . . And their steel cuts true and does not snap. Today we use them on the *Anglais*, but tomorrow . . . May our grandfathers' spirits give us guidance."

"We shall see," Kasak said, unconvinced and mimicking his father's earlier reply. The brash young warrior had witnessed firsthand the French cannoneers at the siege of Fort William Henry, how the iron guns eventually broke the walls and then the courage of the defenders and forced them out, and put them within reach of Abenaki tomahawks. "But why do you stand here? Who are you looking for?"

The war chief lifted his gaze to the way south. *The beast awaits.* "Send runners to the Huron, the Seneca, and

Chippewa. Have them carry belts of wampum to our brothers and tell them to gather with us at St. Francis Village, above the Place of Thunder. Tell them we seek to hold council with all the People of the Green Mountains, and that we seek to unite with our brothers and strike the white eyes with one hand.

Now it was Kasak's time to worry. He frowned and stepped back and for the first time realized his father was dressed for the trail, armed with a rifle and 'hawk but little else. Atoan intended to travel light and fast, trap what food he might need along the way, and live close to the land that he knew would sustain him.

"I have walked in a dream. The One Spirit, *Mahom*, has shown me what I must do. *Kiwaskwek* must die. Or we must die. One or the other. But to kill the beast, I must know him first."

"Then I will go with you," Kasak flatly stated. He had fought Stark once, briefly, remembered his humiliating defeat all to well. The deer hunter still had claim to the young warrior's life.

"No," Atoan retorted, more sharply than he had intended. "It is for me to go alone."

"Why?"

"I have spoken," Atoan said in a tone that demanded obedience. He looked past his son, saw that more of the Abenaki had begun to stir and venture out into the cold. Soon all the fires would be rekindled and the day begun in earnest. These things were good. He took courage in them. His gaze settled on his troubled offspring. He placed his hand on Kasak's shoulder. "Why?" he gently repeated his son's grave question. "Because it was not your dream."

20

"I saw it move beyond the campfire, just a shadow, mind you. But I sensed it was stalking me. I waited a mighty long time, until a powerful thirst came over me. When I could not stand it any longer, I rose up and headed off through the forest." A half circle of firelit faces surrounded the big man whose powerful torso strained the seams of his homespun hunting shirt. A shaggy, silver-flecked mane framed his rugged countenance, and when he shook his head, it was as if some beast of the woods were stretching and testing the air for scent. Bold, indomitable, seemingly fearless . . . this was a man.

"Bloody hell if it didn't follow me down to the creek bank," Big John Stark continued, playing the account for maximum effect. "I'd take a step or two, and hear it move. I held up and give a listen and there it'd be, not just keeping pace, but closing in. And me with damp powder and no way to fire a single shot."

The tavern was eerily quiet, the usually noisy gathering held spellbound by the tone and tenor of the tale-teller's voice. Each of the listeners pictured the encounter in their own way, personalizing the terror.

"I knelt and slaked my thirst and when I stood, the clouds parted and the new moon shone big and round and bone-white, and lit the night, clear as day. And that's when I saw . . . it. . . ." said Johnny Stark, in a gravelly voice, the legacy of a bout with the grippe that had laid him low for the latter part of December.

With the year coming to an end, he'd only recently thrown off the malady. He coughed now and then, but he was gaining strength every day thanks to Molly's expert tending and Aunt Charity's breakfasts. Every morning a hearty bowl of Indian meal served steaming hot with molasses and butter and washed down with strong black tea or hard cider, what man wouldn't mend on such a regimen? But despite the winter's lull, and his own congested lungs, Stark never doubted come spring he would once again carry the war to the French along the Great War Path.

"Well what was it? Man or beast?" Locksley Barlow blurted out, his youthful features flush from the copious amounts of rum he had swilled to guard against the chill of night. Beyond the walls of Kit Fox Tavern, the north wind prowled, swirling the sodden snowflakes as they drifted down. Unseen fingers tapped the signboard hanging over the front door. The wooden placard swung to and fro, chains creaking as the iron links scraped against the wooden pole from which the signboard dangled.

The wheel-rutted streets of Fort Edward were for the most part deserted. There was no one without the comforting log walls to read the weathered words inscribed upon the bill and those within the tavern knew by heart the greeting scrawled upon the signboard's ashen face.

KIT FOX TAVERN

**OH WE CAN MAKE LIQUOR TO SWEETEN OUR LIPS,
OF PUMPKINS, OF PARSNIPS,
OF WALNUT TREE CHIPS.**

It was a grand night for keeping close to a hearth and cleaving to the light, for there might be ghosts abroad this night, or so the gray wind warned with a moan and a sigh.

"A beast," Stark replied, his gaze sweeping across the faces of the men and women gathered around his table, their features reflecting the flames that leaped and danced as the embers crackled within the confines of the hearth. The tavern crowd was made up of Rangers and townsmen. The young men like Locksley Barlow were gathered close at hand. While Sam Oday and Moses Shoemaker, the older men sat off to the side, enjoying how these younkers sat poised on stools and ladder-backed chairs, enraptured by Stark's exploits.

Tess McDonagel, the proprietress, full-breasted with a toothy smile and an earthy sexuality that a man could bloody near drink in like they did her hot-buttered rum, made her way through the crowd, refilling the pewter mugs of her customers from a heavy stoneware pitcher. Her favored drink for a night like this was made with rum from the Indies steeped in a black kettle with heavy cream, butter, molasses, sugar, cinnamon and clove.

But as Stark progressed with his account, even Tess paused in her rounds, eyes wide, full lips slightly parted, astonished by the story. She was just about the finest-looking lass in the settlement and there wasn't a man jack among her patrons who didn't think so.

Just *about* . . . indeed. But there was another who could hold her own with the likes of the buxom tavern keeper.

Molly Page lingered near the front door, a bemused expression on her face as she watched Johnny Stark "hold court." Even in her woolen hunting shirt and buckskin breeches, she looked lithe and sleek as a bobcat, with fire in her eyes and courage in her heart. Molly knew she had won the respect of this lot, no matter that she marched to a different drummer and favored a starlit sky to a roof above her head and the wind in the branches of the sugar maples to gossip circles and quilting bees.

Who didn't think her as desirable a woman as Tess? Maybe even more so, for this woman shared the dangers of the wilderness trails. And the Indian fighters knew first-hand that Molly could hold her own in battle. The Rangers doubted there was another woman like her in all the colonies. She made them proud. And Stark made them envious. Everyone knew how Molly felt about their rawboned leader. Any man would give his right arm to be loved like that, by such a woman.

Molly rolled her eyes and shook her head. She had

heard this story before. Johnny Stark was in his element now, keeping his audience transfixed with his account. Had he no shame? Well, no. Not when it came to telling his tall tales.

"What kind of beast?" she called out, from the back of the room, playing her part. And in truth, seeing him up and about after his illness lifted her spirits. She had grown accustomed to his presence in her brother's old bedroom. But he had mended. And Stark was determined to return to his cabin tonight after spending almost two weeks as Uncle Ephraim's guest.

And Molly intended to be there in his cabin, to give him a proper welcome when he arrived, promised herself to see that his bed was turned down and perhaps, "improperly warmed," that is if the *spirit* moved her and she decided to throw caution and her reputation to the wind. Then again, being alone with Johnny Stark made her feel anything but *spiritual*.

"A wolverine, from nose to tail near as long as a full-grown man is tall," Stark said, right on cue. "With claws like skinning knives and fangs like a devil's grin. And there I am, knowing full well if I turn my back the old devil will tear into me worse than any heathen. So I snapped Old Abraham and, bless my soul, it was the only time the rifle failed me."

"Should have kept your powder dry," one of the older men called out.

"Aye and it was a lesson learned too late for the devil bared its fangs and lunged at me before I could dust the pan with gunpowder."

"You were done for," another of the younger men observed.

"What did you do, Johnny?"

"I knelt down and scooped up a handful of mud and threw it smack-dab into that glutton's mouth." Stark acted out the scene before the fireplace, kneeling and sweeping his right hand forward. "Then another handful soon as it cleared the first. And that's how we passed the better part of an hour, me throwing mud in the brute's mouth every time it charged. Longest hour I've ever spent."

"You finally get your smoke pole primed?" asked Oday, his speech slightly slurred. The buttered rum was taking its toll.

"Didn't need it," Johnny replied. "After an hour I had that wolverine so filled with mud its belly was dragging the creek bank. It could hardly waddle much less run me down. So I just headed on back to my camp, gathered up my blankets and possibles bag, then I walked on out of there." The audience started to relax, then realized the story hadn't ended. "Well, sir, about half a year later I was hunting the same hillside and tracked a white-tailed buck down to that very same creek bank and there she was, the wolverine, and the critter was standing there, just like I remembered her only . . . the mud she had swallowed had dried solid, shriveled her up and turned the creature into a little statue. There it was, a *fiercesome* sight despite its size, even dead, hunkered in a crouch, teeth bared and hackles raised."

He reached into his belt pouch and brought out a small figurine of a wolverine he had whittled while confined to bed at Uncle Ephraim's. He tossed the figurine into Barlow's outstretched hands. The Ranger caught the small carving and held it aloft like a trophy, then realized he'd been duped and the image he held had been carved from wood, had never breathed air or howled on a moonless night.

"Oh the devil, you say," Barlow grumbled, knowing he had been taken in by the story and the storyteller. The crowd erupted into laughter. Tess breathed a sigh of relief, dabbed her upper lip with the hem of her apron, then took up her stoneware pitcher and continued to distribute her libations.

Stark glanced up and saw Molly wrap a coarsely woven scarf around her head to protect her ears from the wind's wintry bite, and then give him a come-hither wave of farewell. He knew where she was off to and planned on joining her soon. He leaned forward to the mastiff and scratched the animal behind the ears and whispered softly in her ear and to the surprise of the men around him, the great hulking canine hurried the length of the room, nudged the door open and vanished into the night.

"Now, where was I?" said Stark.

And Tess leaning forward to reveal the creamy mounds of her bosom barely encased by her sleeveless cotton bodice answered in a sultry tone of voice, "I can think of a place, Johnny Stark." And she glanced toward the ceiling as if indicating the bedroom above the tavern that she called home.

Stark looked toward the door. His stomach growled. By golly, he was downright gut-foundered after all that talk. Molly would be waiting for him in his cabin. He was certain of it. But why hurry? He'd spied a joint of beef sizzling over the flames in the hearth. And Moses Shoemaker and Uncle Ephraim had just produced their fiddles. There was music and laughter . . . and Tess McDonagel. From the sound of the moaning wind, it promised to be a long cold night.

So where was the harm in just one more flagon of rum?

21

Molly never saw it coming, not till the last second when a trickle of moonlight through the diminishing flurries revealed a glimmer of the brass butt plate of a flintlock pistol speeding toward her out of the murky interior of Stark's cabin. She worked the latch and crossed the threshold and was standing just inside the doorway when her assailant made his move. Molly tried to swerve and push herself out of harm's way but could not avoid the gun butt. It struck the side of her head, her right temple received a glancing blow. Stars exploded before her eyes, a lightning bolt of white-hot pain crackled inside her skull.

Molly groaned and stumbled to the side, crashed into a table, sent an assortment of tinware cups and plates clattering to the floor, then knocked over a chair as she tried to break her fall. She fumbled for the pocket pistol tucked in the wide leather belt circling her waist, her hands clawed beneath the folds of her great cloak as she tried for the gun with her fading strength.

"No, you don't," said a familiar voice.

Even injured and near unconscious, she recognized Cassius Fargo. But then she had made a point of studying this one, sensing the harm he meant to the man she loved. Fargo read her actions, growled, and darted toward her. He batted the pistol from her grasp as she struggled to bring it into play.

Molly clawed at his bearded features, left a streak of blood to clot in his silvery stubble and caught a backhand in reply that split her lip and left a trickle of crimson at the corner of her mouth. The woman reeled from the blow.

Still, having the foresight to see the front door was ajar, the woman made a desperate lunge toward the swirling snowflakes that rode the night wind like miniature sailing ships, their sails unfurled and beaconing crystal white against the dark.

Fargo caught a fistful of red hair. His left hand clutched at the back of her hunting shirt. The fabric tore as he overpowered the stunned woman and savagely yanked her about and manhandled her away from the doorway and then dragged her into the room and flung her onto Stark's bed. The walnut frame creaked and groaned from the force with which she landed on the patchwork quilt and goose-down mattress.

Molly tasted blood. The pain was riveting, it took her breath away.

"I was expecting Stark, what with the rum he was swilling. Figured I'd have his measure." Fargo's hungry eyes lowered to her torn shirt and what he could see of her breasts. The sight of that sweet flesh gave him another idea. Stark set quite a store by this one. Scratch her and the son of a bitch would bleed right enough.

"Where's your man now? No one's here to stand for you, Molly Stark. Always meddling where it don't concern you. Well see here . . . you don't look so full of yourself."

"Lay a hand on me and you will rue the day," Molly exclaimed, trying to cling to consciousness. Her head throbbed, the room reeled like a ship's cabin in a squall. The pain was almost more than she could bear. Her eyes moistened and despite her resolve a tear spilled down her cheek.

Cassius glanced to the side. Ford was watching him, standing just in the shadows of his brother's own twisted ego. *"Come on, Cassius, if you can't take Stark, at least take his woman,"* said the ghost. *"That'll kill him sure as if you put a bullet through his heart!"*

"I'll make a romp in your bushy park and be well on my way back to Cowslip before any man's the wiser. The devil take you all, says I."

"You're a fool, Cassius Fargo. There will be nowhere you can hide."

"No. I have kin in Cowslip. Any man . . . or woman . . . come asking for me, they'd play the fool to chance it. But who's to know for sure. I'll take my pleasure and afterwards see you tell no tales." Fargo slowly advanced toward the bed, the baleful moonlight streaming in through the open door played off her wide-eyed features. "You've a pretty mouth, Molly Page. I warrant I can find use for it, better than what you've put it to." *Look at her. See her eyes, Brother Ford. Like a wounded doe in my gunsight. Such pretty skin, how the moon makes her pale.* He shivered. Damn gust of wind. He turned and stared at the open doorway and then with a wink in Molly's direction muttered and tugged on the front of his breeches. "Don't want to freeze it off, not when I can put it to such good use."

He was halfway to the door when the mastiff bounded into view. Duchess sniffed the air, recognized Fargo, curled her lips back and revealed two brutal-looking rows of teeth as she snarled. Then two hundred pounds of canine fury bounded toward him. Fargo shrieked as the animal knocked him to the floor. Those powerful jaws tore a patch from his thigh as he fell to the side, leveled his pistol, and fired. The muzzle of the barrel was close enough to singe the animal's flesh. Duchess yelped as a .50-caliber ball ripped through the mastiff's side. Duchess sagged to the ground momentarily pinning Cassius to the cabin floor. He kicked free and scrambled out of harm's way, stumbled free and winced at the ragged wound that streaked his thigh with crimson. He glanced around intending to join Molly on the bed. But Molly Page was no longer lying supine, stunned, on the coverlets. While Fargo was occupied with the masitff, Molly had staggered over to the fireplace, reached the hearth and the long rifle John Stark had hung over the mantle.

Molly thumbed the hammer back on Old Abraham and steadied herself against the back wall as she drew a bead on her attacker. "I'll send you straight to hell," she exclaimed in a voice thick with pain and barely controlled rage.

Cassius took one look down that long barrel and lunged for the door, bounding across the room and ducking out into the night.

Molly let him go.

For one thing, she didn't have a clear shot, not with the world caving in on her, like a veil of black gauze draping over her eyes, dampening every sound until all she could hear was her own breathing, her own heart hammering in her mind. But she clung to the world, refused to surrender to the pain and the dimming of the light for fear the brute might return and finish what he had begun.

She would never know how long she waited like that, refusing to surrender to the oncoming void. It seemed like an eternity. And then, at last, John Stark loomed in the doorway, blocking the moon's cold-white glare. She heard him call her name as if from far away and watched him rush toward her and catch her as she collapsed into his arms.

"Oh my God! Molly! Molly!"

His gaze swept the room, taking in the critically injured mastiff, Molly's torn clothes, the overturned furniture, the acrid smell of gunsmoke. He tenderly brushed the hair away from her face as he cradled her bloodied head in the crook of his arm. Fear turned to horror turned to a quiet, seething rage.

She knew what he wanted. But Molly held her tongue. She didn't want him plunging off into danger. But his eyes fixed her, held her suspended above a pool of precious oblivion.

"Who?" he whispered, struggling to contain his emotions.

Her bruised lips formed the words. He leaned down until he could feel her breath tickle the inside of his ear. And then he heard.

"Cassius Fargo. . . ."

22

Molly opened her eyes and focused on the ceiling of her bedroom, on the slanted sunlight pouring in through the cracks in the shuttered windows, and on Big John Stark sprawled in a chair by her bed. Garbed in his knee-length green hunting shirt, brown fly-front breeches, his long legs stretched before him like fallen timber. His forest green Scottish bonnet was tilted to the side, riding high on his sun-bronzed forehead and the shaggy ginger mane that framed his craggy features.

"John Stark . . ." she said in a faint voice.

He stirred, coughed, straightened his bonnet, ran a hand across his crooked countenance. He studied her for a moment half expecting to find her delusional. But her gaze held. She even struggled to sit upright though rightly failed, groaning as the dull ache in her skull threatened to break loose in a wave of full-blown agony. She settled back on the pillows and dutifully remained still. John's expression brightened.

"Thank God," he said.

Molly got the feeling that perhaps opening her eyes and recognizing the man she loved caught him off guard. She had no way of knowing the blow on her head had come close to ending her, had no memory of the times during these long hours when she had slipped in and out of her fevered state. In fact, three days had been blotted from her life and Molly would never get them back.

"You look as if you've seen me somewhere before," she said. Her reply alarmed him, but only for a moment. He caught the hint of a smile tugging at the corners of her mouth. And the sparkle in her sea-green eyes took on an impish gleam.

"Every man has seen you somewhere before . . . somewhere. . . ." Stark replied. "But finding you, now there's the trail. A man has the hope of a woman like you before he closes his eyes at night. A man dreams of a woman like you, at his side, to run the river with, to stand with him against the night."

"Why, Johnny Stark, you have the soul of a poet," she drily observed in a voice that was little more than a whisper.

She glanced around the familiar confines of her bedroom in the house where she lived with Uncle Ephraim and Aunt Charity. All was in its proper place, and the cheery fire in the hearth embraced her with its warm glow. Then the reality of what had happened came rushing back and her hand rose to her bandaged head. The pain had lost some of its edge, had dulled to a grinding ache, and there was a faint high-pitched buzzing in her ears as if she were being circled by a swarm of angry bees.

Molly glanced at the man whose rangy frame threatened to shatter the hand-hewn chair on which he'd kept his vigil, only relinquishing his place when Aunt Charity threatened to shoo him away with a broom. Their eyes met. And Stark began to answer her unspoken questions.

"It's been three days since I . . . found you."

"If it wasn't for Duchess . . . she saved my life, Johnny," Molly weakly told him, with an ungainly glance about the room. She had hoped to find the big mastiff curled by her bedstead.

"She's dead," Stark said, his features hardening. "I tried but I couldn't save her," he bitterly added, recalling the long walk back from Fort William Henry with the great beast draped across his shoulders. He rose from the chair to loom over the bed. "Cassius lit out that same night. I dare say he's returned to Cowslip by now. All the Fargos hail from east of Greylock Mountain. But I'll run him to ground. I just couldn't leave until . . . well . . . with you . . .

so stricken . . . not knowing whether you would. . . ."

"Let me mend, Johnny, and I will accompany you," the woman replied, struggling to sound stronger than she felt. She reached out from beneath the quilt and caught his rough hand. His grip was strong and reassuring. But judging from his expression there was no way on God's earth he was going to hold off his pursuit any longer than necessary.

"You're a firebrand, Molly Page. There's not another woman like you in all the colonies, I warrant. But there are some trails I must walk alone. And this is one." He leaned forward. "Are you here with me, Molly? Truly. Look me in the eyes, lass. Do you know where you are?"

"I know I am in bed," she drily observed. She remembered his recent bout of illness that had laid him low. "One of us or the other is always in bed. But never together." She squeezed his hand.

"Bold talk is poor bluff without action. Perhaps we should seek out a parson before you speak further."

Molly placed a hand upon the bandage covering her skull. "Saints preserve me, either I am addled or I do believe the man proposed." She sighed and sank back against the pillows. "And it only took a cracked skull to snare you."

"Snare indeed," he scoffed. "I walked willingly into your camp the moment I first laid eyes on you. Only the time wasn't right, Molly, with the war and all. And I figured a man should have more to offer a woman than a cabin on the back acre of her uncle's farm."

Molly glanced aside at the bayberry wax candles on the small four-poster table alongside her bed. She inhaled and caught the scent, sweet and fragrant and ripe with memories of languorous spring days. Not that there had ever been peace. Fort Edward was too far west for that, and a thorn in the side of the French and Abenaki. Every Ranger and townsman and farmer knew Atoan and his ally, the French officer named Barbarat, would not rest until the last English soldier and colonial settler was driven back across the Adirondacks. How could any man or woman think of love in such a time? The deliberation took too much effort, it tired her out.

"I shall rest," she said. Stark's eyebrows arched with concern. "And when I wake, I intend to remember everything that's been said between us." He relaxed. *She would have none of that. The young woman intended to hold him accountable for all that had passed between them.* "Everything," she pointedly repeated.

23

"Praise be to the Good Lord," Aunt Charity exclaimed, rising from her ladder-backed rocking chair. Stark had only just brought the good news downstairs that Molly had recognized him and even managed a brief exchange. "Perhaps I should stay upstairs? No. The dear will need her rest. . . . Oh my . . . it is all I can do to keep from hurrying to her side." Charity Page rubbed her plump hands together, pursed her lips and shook her head as if continuing to engage in some inner dialogue, weighing the merits of whether or not she ought to take up the vigil Stark had just abandoned.

"Later, there will be time for making a proper fuss over her, Mother Page," said Ephraim, rescuing his wife from her indecision. "We can do more for Molly by getting back to our lives. If our niece recognized this big rapscallion then I warrant she is back among us and the worst is over for her. Now all she needs is food and proper sleep."

Ephraim nodded sagely and leaned on the mantle. He acknowledged their other guest with a wave of his hand, beckoning Robert Rogers to warm his hands by the fire. Page stood aside as he glanced at the commander of the Ranger company who had only recently joined them on his way back from a meeting with Major Ransom. Rogers clapped Stark on the shoulder and then with a nod in Ephraim's direction, knelt and added a log to the blaze.

"Your niece is a remarkable young woman," Rogers said to Ephraim, positioning the log on the andirons. He was tempted to add that Johnny Stark was a fortunate man to have someone like Molly Page so enamored of him. Like so many of the red-blooded young deerstalkers who comprised the Ranger company, Robert Rogers too had experienced a twinge of envy at the sight of John and Molly together. What man of flesh and blood wouldn't wish such a woman to stand at his side?

Ephraim nodded and took a moment to turn away and dab his eyes on the sleeve of his shirt, then wipe a hand across his wrinkled features. Despite the warmth flooding into the room from the crackling flames, the older man shivered. Ephraim's cheeks were flush from a chill that had set in his bones with the first snowfall and that no amount of heat could rebuke.

He kept a woolen shawl pulled about his bony shoulders these days although every time he stooped near the fireplace, the woven hem trailed dangerously close to the flames. Charity cautioned him at first and continued to nag her husband until he removed the shawl and draped it over the back of the wing-backed chair he had freighted over the mountains from Boston.

"And bless you, Johnny Stark," said Charity and embraced the frontiersman who towered over her.

"What for, little mother?"

"Why, for bringing me such good news from Molly's bedside," she said, then turned toward her husband and gave him a kiss on his forehead.

"Now, woman, gird thy loins and behave yourself," Ephraim fussed, his wrinkled features reddening. Page came from stoic stock and was obviously embarrassed by his wife's open display of affection, considering it more of an affliction if the truth be known. In private was another matter entirely. He waved her off with an air of good-natured discomfort.

"See here now, you've ignored our needs long enough. You've grown men to feed, wife."

It was an articulate reprimand that Charity pointedly ignored. She brushed his protestations aside, overpowered his defenses and gave the venerable old gunsmith a kiss and a tug on his white beard for good measure before trundling off to the kitchen to prepare the day's meal.

"Come along, Father Page," she said, leading him by the hand. "Leave Johnny Stark to Major Rogers's care. I am sure our guests have important matters to discuss."

Charity had already set another loaf of brown bread in the oven box and dare not leave it unattended for long. There was a spring to her step now, by heaven, she almost bounded across the floor. Molly was on the mend, she just knew it. Ephraim was quite correct, not that she would admit it to his face, but it was high time she eased back into her role of caring for those who lived beneath her roof.

Now, what was it? Yes, the baked beans. I'll need to add an extra dollop of molasses and brown sugar to the pot. Molly likes them thick and sweet.

The farmer's wife silently congratulated herself for being clever enough to save a portion of the salt pork aside rather than add it all to the beans. A quarter of the inch-thick slab would provide a hearty flavor to the parsnips and wild onions she intended to boil in a separate pot.

The kindly woman hummed to herself as she went about her labor of love. Hungry mouths to feed, grown men to care for, her niece to comfort and fuss over gave her a sense of purpose. Ephraim understood how his wife felt. The way she tripped about the kitchen, it was as if some terrible burden had been lifted from Charity's well-rounded frame.

His own heart felt lighter as well. The howling wilderness had already claimed his only son. Losing Molly would have been intolerable. Still he glanced longingly in the direction of the front room. He hated being kept in the dark. Whatever was said beneath his roof ought to be proper for him to overhear.

"See here. You've no work for me in here, woman," he said. "My place is. . . ."

"Not in that front room," Charity finished. She placed her fingers to her lips and motioned for her husband to be quiet. "There is unfinished business between those two. Could you not tell?"

"Aye." The gunsmith scowled and scratched his beak of a nose. "That's precisely why I wanted to remain."

Charity sat him down at the long wooden table that dominated the center of the kitchen and handed him a stag-handled knife and a stack of parsnips and wild onions fresh from the root cellar. But even as she went about her own task, checking the bread in the oven box, stirring the beans in the black iron pot hung above the flames in the kitchen hearth, she strained to listen, infected by the same curiosity that tormented her husband.

"Sam and Moses and the lads will rejoice that Molly is back among us," Rogers said. He plucked a length of burning bark from the hearth and touched the flame to the bowl of his pipe. Soon a trail of tobacco smoke curled up to wreath his features. He tossed the bark into the fire. "Will you carry word to them? And I am certain Major Ransom will want to be informed. He too showed no small concern for her plight. Even Sir Peter Drennan has sent his condolences."

"I shall thank you to bring the news to the lads for me, I daresay most of them are still gathered 'neath the sign of the Fox. Tess is no doubt anxious to be quit of them. Men like Moses Shoemaker tend to have a shallow pouch. The only silver he's seen is in his dreams."

"There has not been a moment of boisterousness since Molly's . . . attack. Sam Oday, Moses, even a rake like Locksley Barlow have kept a grave watch. But knowing Molly Page has regained her senses will set them a'right." Rogers frowned. "But the word should come from you."

"The day is still new," Stark said. He donned his great coat, slung his possibles bag and powder horn over his shoulder, took up pistol, tomahawk, and Old Abraham. The .50-caliber Pennsylvania long rifle was primed and loaded and seemed an extension of the big man. "The warmer temperatures ought to have cleared the hillsides of snow except where the shade lasts. I hate to waste the daylight for I can be well down the trail before nightfall."

"See here, John," Rogers cautioned. "Major Ransom has ordered every man to remain within the settlement. We need every rifle until the reinforcements his lordship promised arrive."

"One gun won't make a difference."

"Yours will."

Stark wasn't buying into the major's argument. Before Rogers could react, Stark brushed past him and headed for the front door. The smaller man caught him by the sleeve of his hunting shirt. "Damn it, Stark.

Stark scowled, lowered his gaze to Rogers's hand where the major gripped a fistful of his loose-fitting shirt. Then he locked eyes with his friend from whom the Rangers took their name. Robert Rogers nodded, shrugged, hoping to save face, and released his hold.

"See here, Johnny. You are so damn provincial. England and France and Spain are at each other's throats. War has spread across the high seas, to Africa and India . . . my God. Don't you realize, this is a struggle for empire. And we have the opportunity to play a major part."

Stark looked away a moment, crossed to the window, peered out through the shutters, then glanced down at his large strong hands. His flesh was weathered to a leathery tan. These hands of his could hold a rifle steady, grasp a tomahawk. They'd worked a plough, cleared rocks from the land, his land, been clasped in prayer, and raised in a clenched fist to cry defiance.

"I don't give a tinker's dam about empires. These are our colonies. This is our land. I'll not speak ill of Major Ransom, but you're a fool to think we are any more than pawns to be used by the Crown. To hell with empires. This land has been fought and paid for with our sweat and blood. I fight for me and mine."

"Nevertheless, my headstrong friend, you have been ordered to remain in Fort Edward," said Rogers.

"The devil take you and your orders!" the big man

snapped, color creeping into his sun-bronzed features. "There's a time to follow the footpath along with everyone else and a time to blaze your own way."

"Ransom will toss you in the stockade for this." Rogers began to rub his forehead. This obstinate long hunter was a headache. There was simply no reasoning with the man. "Then again, Cassius Fargo or one of his cousins might shoot your lights out. You'll find no friends in Cowslip."

"I won't be looking for any." Stark worked the latch on the door, swung it open and sucked in his breath as a gust of cold wind flooded the sitting room, ruffled the lace-trimmed cloth that covered the end tables, set the tongues of fire lapping at the firebricks. Stark heard the sound of a pistol being cocked behind him. He glanced over his shoulder. Robert Rogers had drawn his pistol and leveled it at the towering individual in the doorway.

"I could stop you," Rogers said, eyes narrowing.

"I don't think so," John Stark quietly replied, staring at the pistol. His own grip tightened on the rifle in his hand but he had yet to raise the barrel to answer the threat. His smouldering gaze read Robert Rogers like a book. In the silence, Rogers reached his decision. He had wealth. He had authority. And he wasn't about to throw it away because Johnny Stark wanted to exact retribution on Cassius Fargo.

Rogers lowered his pistol and returned it to his belt, taking care to lower the hammer back onto the frizzen. "What the hell . . . you want to run afoul of the British, so be it. Do what you've a mind to. But I say the devil take Cassius Fargo."

"He'll have to wait until I'm finished with him," said Stark. He ducked beneath the door frame and vanished into the morning light. In his wake, a slight sudden laugh drifted in on the wind. It was a sound devoid of mirth, cold as gray bones, and inviting as the creak of a coffin lid.

24

"Before you leave your encampment, send out small parties to scout round it, to see if there be any appearance or track of an enemy that might have been near you during the night."

Johnny Stark was not alone, nor had he been alone since leaving Fort Edward, of that he was certain. He rubbed the back of his neck. The tingling just beneath the skin, an inch below the base of his skull, never lied. Someone or something had been following him for the past two days. He was being shadowed, or stalked. And it was time to turn and face whatever haunted his path.

He'd ruled out Cassius Fargo. The brute would have called attention to himself, blundered into view, erred somewhere along the trail that wound over Greylock Ridge. And an Abenaki war party would have fallen on him like a pack of wolves his first day out from Fort Edward.

Then who? Or what?

He needed to know. To that end Stark made camp on the eastern slope of the Greylocks, chose a small patch of cold-cleared ground and built a fire along the banks of White Creek, a narrow, frozen-over rivulet that cut through the glacier-carved valley, worming its way around great gray boulders left in the wake of receding walls of ice in ages long past.

As the sun lowered over the western hills, he built a tidy pyre of brittle tree limbs, coaxed a merry blaze out of the dry branches, then after checking his back trail, fixed a

bedroll so that it appeared he was asleep by the flames. The
Ranger steeled himself against the chill as he left the circle
of warmth and crept off to conceal himself under a deadfall
of decaying leaves and the brittle stalks of jack-in-the-pulpit
and green dragon that flourished near the creek, in patient
slumber, waiting for the distant spring.

He dug a depression beneath in the humus and lined it
with a flap of buckskin upon which he placed a half-dozen
glowing coals and covered them over with another piece of
hide. The warmth was a welcome comfort against his chest
as he stretched out, settled down for what he assumed was
going to be a long and probably unproductive vigil.

Shadows lengthened. Night spread across the fertile
landscape, transforming the forested slopes into a marching
onslaught of cruelly barbed legions that threatened to sweep
across the creek and engulf the hapless little campsite.

Stark waited, allowing the stillness to settle on him like
sheltering wings, disguise him, seduce him, transform him
into something that was once a man yet more than a man.
For his untamed heart beat in accord with the pulse of the
wild country, its blood his blood, its dangers his own. He
was part of the frigid air that braced him, part of the embers
whose warmth seeped into his bones; glance in his direction
and see the earth and the hills and the debris of winter and
not a man on a mission, a man with blood in his eye and
his hand upon a gun.

He lost all track of time . . . lost himself in thoughts of
Molly, in plans for spring forays against the French once
the lakes thawed, lost himself in the threat of what lay
ahead for him. Cowslip, from what he could recall, was an
isolated little farm community another five-hour walk to the
east, in a narrow valley hemmed in on both sides by granite
bluffs masked by rows of elegant maple trees and trailing
vines that spilled across the rim.

Lost in his thoughts, in the speeding hours and minutes
of uncertainty, he failed to notice a patch of shadows stir
on the edge of night, glide effortlessly, soundlessly and
materialize into a man born of darkness until the buckskin-

clad individual entered the circle of firelight. Stark's blood ran cold and he caught his breath to keep from exclaiming aloud.

Atoan!

What was this? Had the man come alone? Where were the howling heathens who comprised his savage horde? Fortunately, any plan he had to murder Stark in his sleep was due for a swift and sudden reversal. Stark remembered the gauntlet, the deaths of his friends. The ghosts of his massacred countrymen whispered in his ear, their voices keening on the winter's night.

The frontiersman eased his rifle forward. He had a perfect shot. Old Abraham slid across the snow-patched humus. Stark took care not to break or rustle any of the dry stalks in his line of fire.

But to Stark's surprise, Atoan did not fall upon the bedroll with his tomahawk and knife. Instead the Grand Sachem squatted by the fire, drew his heavy woolen blanket around his shoulders, and leaned on his musket, his sharp features in repose. The warrior studied the "huddled form" across from him, on the opposite side of the campfire, his gaze swept the surrounding woods, drifted across Stark's hiding place and passed on.

The Abenaki added some more branches to the fire. The flames leaped upward, the blaze reborn. Atoan removed his pipe from a pouch slung across his shoulder and proceeded to fill the bowl with tobacco smoke, wholly unconcerned that by his actions he presented a prime target for the marksman out beyond the light. But Stark, tempted as he was, could not bring himself to take the shot. Curiosity stayed him.

"*Kiwaskwek*, I have lit the pipe of peace, I have breathed smoke to the four winds. This ground is sacred. Come into the circle." The Grand Sachem placed his weapons aside. Johnny Stark considered his options. Atoan had courage, there was no disputing it, too much courage to be shot down from ambush. So Stark rolled out from concealment, brushed the matted leaves and mud from his hunting shirt and sauntered out of the woods and into camp. He knelt opposite the Abenaki warrior. This was the second time they had come face-to-face. The first time there had been screaming and chants and brandished weapons and cries for blood.

And there had been death.

"You call me beast." Stark accepted the long-stemmed pipe from Atoan's hands and raised it to his lips four times, exhaling to the north, south, east, and west. "Why is this?"

"You are the one who slays my people. You stalk us like the beast of the forest. The *Anglais* call you John Stark." Atoan leaned toward him, frowning as he received the pipe back into his hands. "But *Mahom* has whispered me your real name. He has told me who you are."

"There is blood on your tomahawk as well." John Stark sat back on his heels and keeping a close eye on the Abenaki's empty hands, set his rifle down at his side. "You are the beast to my people."

"We have made war, one upon the other."

"I have not killed your women and children as you did at Fort William Henry," Stark coldly replied.

"Yes . . ." Atoan said, sucking in his breath, choosing his words with care, a note of resignation in his voice when next he spoke. "Once this was the land of the Abenaki, beyond the Great Water to the North and down beyond the Carrying Place where the *Anglais* flag flies above Fort Edward. The Redcoats and French came from where the sun rises, they chose to make war upon each other in our land, each of them invited the Abenaki to join. The *Anglais* soldiers brought gifts to my people, warm blankets for when the snow comes. We accepted the gifts. And soon after, the white man's spotted sickness spread among my people, and it did not care who it killed. The woman I took to wife, my children save for Kasak, I lost them all to the sickness. We burned the blankets but it was too late. Day after day the death chants were sung out until there seemed no end to them, until what was left of the People of the White Pines sang with one voice. And wept with one heart."

Atoan's facial expression never changed, but his voice wavered for a moment, and his dark-eyed stare was filled with smoldering resolve.

"Then why are we not trying to kill one another right now?" said Stark.

"Because I walked in a dream and *Mahom*, the Grandfather Spirit, whispered your name in my ear. And I am puzzled, *Kiwaskwek*. You are not like the others. When the earth mother wakes from her winter sleep, you listen to the warm, hear the windsong and that which is beyond hearing. You see the trail, but you also see the spirit of that which left the trail. How is this so?"

"Perhaps I too walked in a dream."

"Yet you are not one of the people. How can you know where you are going?"

"Just because I wander doesn't mean I'm lost."

Atoan nodded. The reply made sense to him. And it troubled him. He would carry Stark's words within him. "I watched you leave the *Anglais* fort. Alone. Where do you go?"

"To kill a man who harmed the woman I will take to wife."

"I shall not interfere. It is good to see you *Anglais* hunt one another." Atoan grew quiet for a moment, then slowly reached for his weapons. Stark tensed. Atoan laughed softly and returned to his original position, then stretched out on his blanket. "I was going to leave, but we have a good fire and the night is cold. I shall go in the morning. Let it be said, *Kiwaskwek*, that we met as enemies, but we shared a campfire as. . . ."

"Friends?" Stark interjected, somewhat doubtful. This man would never cease his war until the colonists were all killed or driven back into the sea.

"Brothers," said Atoan. "Bound by what we must do, the paths we must walk. Brothers bound by blood."

Stark reclined upon his own bedding. He lay on his back, looked up at the black heavens strewn with stars, unimaginable in number, gleaming bright. And he thought how remarkable it was to be sharing a fire with one who was his enemy and yet. . . .

Robert Rogers wouldn't understand, nor poor Ephraim Page, certainly not Ransom, none of the soldiers or the Ranger company or the colonists. Perhaps the great tragedy of this war is that there was guilt enough for all. Maybe one day men would find a way to acknowledge a common pain, and come together into the light, and find a common sacred ground.

"Twice I had you in my gunsights yet I stayed my hand." Atoan's words drifted on the wintry stillness, punctuated by the crackling flames. "I tell you now, twice I have spared you just as you gave me back the life of my son. Now it is ended, *Kiwaskwek*, and all that connects us is what lies ahead, not what has gone before. When next we meet, I think it will be for the last time."

John Stark opened his eyes at first light. It took him a moment to recognize his surroundings. The night before had been like some strange dream. The Ranger glanced across the blackened patch of earth and the smoldering embers of the campfire and found he was alone again. Atoan had returned to the forest, disappeared back into the howling wilderness to await the day that would bring the two of them together, *for the last time*.

"So be it," said Stark.

25

John Stark climbed the last ridge, cut through a stand of white pines, then crossed the summit, and began his descent. He cut across the downslope where patches of snow clung to the shade and made his way to a wheel-rutted path worn in the earth that descended the grade in a series of gradual switchbacks until it straightened out on the outskirts of the farming community.

A pair of stray dogs and a flock of geese announced his arrival, abandoning the safety of their respective domains to sound the alert for all of Cowslip to hear. Heifers in their pasture looked up in lazy wonderment, then returned to cropping the yellow stalks of dry grasses revealed by the recently departed snow. By afternoon, the temperature had climbed to well above freezing. Rivulets in the mud marked the legacy of melting snow.

The sun was behind him now, riding high over his left shoulder in a cloudless sky. His shadow stretched before him on the ground, sunlight warmed the back of his neck, his cheeks were flush and, despite the chill, perspiration beaded his upper lip. His long-limbed strides made short work of the descent to the valley floor.

As if to remind him that winter was far from over, an icy gust tried to steal the Scottish bonnet he wore snugly over his unruly mane and tugged at the heavy folds of his sea-green cloak till it flapped like the wings of some great bird of prey. It was an apt analogy for the man. Indeed, his hunt had brought him this far and grim resolve would carry him further.

Stark sensed he was being watched, imagined the faces

behind the shuttered windows of the cabins haphazardly scattered throughout the valley without any semblance of order or planning. A few homespun-clad farmers appeared in their doorways, paused with arms folded or leaning on their own long guns while they took the measure of this new arrival.

To them, there was only one man who fit the size and cut of this stranger who so boldly marched through the settlement. It was rumored the Abenaki had a name for him, that they frightened their children with his exploits and that the French had a price on his head. But here in the colonies he was simply trouble on the prowl and a bad moon rising. He was John Stark, man and legend rolled into one.

His audience quickly retreated inside as if unwilling to attract attention to themselves. Everyone in Cowslip knew why he had come. The Ranger and Cassius Fargo had crossed one another back in Fort Edward.

Cowslip wasn't much. But the Fargo clan was well represented hereabouts, much to the chagrin of most honest, God-fearing folks. Fargo and his cousins and distant relatives weren't exactly held in high esteem. But they were a mean bunch to cross. And Cassius was the worst. But whatever their sympathies the townsmen wanted no part of the drama that was about to unfold.

John Stark paused in the middle of the settlement to catch his bearings. There really wasn't much to the place, a cluster of farm cabins, a crudely built blockhouse in which the locals might take refuge during a raid, a blacksmith's forge and a long, low-roofed meetinghouse, and there beneath the spreading limbs of a towering oak, the Hound and Hare Tavern that offered lodging, food and drink for the wayfarer.

Stark had come this far but he'd need help from here on out. The way to Fargo's farm began at the tavern. Someone was bound to know the whereabouts of Fargo's homestead. There must be someone in the settlement who wasn't related by blood or marriage. On the other hand the likes of Cassius Fargo and his cousin folk might have the locals intimidated into silence. Stark had the unsettling impression he was placing one foot in a trap and following it with the other.

The pack of mongrels was becoming a nuisance. It was a struggle for the Ranger to ignore the dogs yipping at his heels, but he managed to hold to his course and head straight for the tavern. By the time he reached the low-roofed stone house he'd had enough. He slowed his pace beneath the shadow of the tavern's signboard, a cracked and knotted plank of wood decorated with an artist's rendering of a hound about to pounce on a hapless hare as it attempted to scamper off through a few strokes of hastily-etched reeds.

Without warning, Stark stopped dead in his tracks and whirled about to confront the dogs. The big man's features crinkled into a war map of unabashed menace. He growled low and deep in his throat. The strays stared wide-eyed for a moment then slunk away, whimpering and yipping as they went. Stark nodded, satisfied, and ducked through the doorway into the shadowy interior.

A hunter knows his prey, studies the terrain. Is there a way out? Is the animal cornered and more likely to turn with his back to the wall and confront his pursuer? And is this the den or a cold trail and a blind lead?

The tavern was smaller than the Kit Fox in Fort Edward, a few long board tables filled the center of the room. Another five smaller tables were made from upturned barrels fitted with a round wooden top. Stark paused to allow his eyes to adjust to the smoky interior. The chimney was not drawing properly and evidently, every time someone entered, tendrils of soot-gray smoke were drawn into the tavern to collect near the bark-bristled rafters.

Stark's intrusion ended the conversation among the patrons. The long tables in the center of the room were occupied by a gathering of farmers and wayfarers who fell silent at the sight of the Ranger looming in the doorway.

Stark took in the scene, scrutinizing his surroundings with the caution of a man who had just entered a wolf den and wasn't sure whether or not it was still occupied by a pack of feral beasts.

He glanced in the direction of a balding, heavyset individual standing behind a hand-hewn maplewood bar. By his placement and the air of authority in the man's bearing Stark could only assume this was the proprietor. The tavern keeper, framed by two enormous barrels of ale, looked to be twenty years Stark's senior. He frowned at the newcomer and then set his bung hammer and starter aside on the bar top and folded his arms across his thickly-muscled chest.

The patrons looked to be farmers, tradesmen, or freight haulers dressed in nankeen shirts and woolen trousers. Three men at a table toward the rear of the room caught the Ranger's attention. The three were clearly younger than Stark and bore a certain resemblance to Cassius Fargo. Judging by the slope of their shoulders and their close-set eyes and square, flat faces, Stark was certain the three had Fargo blood flowing through their veins.

One of the three, the more nervous of the lot, remained at his table nursing a tankard of ale while his two companions bestirred themselves from bowls of venison stew and torn crusts of bread. They stood and exchanged a few softly spoken words of wisdom to their agitated companion who nodded and gulped his ale in hopes perhaps of finding his courage in the bottom of the pewter cup.

The other two nonchalantly followed Stark as he approached the sour-faced tavern keeper. One had pockmarked ugly features, the other had fairer features but also the mean, confident eyes of a bully. There was a swagger to their walk, an air befitting some figures of importance. Stark guessed a man like Cassius Fargo and his kin were accustomed to the deference of other men, a quality they'd find lacking in John Stark.

If the two were put off by his size, though, they did not show it, taking comfort in the fact that they were among their own. "Pockmark" took the right side, "Bully" leaned his elbows on the bar about six feet from Stark's left, both stared toward the kegs of ale, taking care not to even glance in the direction of the man they had just flanked.

The tavern keeper chewed the inside of his lip, in thought, then scratched his grizzled jaw and addressed the Ranger, as Stark placed Old Abraham upon the bar and rested both hands on the rifle barrel.

"We have no rooms today. What we have are taken."

"Not looking for a room," Stark said.

"There's ale and the mistress has a venison stew over the fire yonder. Take you a wooden bowl here and help yourself. No man can say Irish McQuade ever turned a man back into the wilderness with an empty belly." The tavern keeper turned toward one of the barrels to his right. Stark reached over and caught him by the shoulder.

"Neither drink or meat, Innkeeper, but a simple word or two to point me in the right direction from your doorstep."

"Indeed? How so then?"

"I have come for Cassius Fargo." There, it was said. If the room was quiet before, it was positively tomblike now.

Bully, the man to Stark's left, spoke up. "Our cousin said to keep a look out for the likes of you. We know you, John Stark. But the only weight that name carries is what's tucked in your boots."

"The same boots that better carry you out of here and out of Cowslip," said Pockmark. And to make a point he allowed his coat to part to reveal the curled walnut grip of a pistol tucked in the broad leather belt circling his waist.

Stark glanced to either side and then focused on McQuade. The tavern keeper shrugged and grinned. "No one will help you. You see how it is," he flatly stated.

"I have come for Cassius Fargo . . . *that's—how—it—is.*"

"Just who do you think you are?" Pockmark blurted out, his hand drifting toward the pistol.

Stark fixed him with a stare. "Justice."

Bully made his move, grabbing for his pistol. Stark, with his hands on the rifle, jammed the tip of the barrel into the younger man's throat. Bully staggered back, gasping for breath. In the same motion Stark stepped back and caught Pockmark right between the eyes with the brass butt plate. Pockmark dropped hard, bounced his head off the floor and lay still. Stark let momentum pull him in a complete circle and swinging the rifle slapped the barrel up alongside McQuade's head as the tavern keeper reached for a blunderbuss he kept beneath the bar. The weapon discharged with a thunderous roar, blowing a hole in the top of the maplewood bar. The tavern keeper groaned and slumped forward onto his knees.

Stark snatched the bung hammer from the countertop and descended on Bully like some wrathful Norse god. As the choking man tried to bring the flintlock into play, Stark batted the weapon from the cousin's grasp. Bones snapped. The gun dropped. Bully yelped and collapsed in agony, cradling his broken hand.

Stark whirled to confront the rest of the room. He brandished the rifle in his powerful right hand, and in his left, a lethal-looking twin barreled flintlock pistol, cocked and ready to fire. Silence . . . broken by the sobbing cousin at his feet. Stark was tense, primed as his weapons, ready to take on one or all.

But no one moved.

The locals averted their eyes, stared at the bowls of food or tankards of ale or the blank boards of the tabletops before them. Stark slowly turned and advanced on the last of the cousins, the nervous one who had not stirred from the back of the tavern.

Step . . . Step . . . Step.

And then, nothing.

Looking up into the face of this berserker looming over him, Cassius' cousin only had one thing to say.

"I can draw you a map. . . ."

26

Cassius Fargo hoisted the carcass of the white-tailed buck into the air and tied off the rope around the tree trunk. The buck hung suspended with its hind legs a foot off the ground. Earlier that day, just before noon, Cassius shot the animal while it grazed on the dried corn Fargo had scattered over a hillside just over a ridge behind his cabin.

The animal's glazed stare beheld its killer with mute wonderment. A few handfuls of seed corn had lured the graceful creature to its death. Cassius indulged himself with a silent moment of congratulations. It had been a splendid shot. But then all his kin had a way with a smoke pole. Still, Cassius liked to think himself the cleverest of the lot and boasted about his marksmanship.

With the buck swaying from the oak limb like some unfortunate miscreant dangling from a gallows, Fargo set to work. He sliced the carcass from groin to throat, took care to avoid dulling his blade on the breastbone, then sawed clear through to the left of the sternum and had to reach up inside for the lungs and heart.

He sliced through muscles and fibrous white tendons, then scooped the organs out with his hand. Before long the hunter had a pile of steaming entrails at his feet. Dark blood stained the patch of snow here where the shade lingered longest. The heat of the organs melted the ice crystals and their pink runoff soaked into the hard-packed earth.

A breeze stirred.

"What's that?" Cassius said, glancing over his shoulder toward the side of log house and the uneven ground where he and Ford and their father had started their first well, the one that had buried Pa alive.

"Just you stay put, you old devil. Ford ain't coming back. You know that by now. Look about yourself, there amongst the brimstone, he ought to be dancing with the devil right alongside you." Cassius Fargo shook his head, some vague protest seeping through his skull like an afterthought. "Damn you, I said look about. You'll see him. Why bother me? I got to cut up this buck before the meat spoils."

Fargo scowled and surveyed the family farm, the fallow fields, the empty barn with a loft, a cold smokehouse with its naked beams that should have been groaning beneath the weight of wild game and slaughtered hogs. There was a lot of work to do if he planned to last out the rest of the winter at this homestead. And stocking the smokehouse was a high priority. His belly was already rumbling.

These late winter preparations were too much for one man alone. But he had kin here and that made all the difference. He could count on his cousins. They'd stand by him. That was the way of things in Cowslip, the Fargos ran together like a pack, cross one and you crossed them all. The folks in the settlement knew it and didn't get out of line.

"We served them well," Cassius said aloud considering Cowslip and those who had come to make a life for themselves in the valley. "When injuns showed, it was always Pa and Uncle Jesse who were the first to fight. And the rest of us marched right along with 'em as soon as we could hold a smoke pole of our own. By heaven, it was Fargos who stood their ground when others turned tail and ran, Fargos who fought and bled and drove off the heathens, every mother's son and made these woods safe for Christian folk."

Standing ankle-deep in gore, Cassius continued to plead his case to the uncaring sunlight while he continued to skin the carcass. The voices in his head were as real to him as the warm red flesh beneath his hands. "I'll *brain tan* this. Yeah, I know, Pa, I'll make sure the brains are smoked first. I learned it, not like Ford who always rushed his way through. I can soak the hide in the rain barrel till I'm ready to brain tan it good and proper."

Cassius paused to survey the homestead, wiped the sweat from his brow and inadvertently smeared his features with the blood of his kill. The three-roomed log house dominated the center of a broad open clearing dotted by the stumps of trees like so many flattened tables in the field. A ramshackle barn built of stone and weathered timber stood off to the side, about twenty yards from the cabin. It was empty now for the most part, home to the mice and squirrels, but in better days the barn had stored winter grass and sheltered a pair of stout oxen from the elements.

It would again, Cassius resolved.

A twig snapped behind him. The hunter dropped his knife and reached for one of the pistols tucked in the wide leather belt circling his thick waist. His gaze narrowed. The pistol barrel slid from the belt. Then a calico cat leaped from the shadows into the sunlight, broke from cover and chased a field mouse out of the shadows and into the sunlit field.

Fargo relaxed his grip on the weapon and took comfort in the broad open pasture surrounding the homestead. It had been necessary to force the forest back from the house so that a man could watch the approach to the farm. Except for a cluster of oak trees alongside the cabin, Cassius was surrounded by nothing but about two hundred feet of weed-grown field and a clear field of fire in every direction all the way to the forest's edge. Anyone emerging from the woods with its stands of maple, pine, and white oak would present an inviting target as they approached. There was no way Cassius Fargo was going to be surprised by an unwelcome visitor.

It felt good to be back home, away from Fort Edward with all its travails and temptations and soldiering. The hell with Rogers's Rangers, with Major Ransom and the royal regiment, and the fool lot who marched to the drum of Big John Stark.

Let the cursed militia take the war to the French. A man need only defend his place. Cowslip was fine, just fine. The valley was world enough for him. And any man who came prowling around, looking for trouble, be he red or white, would get more than he bargained for.

Come springtime Cassius intended to bring some of his cousins over and break ground for a decent garden. He paused a moment and ruefully considered his mistakes, how he should never have abandoned the homestead for soldiering. It had been brother Ford's influence and poor fodder of an idea to be sure. It had done nothing for either of them but make the homestead fall into disrepair. And adventuring had cost Ford his topknot. What a waste.

This valley was home. His kin were here. And the folks in the settlement knew well enough to give Cassius a wide berth when he needed it. What man could ask for more? And once he had rechinked the cabin walls and put some game in the smokehouse and brought over the cows and oxen Uncle Jesse had tended for him, Cassius might just see about fetching himself a wife, maybe from over the mountains.

Cassius stepped back from the carcass, once again dabbed his blunt features with the sleeve of his shirt, tossed the skinning knife aside and sauntered over to the rain barrel and splashed his face with water. He knelt for a second and rummaged behind the rain barrel and produced a brown ceramic jug. He uncorked the hard cider and tilted the spout to his lips. The spirits burned all the way down, but it was a welcome warmth that reinvigorated the man. He felt energy returning to his stocky frame and muscled limbs. Butchery was hard work by any standard. But he took a moment to catch his breath, studying the remains of the deer hanging from the tree limb, then his eyes focused beyond, to the site where the well had caved in on his father and ended his tyranny.

He grinned. "I showed Miss Molly Page a thing or

two." He scowled at the earth. "I would have had her, save for that damn mongrel dog. I took her measure though, taught her there was a price to pay for the way the harlot lorded around like she was royalty, just cause she opened her legs to Stark."

He clenched his fist, hearing his father and brother mock him from the grave. "I'm not afraid of John Stark. The hell I am. Let the bastard come, says I. He won't cast such a long shadow in this valley. The Fargos will teach him humility!"

Cassius stood over the mounded earth. His father had been leather tough. And that was how he raised his sons. "You hear me, Pa? I will fear neither man nor beast. As for John Stark, just let him come. Why I might even welcome it. I'll give him what his whore got and more. You'll see." He kicked at the mound and started back toward the carcass.

Fargo retrieved the skinning knife, hesitated, a man torn by some internal monolgue, harangued by the spirits of the dead, and stared at the bloodied flesh. His father and brother were amused. Damn them, amused. . . .

Cassius growled and plunged the knife into the flayed flesh before him.

"You heard me! I'll show you. I'll show you both. Just let him come!!"

It was at that moment he heard the familiar sound of a hunting horn reverberate among the distant trees, drift ominously from the forest's edge like a thinly-veiled threat across the barren fields, that single dreadful note announced in its own way, a reckoning was at hand.

And Cassius Fargo . . . in that single awful moment of recognition . . . heard his father's ghostly admonition. "*Be careful what you wish for. . . .*"

27

Maybe I shouldn't have announced myself, Stark thought, second-guessing his bravado as he glanced down at the hunting horn that dangled at his side. Still, he suspected that Fargo, brought to bay on his own land, might find the gumption to meet his enemy head on. The Ranger waited in the emerald shadows, studied the homestead out beyond the field, took his time, wanting to give Cassius every opportunity to face him like a man.

It was midafternoon and most farms would have been alive with activity, more especially since this midwinter's day had dawned milder than the ones before. There were stumps to be cleared, oxen to care for, repairs to be made. But the only sign of the owner's presence hereabouts was the deer carcass that swayed from the spreading branch of the oak tree alongside the log house, near a wheel-rutted path that led past the homestead to the two-story barn.

"Appears Cassius has made one kill today," Stark muttered beneath his breath. "I'd best be careful he doesn't make another."

The Ranger checked his Pennsylvania long rifle. It was primed and the hammer had been fitted with a fresh flint, the same for the double-barreled pistol tucked in the broad leather belt circling his waist. Stark shrugged and stretched, then glanced over his shoulder at his back trail. The flesh between his shoulder blades tingled, the way it always did when he sensed he was being watched, by the forest folk, the wild creatures of the piney woods, or perhaps Atoan was concealed somewhere among the ancient secrets of the trees. But the Grand Sachem was a reckoning for another day. Right now Stark needed to concern himself with only one thing . . . survive the afternoon.

The Ranger removed the dark green Scottish bonnet he favored, brushed back his leonine mane from his chiseled features, set the bonnet in place, thumbed a silver-flecked strand of hair beneath his brim. His brow furrowed. Frowning, he spied a squat, powerfully-built figure appear in the doorway of the farmhouse. Cassius Fargo, rifle in hand, strode out into the yard and held his long gun up above his head and called out in a coarse voice.

"I have been waiting for you, John Stark. But you have come a long way for nothing. This is my land, and you cast no shadow here."

Words words words . . .

His challenge hung upon the north wind, drifted through the tempering sunlight, fell upon deaf ears. Stark had not left his lover's side, refused the order of his superiors, braved a solitary passage over the mountain and run his prey to ground for the purpose of prattle!

And yet it was a sobering thought. Never before had John Stark set out for a killing. War was one thing, to strive and conquer and take a life in the heat of battle; a man could put that behind him. But this . . . was a dark and bloody business. And for a moment he even considered leaving well enough alone. But Fargo had a poison in him, and as long as he lived, neither Stark nor any of his loved ones would be safe.

Molly . . .

Cassius Fargo had tried to kill her. And that must not stand.

Stark tightened his grip on Old Abraham, its walnut stock and iron barrel were a reassuring weight in his hands. Then he started forward, abandoning the edge of the forest to set out across the killing field, his long-legged gait gobbling the distance. Aware he presented an inviting target, Stark increased his pace.

Fargo raised his rifle. Smoke blossomed from the barrel. Stark waited until the last second, darted, swerved,

heard the whine and felt the rush of heated air as a .50-
caliber lead slug traveling at eighteen hundred feet per second missed him by a whisker.

The man by the farmhouse began to hurriedly reload,
ramming powder and shot down the barrel as Stark raced
across the fallow meadow, leaped a stump, took a deadfall
in stride, then almost lost his footing on a patch of moist
earth where the melted snow had pooled and regained his
stride. A rabbit scurried out of harm's way, darted across
the field toward its lair. Stark increased his efforts, closed
fast now, an oncoming storm of retribution and death.

Fargo sighted along his rifle but before he squeezed
the trigger Stark snapped Old Abraham to his shoulder and
fired. Cassius flinched despite himself; "Damn," he cursed,
as he inadvertently fired his flintlock on reflex. Duck and
cover spoiled his aim. An alarmed expression replaced the
look of resolve he had worn like a mask. Fargo fumbled
with his rifle. He had to reload. *Best hurry, brother Cassius!
Time for a reckoning. He sent me under, don't you let him
do you the same way!* Fargo shook his head as if to clear
his brother's admonishment from his mind. And how close
was Stark? It was said the big bastard could bloody well
outrun a horse. But that had to be more brag then fact.

The farmer from Cowslip chanced a quick glance in
the direction of the field. Cassius paled as he saw Stark far
closer than he expected, reload on the run, a skill many of
the Rangers had mastered and one that often meant the
difference between life and death. Fargo's hand trembled
as he jammed the ramrod down the barrel, tamping the
gunpowder in place. He dug in his shot pouch for a rifle
ball, fumbled once again for a patch. He would still need
to prime the weapon.

"Not enough time, Cassius," he heard his brother caution from the recesses of his own bedeviled imagination.
But his brother's ghost skewered the problem. Fargo didn't
have enough time. Not nearly enough. Stark would be on
him before he could bring his gun to bear. So the man chose
a different tack.

Cassius spun on his heels and sprinted for the safety of his house, vanished through the open doorway, slammed the heavy oaken door in his wake, and slid the bolt home with Stark fast on his heels. The big man loosed a war whoop as he rushed the entrance and hurtled his powerful shoulder against the door. The sound of that impact cracked across the clearing but the stout construction held.

Stark staggered back, ignored the pain that shot through his shoulder. He glanced to either side, took care not to bring himself in line with either of the shuttered windows and their firing ports. He retreated just enough for what he had in mind, drew his pistol and fired point blank, blasting apart the top leather hinge and then the lower one. He returned the pistol to his belt, lowered his shoulder and lunged forward yet again. With the leather hinges shot away, the door gave just enough to shatter the bolt. With a crash and a clatter it fell onto the floor. Stark darted across the wooden planks, his great frame bowed forward. Crouching, he held his rifle poised to meet any threat.

The Ranger eased into the front room. The shuttered interior was gloomy and thick with menace. He carefully picked each footstep, made his way past hand-hewn furniture that was plebeian but serviceable, although a rocker near the hearth showed real craftsmanship. One member of this sorry lot had talent; although it was a mystery to Stark which of the brothers had turned his hand to the plane and the lathe. Not that it mattered now. He wasn't here for a lesson in woodworking. This was a day of reckoning.

He checked each bedroom. They were much the same with their log-framed bedsteads, square, solid-looking wash stands and chipped basins, foot chests for clothes, one of the rooms boasted a small writing table by a shuttered window. He proceeded into a dining room with a massive table that could have seated half a dozen grown men. The marred pine surface had been thoughtlessly whittled on. One wall was obscured by a cabinet that sported a haphazard collection of pewter ware, mugs and cups and plates, a pair of wooden trenchers, various knives and forks. Stark noticed a trail of bloody footsteps on the wooden floor, just a smear here and there, but a telltale sign of someone passing. Was Cassius wounded?

Stark knelt and dabbed his fingers into the stain. Cool to the touch, and sticky, not a fresh wound. He remembered the carcass outside. No doubt Fargo had stepped in a puddle of entrails and tracked the mess into the house. Stark eased down a shortened hall and entered a large kitchen that dominated the rear of the house save for a pantry at one corner.

The tabletop was littered with stale chunks of brown bread, a few strips of jerked venison on a wooden platter, a stoneware plate held a half wheel of good Christian cheese partly concealed beneath a flap of sailcloth, and close at hand, a carving knife, a stoneware jug of hard cider and an overturned tankard with naught but a spreading smear radiating out from the lip.

The backdoor was agape.

"Damn . . ." Stark muttered beneath his breath. He leaned his rifle against the edge of the table and took a moment to attend his pistol. Then once more, *loaded for bear*, he tucked the pistol in his belt and edged toward the doorway. Carefully he eased past the doorsill, checked to the right and left, paused to study the open field behind the house.

He could discover no visible tracks. The soil was rocky at best and given to weed. But even the dry yellow stalks looked undisturbed. And he knew firsthand after almost losing his footing in the field, the ground was not as hard as it looked. What with the milder temperature and steady sunlight, the snows had melted, leaving patches of moisture to soften the topsoil. If Cassius had escaped into the backwoods he would have left a mark upon the meadow.

No, Fargo was still hereabouts, somewhere, biding his time, waiting for a single sweet shot, the one that couldn't possibly miss. Stark made his way along the rear of the farmhouse, peered around the corner, studied the trampled earth, and glimpsed a pair of boot prints that appeared freshly formed. They pointed in the direction of the barn.

The loft door was open. He ducked back and centered his thoughts, recalled an image of the farmstead when he first arrived, in his mind's eye, the tableau formed, the farmhouse, the empty yard, the wheel-rutted path and freshly-gutted deer carcass, and beyond, the barn, its roof needing repair, the double doors left ajar but the loft door shuttered.

Yes, he was certain of it.

Now there was only one thing to do. He leaped past the corner, hit the ground running flat out. A cloud drifted before the sun. A murder of ravens exploded from a hole in the barn roof, disturbed by what? Or whom? Cassius mucking about for a better shot? Stark fired from the hip. Old Abraham bellowed thunder, spat flame and sent a rifle ball flying through the loft window forcing whatever marksman might be lurking in the shadows to leap out of harm's way.

Johnny Stark ran for all he was worth, ran like his life depended on it . . . and it did. He heard the crack of a rifle and steeled himself for an impact that never came and saw the cool dark recesses of the barn open to him and then he was inside.

Safe?

Hardly.

A pistol shot from above. Wood splinters spattered his face. He dove to the left and found momentary refuge in a stall beneath the loft which ran lengthwise and was about half the width of the barn. Hidden from sight, with his back to the wall and staring up at the underside of the loft, Stark wiped the blood from his cheek and gingerly plucked the splinters from his flesh.

What passed for silence was broken by the sound of wooden ramrods rasping against metal and the faint whisper of gunpowder sprinkling down the length of an iron gun barrel, the unmistakable punctuation of hammers cocked . . .

"You came close," Fargo's voice drifted down from above.

Stark scrutinized the planks overhead, began to maneuver beneath the loft, drifting toward the back. The sound of Fargo's voice indicated the man was on the move. "Have I nicked you yet?" He waited for a reply. "Maybe you're bleeding, eh?"

Stark shifted his rifle to his left hand, took the pistol in his right. He glimpsed movement between the cracks in the wood. A few wisps of straw drifted down, disturbed by Fargo's steps. In the barn below, Stark kept pace, an unseen stalker.

"Speak, damn your eyes!" Fargo's voice sounded shrill now. "Bleeding, that's it. Or maybe dead."

Stark froze, fingers tightening around the trigger. His left arm began to tremble from the weight of the long rifle. But he held his fire. Bided his time.

"Are you dead, John Stark?" Cassius chuckled. "Well, if not now, soon." He was on the move again and the man below climbed over the side of a second stall and then eased through the broken slats of a third.

"You should have stayed in Fort Edward, stayed with that tart of yours," said Fargo. He found an inch-wide gap in the floor planks. He paused and was rewarded with the sight of Big John Stark stepping into view. "But I showed her a thing or two and took her down a notch. She'll remember Cassius Fargo." Stark glanced up and saw a patch of homespun shirt and the glimmer of a hate-filled stare. "All the more so when I ship you back in a box!"

A section of the floor exploded in Stark's face. He returned the fire and blasted another section back at the man above him. The two men moved in line with one another, screaming as they emptied their guns, blowing holes through the loft floor, shards of wood flying off in all directions as they blasted away at one another with pistols and rifles. The air filled with thick clouds of powder smoke. The sound was deafening.

Then it ended.

Cassius Fargo's body crashed to the dirt floor, bones snapped, limbs flopped and lay still, leaving him sprawled lifeless in the terrible haze, staring with sightless eyes, his features awash with blood from a terrible head wound. Another slug had torn through his chest and left a gaping hole in his back.

The hunt was ended.

Now all that remained was a ringing in the ears, burning eyes, the stench of mortality, and a killer with a heavy heart standing over his victim amid the settling benediction of the straw-stained dust.

The Big Leaf Moon

1758

28

> "If you are to embark ... chuse the evening for
> the time of your embarkation, as you will then
> have the whole night before you to pass undiscov-
> ered by any parties of the enemy."

The feast began as soon as Major Ransom pronounced the
couple married. While Molly Page Stark beamed and
John Stark sheepishly grinned, his fellow Rangers led by
Robert Rogers and Locksley Barlow emptied their rifles
into the air. Sam Oday's blunderbuss sounded like a cannon. Moses Shoemaker dabbed at his grizzled features and
then barrelled his way through the gathering of townsmen,
soldiers of the Regiment and green-clad Indian fighters who
had ventured down to the banks of the Hudson to join in
the celebration, for this was a happy union and a time of
joy after a winter that had brought them to the brink of
tragedy.

Molly was hale and hearty after her ordeal, having re-
covered from Cassius Fargo's despicable assault. During
the months after his return from Cowslip, Stark had kept
close to the settlement, broke ground with Ephraim Page
and suffered other men to patrol the woods while the "beast
of the Abenaki" added a kitchen connected by a covered
dogtrot to the rear of his cabin and made the place fitting.
By the time the ice broke and the river currents carried off
the floes, Big John Stark was prepared for the happy day
when he would join his life and fortune to the woman who
roamed the forests at his side. He would take Molly Page

to wife, to have and to hold, to walk the trail of life together until death.

No one had asked Stark about the fate of Cassius Fargo and the long hunter offered no account of what had transpired but word reached the settlement despite Stark's reluctance to speak on the matter. A freighter hauling goods over the mountains from the eastern cities had passed through Cowslip and, along with an itinerant tinker come to ply his trade, carried the news of Fargo's untimely end, to which the inhabitants of Fort Edward added "well-deserved" and let the matter drop.

John and Molly were married by the river they loved, on a knoll where the dogwoods bloomed. Their cathedral was a landscape of rolling hills thick with oaks and maples adorned in broadleaf raiments of amber and green that swept up from the riverbank and fringed a meadow carpeted with the pinks, blues, and pearl-white bouquets of bloodroot, trout lilies, and lady's slipper.

The hills teemed with wild game and the hunting had been good. White-tailed deer and brown elk had returned to the wooded hills to graze upon the witch hobble and wild turkeys frequently flocked to pristine vales where wood ferns sprouted 'neath a shading canopy of hemlock, spruce, birch, and white pine.

The local hunters had been busy replenishing the settlement's smokehouses. But it was the sure-eyed skills of Molly Page and Big John Stark that provided a substantial part of the wedding feast. While other lasses might have been embroidering their wedding finery, Molly had followed her husband-to-be out among the hills, rifle in hand. Nor had they returned empty-handed. No less than three cookfires crackled and snapped in the afternoon. Greedy flames lapped at the spits of roasting venison, pheasant, and turkey.

Moses Shoemaker made the rounds of each blaze. He had personally appointed the men tending the fires. The irascible old Indian fighter admonished each of his men to keep the flames steady and to see the meat was basted with an anointing of fat drippings and honey. He took care to sample a cut from one of the roasts to satisfy his concerns that all was ready and waiting for the hungry revelers to descend upon the banquet.

Shoemaker might be in charge of the game cooks but Charity Page was the self-proclaimed marshal of the feast. Under her tutelage, tables were arranged, groaning boards set aside and weighed down with platters and bowls of English pudding, brown bread, johnnycakes glazed with maple sugar, tureens of succotash, and blueberry pies. Children wielding makeshift fans were instructed to keep the insects from swarming the foodstuffs. The treats were too tempting for many of the young ones who pilfered the trifles when no one was looking.

Ephraim stood at his wife's side. The gunsmith was clad in his best frock coat and embroidered waistcoat, the front of which was concealed beneath his snowy beard. His features crinkled as he flashed a good-natured smile in the face of their loss. "Well, good wife, it is a good day."

"To think our precious niece is finally married. I prayed I might see this happy day and yet now that it has come to pass, I can only think how I shall miss her about the house." Charity used her apron to wipe the moisture from her eyes. "First Abel and now Molly. I love her like a daughter, I swear I do."

"Take comfort, old dame, I daresay Molly will not be a stranger to our door. She knows her husband has another calling. The wilderness howls in his veins. I doubt he will ever be fully tamed. More's the better for we will need his kind," Ephraim replied. "The drums will sound once more along the War Path. The French will loose their dogs of war." Page caught himself before he added, "and God help us" and silently rebuked himself for calling up such a dark cloud to dim the brightness of this blessed day.

Still, the gunsmith wasn't alone in his anxiety. Of course, spring was a time of renewal and rebirth, when the world walked in beauty. But no one on the frontier was fooled by the grandeur. Now that the river ran free and the wind blew fair, so the rumor of war was in the air and with April already drawing to an end, it was only a matter of time before blood was spilled and the brutal raids began anew.

Time had not dimmed the memory of the fate that befell Fort William Henry. It was whispered that on moonless nights the ghosts walked the forest and lingered, all forlorn, by the banks of Lake George, their endless keening in contrast to the tranquil splash of the rippling waves. Several of the Rangers claimed to have overheard a spectral portent borne upon the rustling breeze. Lo, the ghosts foretold Fort Edward would be the next to fall and the settlement that had sprung up within the shadow of the ramparts, put to the torch.

There were no fools in Fort Edward. It was common knowledge that the reinforcements promised by Sir Peter Drennan had yet to materialize. And though the British forces were massing along the eastern seaboard, here in the wilderness all that stood between the settlements and disaster were the shattered remnants of the 1st Regiment of Foot, and the small but efficient force of Rangers who followed Johnny Stark and Robert Rogers. Still the Colonials refused to abandon their homes and flee to safety. What they had was worth fighting for, and dying for, if need be.

Charity glowered at her husband. "Enough of your gloom, you old *nutmegger.*" She adjusted her lace cap then with a wave of her hands signaled the settlement's musicians to ply their talents. Locksley Barlow with his fiddle, Sergeant Strode with his walking drum, and a trio of Irish fifers from the Regiment began to play a merry jig while the festive throng formed a circle about the newlyweds.

Molly tossed her head, her thick red hair struggled against the ribbons that bound them, her eyes twinkled bright as if imbued with sunbeams glimmering upon an emerald sea. "You're trapped now, Johnny Stark," she called out, tying up the front of the wine-colored apron she wore over her pink-and-white petticoat. She checked the fastened buttons on her matching lace bodice for modesty's sake, then approached the long hunter who glanced about for an escape route. But his fellow Rangers and townsfolk stood shoulder to shoulder.

"Perhaps I'd best break him in for you, darlin'," Tess McDonagel called out with a wink and a grin from where she stood amongst the well-wishers. "It appears the groom might be a trifle shy with you." She placed her hands on her ample hips while the Rangers catcalled and sallied forth with ribald challenges, coming fast and furious as their beloved leader began to squirm with embarrassment.

"Tess can warm him up for you, Mistress Molly," another of the lads shouted.

Tess stretched out her hands and began to sway invitingly. "He'll dance with me, never fear. I'll warm him true. It's not like I haven't taken him around the table before."

Molly stepped forward and blocked the tavern keeper. "From what I hear there's not a man alive in Fort Edward you haven't *taken round the table* before."

The onlookers roared with laughter. Now it was Tess McDonagel's turn to bear the brunt of the teasing. And these rough-hewn dull-swifts were more than ready to dish her out an ample portion of mortification.

But Molly wasn't finished. "And though I call you friend, see you keep a respectful distance from my man, Mistress Easy-Peasy, for I shall keep him *busy* enough to suit his tastes. And mine." A chorus of cheers erupted from the crowd. Tess scowled and spurned them with her flashing eyes and arched expression.

Molly might have added an extra riposte to their verbal duel but for John Stark who clasped her about the waist and lifted her into the air and swung his fiery-tempered paramour into the sunlit circle. She seemed light as a feather in Stark's arms. The musicians started to play a Celtic reel.

"Well met, young wife, will you quarrel or will you join your husband in the reel?"

Molly laughed, a sweet clear sound, and placed her

hands on her shapely hips. "I know you can fight, sir, but can you dance?"

Stark dared her to keep up with him, bowed and took a broad right step and high-kicked to the left to the merry accompaniment of fife and fiddle and drum, his long legs tapped a quick tattoo upon the well-trampled sod. The crowd encouraged him all the more.

And to the delight and grudging respect of his peers, Stark showed them all how a Celtic reel should be danced, with his frock coat cast aside and the pewter buttons of his mid-thigh-length umber waistcoat straining to contain his rippling muscles. Laughing and hollering, he kick-stepped, swung about, plunging left and right, swirling Molly along the perimeter of the circle as she struggled to match his pace.

As they passed Tess McDonagel, Stark reached out and snared the buxom wench by the wrist and spun her into Sam Oday's arms to the surprise and delight of the scarred frontiersman.

So it began, wives and husbands, spinsters and fair maidens, not one woman was left unasked, not one refused an invitation to dance and when the women were all spoken for, the remaining townsmen and Indian fighters either watched and awaited their turn with the ladies, or succumbed to the aromas that drifted over from the long tables where the wedding feast was prepared.

One reel led to another and then to a jig, then back to a foot-stamping, boisterous reel. The music buoyed on the rising warmth and filled the air. The forested slopes marked each wayward breeze. It was as if the wind-stirred branches of the trees kept time with each merry refrain.

"You astound me, husband," Molly said, keeping time with the music. "I daresay you move as nimbly to the fiddle as you do on the trail. What other secrets will you show me?"

"You will have to come to the cabin to find out," said Stark.

"And what will people say?" Molly flirtatiously replied.

"They will say there goes the most fortunate man in Fort Edward."

Molly blushed. His compliment touched her heart, spread through her like warm wine. The big man had a gift for words after all. With a tug and a turn of her wrist she led him from the dance and stepped in close for her words were for his ears alone. "Then take me there."

"But what of the feast?" Stark asked.

"My hunger cannot be sated by food or drink. It requires a more intimate appeasement." She looked at him, guarded, toying, the hint of a smile on her full lips. Stark felt the blood creep to his cheeks. He gulped, took her by the hand and as the reel ended, began to work his way through the well-wishers. Friends and neighbors clapped him on the back or embraced Molly, made for slow going. The circle seemed to tighten for a moment so Stark lowered his shoulder and had to make his own path, with Molly close behind.

Suddenly he burst through the throng, staggered forward and blundered into Major Ransom, very nearly bowling the officer over on his backside. Ransom's aide rushed to the major's defense.

"See here, Mister Stark," snapped Lieutenant Allan Penmerry, the product of a life of privilege and overindulgence. The lieutenant had taken the liberty of inviting himself to the festivities. The youthful officer was determined to make a place for himself as Ransom's second in command. He pretended not to be cowed by the Ranger looming over him.

"Sorry, Major," Stark said as he reached out and steadied the major and kept him from falling backwards. He scowled at Penmerry, an officer he considered to be about as valuable as teats on a bull.

"There, there, Lieutenant," Ransom exclaimed soothing his subordinate's *ruffled feathers.* "No harm done that a bit of straightening won't set to right." The English officer readjusted his scarlet frock coat. Sunlight glinted off the brass buttons that adorned his wide lapel. He was wearing his best powdery white periwig. His features certainly reflected the responsibilities that fate had thrust upon him. His gaze was steady, his eyes reflected the beginnings of a resolute patience and wisdom only the frontier could bring.

Men learned, here. Or men died . . . here. And that was both chapter and verse.

Penmerry went his commander one better. Unlike Ransom's lived-in looking finery, the lieutenant had ventured out among the provincials in his best kept uniform, one he kept tucked away in a trunk at the foot of his bed. He sported a plumed tricorn hat in hopes of lending an air of dignity to the proceedings. But once the fiddle and fifes began to play and the colonials began to gambol about like a tribe of barbarians, he realized all sense of propriety was lost. However he was polite enough to bow in Molly's direction. After all he didn't want to offend a woman who frequently cavorted about in breeches and could outshoot any man in the Regiment.

"I wish you well, milady," said Penmerry.

"Thank you, Lieutenant. And, Major Ransom, I am deeply grateful for your presence. As Reverend Strittmatter has yet to make his first spring foray across the mountains, John and I would have had to wait for several more weeks before proclaiming our vows and he might have turned tail and taken to the forest."

"I am glad to have been of service." The major bowed. He listened as the musicians started another tune, this one of local creation, a broadside ballad heralding the exploits of Johnny Stark. "You have both my blessings and my sympathies," Ransom added, "for I suspect you have joined yourself to both man and legend."

Stark shook his head, frowned at the suggestion. "Locksley Barlow is o'erfond of the hot-buttered rum Tess serves at the Kit Fox Tavern. His ballad has less to do with my exploits and more with the young man's intemperate dreams."

"Hmm . . . so you say," Ransom replied. "But remember, Stark, I was there at Bloody Meadow. You rallied your men and checked the savage advance and drove back the French." Ransom indicated Sergeant Strode and a cluster of British soldiers garbed in green buckskin leggings and hunting shirts adorned with scarlet trim . . . the newly-formed King's Rangers. They were yet to be a match for the long hunters, but they would learn.

Stark noted their presence, with a mixture of pride and deep-seated misgivings. He wondered if the day might come when he would regret teaching these regimental volunteers the ways of the forest. A cloud passed across his spirit, but he willed it away, refusing to surrender to whatever portent it might hold. Major Lucien Barbarat and Atoan were real threats. They had no need of imagined dangers. Suddenly, Molly's hand was in his, leading him away with a fervent but hasty farewell.

Children darted past them, laughing, squealing, nibbling on roasted ears of corn, johnny-cakes, their faces and fingers smeared from the pies they had been assigned to protect. They called out to the big man who answered in kind, addressing each child by his or her name. His bride was impressed. Further up the riverbank and heading toward the cabin, Molly and John tried to avoid the banquet tables but Charity appeared in front of them with plates of food she had prepared just so for the happy couple. She insisted they take a meal because a man like Stark was going to need his strength this night.

"Aunt Charity!" Molly blurted out, aghast.

"Tut tut," the older woman retorted. "I was a young bride just like you. Well younger really. I didn't have to wait on Ephraim like you did on this big 'un."

"Then you will understand when I do this," Stark said. He handed Molly both plates, then scooped her up in his arms, leaned over and kissed the older woman on her plump cheek and continued toward the cabin he had prepared for his new bride. Charity blushed, laughed aloud and waddled off, her round, ample frame all ajiggle the faster she moved.

Stark set Molly down before the front door and nudged it open with his strong right hand. Molly stood in the doorway, caught a glimpse of freshly-chinked log walls adorned with wildflowers and a four-poster bed with a festive-looking patchwork quilt upon a mound of feather bedding. There were curtains on the windows and a cheery fire in the hearth.

Molly sighed. "I had resigned myself to the inevitable, that we would never be alone." She set the plates of food upon a sideboard just inside the door and walked across the room to the bedroom, and turned and looked back at her beloved. She unbound her hair, then started on the ribbons fastening her bodice. "Legend are you?" Her ruby lips slightly parted. "Show me."

John Stark followed her inside and closed the door.

29

He dreamed of smooth flesh and soft supple curves, of warm and willing kisses, he dreamed of fire and storm, of yearning and sweet satiation. He saw yesterday and tomorrow and like any man in love, sensed how precarious and yet how wondrous it was, to be with the one who completed him.

Honey dreams and deep sleep, sunbeams gilded his heart, moon glow defined the room with luminous shafts of opalescent light. All doubts, all uncertainties were transformed, by the ebb and pitch of passion, roiling lust, spent strength, whispered endearments drifting into sleep and silver dreams.

"My beloved. . . ."

". . . beloved mine."

Stark bolted upright in bed, sweat beaded his lip, matted his hair, his muscles tensed, chest heaved, shoulders rose and fell; as he breathed, for a moment gasping, his ears straining to hear, in the silence, beyond the silence, his senses honed by the wilderness searched the nocturnal gloom without the cabin walls.

Molly's hand touched his forearm. Propped on her elbows, the covers fell away from her breasts, temples of desire capped by taut pink blooms, enticing any other time. But not when he had been pulled from sleep by a dire prescience. He glanced in her direction, his expression telling her all she needed to know, that stealth was called for, stealth and a loaded gun.

Stark swung his long legs over the edge of the bed and pulled on his breeches and reached for the double-barreled pistol he'd placed on the nightstand next to the bed. Molly pulled a nightshirt over her head as her husband rose from the bed and gingerly padded across the floor to stand in the doorway. He reached off to the side and slung a leather strap over his shoulder. Now a brass powder flask and shot pouch dangled at his side. He heard a familiar metallic click behind him and looking over his shoulder saw Molly held a horse pistol, primed and cocked in her steady hands. The Ranger nodded. She did the same. He continued across the room, paused at the door to catch up a tomahawk from where he'd left it on the table. He shoved the pistol in his waistband and took up his rifle. Old Abraham was a reassuring weight in his hands.

Now he eased over to the window and slowly, using the most torturous caution, shoved the shutters open with the muzzle of his rifle. With no interior light to distract him, his vision need no adjustment to the night. He glanced at the long-case clock on the far wall, a gift from the local artisans. His eyes drifted up the swaying pendulum and tried to focus on the face and the time. The London-made mechanical workings had been freighted over the mountains from Boston, but the case had been crafted out of rich cherrywood by one of the Barlows.

It had been a wedding gift for his bride and had a melodious way of tolling the hours, not that John Stark needed some English clocksmith to tell him the time, a man who could read the starlit night and approximate the hour by the sateen sailing moon above. A man's aim must be accurate; his reading of the trail and the dangers ahead, precise; for anything else an educated guess would suffice.

It was well after midnight, around three, give or take, and the wedding celebration had long disbanded with the revelers off to home and hearth. All that remained of the previous afternoon's festivities were the empty tables and the recessed, blackened circles where even now a few coals feebly pulsed, like miniature molten orange hearts beating fitfully among the blackened mounds of charred wood.

And there between the remains of day and eventide, delineated against a backdrop of moonlight glistening on the Hudson River behind him, stood a solitary figure, a man of average height, squat, with sloping shoulders, slightly bowed legs. A man alone, yet oddly menacing, standing still as a statue, watching the house.

One of the Fargos, Stark thought, eyes narrowing, jaw tightening. He walked to the front door and shoved it open and stalked outside, striding barefoot down the riverbank, gun in hand and his thoughts shifting from romance to murder. He would not be harried, if he had to send every one of the Fargos home in a basket.

The watcher retreated for a moment, a hesitant step, then wisely held his ground as if realizing in that one instant of weakness that to turn and run meant to die before he reached the water's edge. He held up his hands, palms upward. He recognized the big man advancing toward him, but then he had been watching throughout the day, biding his time, afraid to make his presence known for fear of just such a reaction. His patience, and the spyglass in his coat pocket, helped him locate Stark's cabin. And that was what he had needed to know most of all.

"*Major Stark*, I come in peace," he called out.

Stark stopped in his tracks, looming over the smaller man, pistol in hand leveled at the intruder who had disrupted his wedding night. A Frenchman? "What the devil is this?"

"The devil? *Oui*, my friend, I do bring news of the devil."

"Do I know you?" Stark squinted, studying the man's thick homely features in the dim light.

"*Certainement.*" The Frenchman nodded and removed his woolen cap. "You gave me a gift once."

"This is nonsense?"

"*Monsieur*, I am Benoit Turcotte." The Frenchman continued, nervously crumpling the hat in his hands. "You gave me my life once. I have come to return the favor, *mon ami.* I bring a *cadeau de mariage* of my own."

Something in the way the Frenchman spoke, the flat, almost benumbed tone of his voice made Stark's flesh crawl. He readied the rifle, thumbed the hammer back. One false move . . . "What is the gift?"

"Butcher of Fort William Henry. *Oui*, I bring you the life of Colonel Lucien Barbarat . . . and how to end it!"

30

Benoit Turcotte gratefully accepted the tankard of hard cider Molly Stark handed him. He remembered her from
the ruse that had cost him his bateau and his livelihood as
a *voyageur*. Yes, this pretty one had lured him ashore. Well,
the fault was as much his own and besides, how could one
hold a grudge against such a beautiful woman?

"Merci, Madame Stark," he said. If Molly remembered
him there was nothing about her expression to reveal it.

The Frenchman glanced about at the men Stark had
gathered to hear his story. It was obvious there was no love
lost for the *voyageur* here. Turcotte was grateful he hadn't
been marched to the gallows and hanged for a spy. That's
the treatment Stark would have received in Fort Carillon.
Major Lucien Barbarat favored a free hand with the hang-
man's noose, curse his black soul.

Benoit Turcotte glimpsed his reflection floating on the
amber surface in his tankard as he raised the pewter vessel
in salute to John Stark and his bride of one day, and then
acknowledged the English major, Robert Rogers, and the
Rangers who were congregated around the long, heavy table beneath the spreading branches of a mighty oak. Stark
lifted his own cup in kind.

"Best while you have it, use your breath, there is no
drinking after death," said Johnny.

The *voyageur* chuckled softly and nodded in approval.
He drained half the contents and slammed the tankard on
the tabletop, wiped his mouth on the sleeve of his river-
man's shirt. He stared at the tankard as if it were both
adversary and friend.

There were only a handful of men present, Ransom and his aide, Lieutenant Penmerry, Robert Rogers, looking somewhat chagrined that the Frenchman had appealed to John Stark for sanctuary among his enemies here at Fort Edward. Moses Shoemaker seconded the toast and gulped his cider down. He was drinking "stone walls," a mixture of hard cider and rum. It calmed his nerves and took the sharp edge off the morning sunlight as it filtered through the branches.

Damn but the world was bright in spring.

Like Sam Oday and young Locksley Barlow and most of the other Rangers, Shoemaker had used the wedding celebration as an excuse to play the glutton and drink till his belly near burst. He'd passed the remaining hours before dawn dead to the world on the bed of a freight wagon that someone had left unattended alongside the Kit Fox Tavern near the center of town.

"Don't spill your drink, *jehu*. Your hand is all a'tremble," Barlow chided. He had yet to sleep and was not about to reveal to anyone where he had spent the night.

"Steady enough to shoot your lights out if you sass me ag'in," Shoemaker grumbled, closing his eyes for a moment while the warmth spread through his limbs. "I feel like the Grand Sachem himself is trying to club my brains loose, from the inside."

"From the looks of you, I'd say you tied a knot in the dog's tail last night," said Sam Oday.

"And then some, old friend." Shoemaker wanly grinned. "But not as twined as the young buck here." He nodded in Barlow's direction. "I heard a noise and raised up in time to see the younker arm in arm with Tess McDonagel. And I warrant they warmed the blankets, him toes down and her toes up." He started to laugh then realized there was still a woman present. Moses blushed and knuckled his forehead. "Begging your pardon, Miss Molly . . . uh . . . Stark . . . Missus Stark."

Molly shook her head in mock dismay then tugged his

Scottish bonnet down over his eyes. "As well you should, you old goat."

"Enough of these antics!" Lieutenant Penmerry blurted out. "Major Ransom has agreed to hear what this man has to say. Well then, let him speak. Or I shall summon our escort to clap the Frenchman in irons and return him to Fort Edward to await his fate. For I suspect he has come to spy on us."

"Then he is a damn poor one," Stark snapped.

"One cannot expect an unsophisticated farmer like yourself. . . ."

"A farmer who has saved your life countless times," Molly retorted, color creeping to her features. Fire flashed in her eyes. "Without my husband and others like him, Colonel Lucien Barbarat and his heathen allies would already be at the gates. And your topknot would be hanging from an Abenaki trophy belt."

"Forgive the lieutenant," Ransom said, interjecting a note of calm before matters spun out of control. "Mister Penmerry is anxious to test his mettle in battle. I am certain the French or Indians will give him ample opportunity before the year is out." He clasped his hands before him and sat patiently at the table. "And now, sir, you have had your food and drink for which you must pay with a story. Why have you come here and what do you hope to gain?

"Revenge," said Turcotte. "I have come for revenge."

"Against Colonel Barbarat?" Stark asked.

"The same."

"And to that end you would squander your honor and betray your countrymen?"

"It is honor that has brought me to this table. And as for my countrymen . . . they are all dead." With that, Benoit Turcotte proceeded to give an account of all that had befallen him from the moment Stark had burned the bateaux and left his captives bound but unharmed on the shore of Lake Champlain. He told how the marines discovered them, how Barbarat, in his fury, dismissed Father Jean Isaac's entreaties and ordered all the *voyageurs* hanged, right there by the caves. They were to be made an example of for the rivermen who plied their trade upon the lakes and rivers.

His voice halting, eyes moist, Turcotte described the scene, how one by one his own brave lads were taken out and summarily executed according to Barbarat's orders. *Hang them high*, said the colonel, *hang them high*. The detachment of marines followed his order to the letter, at first. But as the afternoon wore on, Father Jean Isaac administered last rites all the while beseeching the soldiers to disobey their commander's orders and free their countrymen. As the stench of death began to fill the air some of the marines' resolve crumbled. They began to argue among themselves. A struggle broke out.

"*Père Jean* slipped a knife to me, unobserved by the soldiers. Then he stood in front of me, his black robes concealing me from the others, while I cut myself free," said Turcotte, reliving in his mind how he sliced through the bonds looped about his wrists and ankles. "I tried to free my brothers, but alas, I was discovered and was forced to flee into the forest." His tone of voice grew heavy with guilt. "*Les Marines* scattered and searched as best they could but I moved hard and fast. Before long they abandoned the chase and finished off the rest of my friends." The soldiers had suspected the priest but were loathe to do any more than force him to wait in the boat until every last one of Benoit's companions had paid the price for losing their cargo to Stark's Rangers.

"Later I returned," Turcotte told the men around him. "The dead hung from the trees, left for the ravens to feed upon, by order of the colonel. Later I learned that the soldiers reported all the *voyageurs* had been executed. Barbarat thought I was dead. And so I was, to one and all. I drifted to Fort Carillon where *Père Jean* hid me in the church. But I soon discovered it was unnecessary. I meant so little to the colonel . . . once he passed me on the docks and did not recognize me. Why should he? Benoit Turcotte was dead. Not that he ever knew my name."

He checked his tankard and glanced in Molly's direction. She read his thoughts and brought a pitcher over to refill his cup. "I swore I would find a way to make the colonel pay for his conduct." He gulped the cider, looked around at the faces of his audience surrounding him in the sunlight. A gentle breeze tugged at Molly's long hair and ruffled her dressing gown, capturing the scent of cherry blossoms for all to enjoy. But with talk of murder and retribution in the air, the sweet scent of spring went unnoticed.

"The Abenaki spent the winter up north where they gathered with the Seneca and Hurons. Now Atoan has called a Great Council and sent word to Colonel Barbarat to join him at the place the Abenaki call *Tobapsqua*, the Pass Through Rock."

"I know the place," Stark said. "The mountain drops off at the shoreline, as if it was cleaved with an axe, a straight cliff maybe a couple of hundred feet high with nothing but a pile of jagged-looking rocks rising up out of the water below."

"That's the place," Turcotte said. "Now if you cross over Pass Through Rock, on the other side of the mountain, the land slopes down into a valley, bordered by steep ridges, where trees grow thick as bristles on a porcupine. I've heard rumors of caves back in those mountains. When the wind blows through them it makes a moaning sound. The Abenaki say it's the voices of their ancestors and that makes it a sacred place, the Gathering Place. They say wisdom sits there among the rocks and trees." Benoit Turcotte glanced about at the English faces surrounding him. He had their undivided attention now. "Come the end of this month, that's where Atoan and the elders of his tribe will be. I have heard he's called for the colonel to be there. Lucien Barbarat will have to meet with him, he cannot afford to dishonor the Grand Sachem."

"Barbarat will have an army to protect him," scoffed Lieutenant Penmerry.

"No," Stark said. "Not to a Great Council. It isn't their way. Each war chief can only bring a token force, a dozen men or so. The colonel will have to do the same."

"Suppose the Seneca come, the Mohawk, perhaps the Huron," Major Ransom mused aloud. "Then add Barbarat and a detachment of marines."

"I doubt we'd find more than a hundred men in camp." Stark glanced over at Rogers who wore a similar expression. Pass Through Rock lay about a hundred and fifty miles over land. He had taken canoes past it before at night. But none of the Rangers had ever put to shore or approached the valley from the landward side. Now was as good a time as any. The Butcher, Colonel Lucien Barbarat, now there was a prize worth the risk. The ghosts of Fort William Henry still cried for vengeance. Who among the Rangers hadn't counted a family member or friend among the slaughtered dead?

"I cannot risk taking the garrison from the fort. But once we receive reinforcements . . ." Ransom began.

"It will be too late," Stark interrupted.

Ransom's aide cleared his throat in pointed displeasure at Stark. But the major was accustomed to the frontiersman's lack of convention. The man spoke his mind. And at least what he said was worthwhile, so Ransom made a point of ignoring Stark's disregard for rank.

"See here, Mister Stark. Even if I agreed to leave the settlement unprotected and attempted to carry the war to the French, I do not think the First Regiment could traverse these mountains and reach this Gathering Place in time."

"We could," said Robert Rogers, already in step with the big man's thoughts.

"And we will," said Stark.

31

For a day and a half, preparations were made for war, and of the company of Rangers, John Stark and Robert Rogers selected sixty men for the trek north. Two nights later, this band of stalwart souls gathered in the night-shrouded yard of Ephraim's farm. The First Regiment was represented by the presence of Sergeant Tom Strode who had joined the Colonials on their mission, and Major Ransom. The commander of the garrison had made a point of being here to give the buckskin-clad volunteers a proper send-off.

The Rangers made some last-minute preparations, repeating actions they had performed in the day. The raiding party was outfitted with rifles, pistols, tomahawks and hunting knives. Each man carried a water flask, a small pouch of jerked venison and parched corn and Indian *pemmican*, made from pounded berries, nuts, dried meat, back fat, and maple glaze.

From this night on, cold camps were the order of the day for the Rangers dare not risk a fire and alert any Abenaki who might be scouting the mountain ridges to the north. While Charity Page and a number of the ladies circulated among the men, bidding farewell and seeing to any last-minute needs, a word of encouragement, an oil pack of bread and cheese, Robert Rogers made a pretty speech. He invoked their courage and sense of duty; he spoke eloquently and forthrightly of the trial that lay ahead. As the defenses could spare no more than sixty men, the raiding party was going to be outnumbered, but no man expected any less.

"Swiftness and stealth shall be our allies," Rogers concluded. "You are men to walk the trail with. I trust each man to do his duty. And we shall prevail for our king and for England." Several of the Rangers raised their tankards of rum and cider, the last real nourishment they would have until they'd reached Pass Through Rock and seen their mission through to its bloody end.

"Well spoken, Major Rogers," said Ransom. "I echo your sentiments, our immediate survival may well rest on the shoulders of your brave company. I have no doubt but that my French counterpart will attempt to persuade his heathen allies to undertake a full-scale assault upon Fort Edward. And in all honesty, I cannot see us withstanding a siege, despite General Amherst's orders to hold at all cost."

"The French will have more to worry about than Fort Edward before we are through with them, on my oath," Rogers replied. He gazed across the field toward Stark's cabin. He could only imagine the scene within. And it was still any man's guess whether John Stark would emerge alone or with Molly following close on his heels, wearing her buckskins and shouldering her rifle.

All eyes were on the cabin.

"I'd hate to be the one to tell her to stay behind," Sam Oday muttered, sharing a jug with his frequent companions seated across from him. "That isn't Molly's way. But I can tell Johnny wants her to. Plain to see." Locksley Barlow and Moses Shoemaker shared another of the pine benches Ephraim had placed in front of his house. The benches provided a good place for friends to congregate in the shade of the maple trees and share a jug of cider and smoke their pipes on a warm summer's evening.

"Molly must be burning about now," Shoemaker chuckled, staring at the cabin. Sensing movement behind him he glanced over his shoulder as Benoit Turcotte ambled over toward them. The *voyageur* had overheard their conversation. He licked his lips, watching them pass the jug around.

"Elle est une grande femme!" he remarked. "That is
. . . I mean to say. . . ."

Moses looked up at the Frenchman. "I can parley-voo
some." The old Indian fighter handed the jug to Turcotte.
"And Molly sure is a grand woman, ain't no finer between
Boston and Quebec or I'm a sea snake. Now drink your
fill, Frenchie, cause when we set foot on the War Path,
we'll be in for a drought until we run Lucien Barbarat to
ground."

"Merci, my friend." Turcotte was eager to warm his
belly. They had allowed him a day to rest up, no more, and
he was going to need all the strength he could muster to
keep up with the company.

"There you go, calling me a *friend*. Best you know
right up front, me and the lads will be watching you, and
the first time you even so much as step funny. . . ." He
placed a thumb to his neck, drew it across his throat and
as if that weren't clear enough, made a horrid slicing sound.
"Comprenee-voo?"

"I understand, *monsieur*," Turcotte said. "And I will
remember."

"See that you do," Sam Oday told him, patting the
fluted barrel of his blunderbuss. For close-up fighting, the
weapon was as effective as a hand cannon and could clear
a broad swath through a crowd and, at point-blank range,
cut a man in half. The ordinarily good-natured Colonial
spoke in a grave tone of voice this night, his scarred features lending solemnity to his thoughts.

Shoemaker studied his friend. They were seeing another side of Sam Oday. His friends had never heard him
sound so menacing. Something was eating at the man.
Nerves? But he was no stranger to a raiding party. What
was different about this? It was just expected, count on Sam
Oday to keep a level head. The man had suffered his share
of tragedy, buried his wife and family and still he hadn't
broken.

Then Shoemaker answered his own question. This was
no ordinary raid. The Rangers were out for vengeance. And

Sam Oday had much to avenge. His thoughts had to be of
the family he had lost to French plunderers and the savages
who accompanied them. Better to give Oday his space this
night, let him find his own way of dealing with the memories.

Moses resolved to change the subject. All that remained was for Johnny Stark to join them. *But I reckon
he's fighting the first skirmish of this campaign, right this
moment.* He clapped Barlow on the knee as the jug made
its way back into the old man's eager hands.

"Take it from me, lads. I warrant Molly Stark is giving
her man what for. Mark my words. She's cutting that big
timber down to size." The men around him chuckled, just
to think it, the towering Indian fighter whittled down to
size by a mere slip of a girl.

"And what would an old moss-bones like you know
about such things?" Barlow asked.

Moses didn't mind if they scoffed. "You'll see," he
said. "You'll see."

He knew all about womenfolk.

John Stark stood out in the yard in front of his cabin, rel-
ishing this moment of peace, in the dark, in the company
of his doubts and premonitions, perhaps, but only momentarily. The wilderness beyond the hills rushed to his aid. A
sibilant breeze sprang up to defend him, a pattern of flam-
ing stars fell from heaven, vanished in soundless splendor,
in phosphorescent explosions of searing white and fuming
emeralds. The river lapped at the shore, the swiftly flowing
current roiling over rocks, and adding to the symphony of
the restless wind and the stars. How could a man despair?

Once before he had stood alone, defiant against an
Abenaki war party, he had run the gauntlet and hurled his
victory in their faces. Then, as now, he held his vigil with
the wilderness and made his benediction to the untamed
spirits with whom he shared a kinship.

The wind shall guide him. Let him draw upon the secrets of the trees for strength.

"I am here," he said, standing tall, a legend in the night.

Voices carried to him from across the field and he knew it was time. He turned and started back to the cabin, climbed the steps into the civilized light. Stark ducked and stepped through the cabin doorway, to deliver the news that the Rangers had gathered at Ephraim's farm and the hour for departure was at hand.

Throughout this last day, he had been making last-minute repairs about the cabin, as if anticipating . . . well, why not? A man never knew when some Abenaki war club might send him under.

Funny he never worried about it before, not once considered the possibility he might not return. Marriage had made him mortal. He started to say as much but the words died aborning. Molly was dressed in a petticoat and apron. Lamplight and shadows muted the color of her shortgown, a loose-fitting long-sleeved jacket worn in place of a bodice. Her eyes seemed to sparkle, and all the heady joys of springtime were captured in her smile.

Mortal, yes. But in another way, immortal. As if he were somehow connected to the divine in a way he never thought possible. But that was love.

Before her on the tabletop lay Old Abraham, a brace of pistols, his powder horn and shot pouch. Stark was caught off guard by her attire.

"You expected to find me in buckskins?"

"Yes."

"You did not demand I stay behind."

"It is your land, too. And you can outshoot most of the lads."

"Maybe a few," she agreed. "My land . . . and my home."

He refrained from showing his relief or revealing how he had dreaded her determination to join him on the war trail. His expression was easy enough to read.

"Don't worry. I have decided and will not change my

mind," said Molly, placing her hands upon the burled walnut rifle stock. "No, I will remain behind."

Stark was definitely confused. All the arguments he had compiled in his thoughts to keep her at Fort Edward suddenly seemed like a waste of time. And in one way, he was even disappointed. John had come to expect to find the woman at his side.

"Molly . . ."

"No, just listen," she said, her lips moist and inviting, her voice soft, smooth as French silk, remarkably steady. "It is different now. We are husband and wife, joined now by a deeper bond, so that even when we are apart I am with you and you with me. But if I march off with you now, when the shooting starts, you'll be worrying about me in ways you never did before. I might be carrying the seed of our child, who can tell, but by watching out for me you will get yourself killed."

Her lower lip began to tremble. It was all so new to her, being wife and lover and one day, God willing, mother. "There will be other trails and we will walk them together like before. But this War Path, you must go alone, with your company of Rangers." She exhaled softly. "And I must stay." Her gaze hardened. "If the Abenaki come, then Aunt Charity and Uncle Ephraim will need my help. And you, my love, will be avenged."

"Was there ever a man so blessed with a wife like mine?" The long hunter rounded the table and swept her up in his arms. "I swear before God and all that is holy, I will come back to you, Molly Stark."

And after a kiss and then another, John Stark gathered up his weapons of war and left her standing, breathless, but brave in the deafening silence.

32

By morning, Fort Edward was but a memory of fond fare-wells, of cookfires and hastily-filled wooden bowls of corn pudding and maple syrup, of shared embraces, the comfort of friends and the security of the fort's ramparts with its redoubts and cannon placements. But the frontiers-men knew, as well as anyone, walls and grapeshot were a false security. Fort William Henry had boasted the same armaments and it had fallen. All that remained were ruins and ghosts.

Unless something was done to disrupt French inten-tions for the settlement, no one doubted Fort Edward would suffer a similar fate before the summer was out. The *voyageur*, Benoit Turcotte, had set in motion a bold undertak-ing. Every man knew the risk, to mount a surprise attack against both the French and Indians at The Gathering Place below Severed Rock might be considered folly by some. But peril was no stranger to the company of the Rangers.

Major Robert Rogers, Locksley Barlow, even Old Moses Shoemaker kept up an unrelenting pace that de-voured the distance throughout the night and well into the day. The *voyageur* slowed them some. The Frenchman was simply unused to such exertions. He was a man of the river. Half the time he rode on a makeshift sling carried between two of the strongest lads. They might have left him back on the trail save for the fact that they needed him to identify Colonel Lucien Barbarat. And if this was a ruse and they were heading into an ambush, the Rangers wanted to assure themselves Turcotte would be the first to fall.

With short rests every hour, taking food and drink as

they walked, the Rangers kept up their forced march throughout the lengthening hours of daylight. The column was able to move with a certain degree of freedom, fairly certain they were safe from observation because of the two men scouting ahead who left a trail of marked trees and piled stones to indicate the direction the column needed to travel.

A quarter of a mile forward of the column, John Stark and Sam Oday continued to blaze a trail their companions followed. The two scouts remained ever vigilant as they marked the trail for those coming behind them. Stark kept a wary lookout for any sign of the enemy, the simple impression left by a mocassin meant cause for alarm. Using their spyglasses, the two scoured every ridge for a telltale trace of smoke from distant campfires.

Though the forests seemed devoid of French patrols or Abenaki war parties, every hill and dale teemed with life. Wrens and jays and mockingbirds chattered among the branches, gray squirrels scolded their passing, game darted from harm's way. Rabbits scampered from underfoot, disturbed by the intruders. Stark caught sight of a fox, just a flash of rust-red fur in pursuit of ground rodents. Hawks circled overhead, pinned to the azure sky above the breaks, waiting patiently for a kill. Mallards and blue teals nested in the ponds whose spring-fed waters bubbled cool and clear from mother earth.

Late in the afternoon, Stark and Oday found a proper place for camp. They'd marked the trees with their tomahawks and left a trail more than visible enough to lead the Rangers to a clearing concealed by a thick stand of white birch and maple. The two scouts stretched out against an outcropping of speckled granite on a slope overlooking the spring and waited for the column to arrive. Sam Oday was grateful for the rest and he was content to while away the remainder of the afternoon, watching slanted rays of sunlight infiltrate the forest with an army of encroaching shadows.

"These smoke poles get a mite heavy after a long run,"

he said, nudging the butt plate of Stark's long rifle.

Stark nodded. He never stopped searching the perimeter of trees.

"Don't you ever tire?" said Sam. He lowered his head to his hands, the black scarf covering his scarred scalp felt warm to the touch. He tried to suppress the memories of his murdered family. Faces he had long thought dormant had bloomed in the garden of his mind like flowers of evil, opening their petals of loss and indescribable pain, to deprive him of rest and plague the long unceasing daylight hours.

"What is it, Sam?"

"Just thinking, Johnny. Just remembering. I don't know. It comes whenever the winter breaks and the world looks so fresh and full of promise. Then I get to thinking how I'll never see her and the children again."

"I can imagine," Stark said.

"No, you can't."

Stark shrugged. He was not about to argue with the man and his pain. "Not like you, I know, but when Molly was hurt, I damn near went mad. I've stood on the trail you've had to walk, Sam, and I wanted to go no further down it." His expression grew distant, veiled. "I've seen the ghosts of Fort William. I walked among the killing fields, saw our brothers left as food for the ravens, and the women, the children. . . ."

"Enough!" Sam blurted out, his voice tight.

"This French officer, Barbarat, it was his handiwork," said Stark. "If I do nothing else on this earth I shall see that he answers for his butchery."

"And the Abenaki, the Grand Sachem . . . Atoan," Sam muttered, hands clenched around the fluted barrel of his blunderbuss. "Kill them all."

Stark tried to echo his sentiments. The French commander was without honor, a base and merciless adversary. However, Atoan was different, no less fierce, but not the same. He knew the Grand Sachem would not yield, not rest until he drove Stark and his kind back over the mountains.

That was the tragedy of the situation. This land was Atoan's by birth. This land was Stark's by blood. The Grand Sachem wanted him to go. Stark was determined to stay. Thus time and place had made them enemies on a collision course with destiny.

33

Colonel Lucien Barbarat woke with the dawn. His mind was instantly alert, unclouded by the effects of the previous night's excesses. It had been an enjoyable interlude, but a man could not live on duty alone. The Widow Roxanne LeBret had helped clear his thoughts. He had nearly depleted her supply of brandy and sated his lust in her arms. However, Barbarat's appetite for fortune and glory could only be appeased by another mistress, her name was *War*.

He lay still for a moment, watching the honeyed glow fill the curtains. He was content to let a half hour pass. It was comfortable here. The widow's boudoir was half again as large as his officer's quarters within the fort. Her furnishings, unlike the locally-crafted trappings of his own quarters, came from Quebec and had been ferried down aboard the boats belonging to her husband's trading company.

He stretched out his legs, patted the cotton bed sheets, yawned, and silently observed this bed alone was worth half a year's pay for a colonel. Of course, being the officer in command opened up opportunities to feather his own nest. The four-poster was built of natural walnut and painted beech, the footboard was decorated with carved garlands, the headboard's centerpiece was an intricately-inlaid design resembling a basket of flowers with bronze ornamentation. The legs resembled Roman columns.

The wages of a widow's grief paid well indeed, the officer mused, considering the bed, the drawing-room chair, the dressing table against the north wall, the clothes chest and damask-covered settee near the curtains. How fortunate the old merchant she married had proved to be of such delicate health. While Lucien Barbarat estimated his host's personal wealth, outside the window, the settlement of Fort Carillon came alive.

The familiar sounds of frontier life drifted up from the streets: the jangle of a horse in harness, the creaking axle on a milk cart winding its way among the houses, farmers in from the fields selling eggs, cheeses, breads, and onions, and rivermen crying out the morning's catch of lake trout, bass, and yellow perch.

The bells of Saint Elizabeth tolled the morning hour. Father Jean Isaac or one of his sanctified heathens was calling his flock to the holy rites, but they competed with the echo of distant drums carrying over the rampart walls, signaling the garrison of French marines to rouse from sleep, break their fast, or present themselves to the officers for the orders of the day.

Hmm, marching orders. Barbarat began to make mental calculations as to how many men were appropriate to accompany him to The Gathering Place. He mustn't dishonor his red allies. *Merde*, but these heathens were a tricky business. He was weary of placating the savages. But for now, he needed men like Atoan.

General Montcalm was not pleased that Fort Edward was still in the hands of the English. Worse, last autumn's constant depredations by these Rangers had reached the general's ear. In his last dispatch Montcalm made it abundantly clear, he wanted the English and the Colonials crushed, their spirits broken. He wanted them driven back across the Adirondacks. It was a tall order. But if Colonel Lucien Barbarat could not get it done, Montcalm intended to find another man for the job.

Barbarat scowled. He had come too far, risen in rank too fast to let his dreams slip away. He needed his allies, the Abenaki, and any of the other tribes, if possible, the Seneca, the Mohawk. At the Gathering he intended to argue they should bring their warriors and march the War Path with Atoan and the French to destroy the English once and for all, thereby assuring the eternal friendship of the French crown, and Lucien's own good fortune.

But drawing upon the allegiance of a man like Atoan required Barbarat's presence at the Gathering. It required him to leave the comfort of this feather bed and his mistress's house. Barbarat sighed audibly and sat up in bed, lifted the covers, glimpsed a half-moon portion of plump derriere, leaned over and planted a kiss on that patch of pink flesh. He felt a stirring in his loins for the widow and briefly considered malingering in her company.

But duty called him, this time in the form of Madame LeBret's maidservant, Nicolette Perillard, a toothsome little wench, all fluster and giggles in cotton petticoat, apron and lace-trimmed bodice who busily entered the room and drew back the shades.

"Begging your pardon, *mon Colonel*," said Nicolette. "You requested me to draw the curtains at first light."

"That I did, child," he said.

"And, sir, *Père Jean* waits in the parlour."

"The priest? But I only just heard the bells of Saint Michael's."

"*Je ne sais pas.*" The young woman shrugged. "I do not know who rang the bells. But the priest waits for you." She averted her eyes as Barbarat rose from the bed and padded, naked across the floor, caught the maid by the arm, turned her to him, tilted her chin, and then brought her hand to his lips. First he kissed her knuckles, then lowered her hand to his belly.

"*Monsieur!*" Nicolette exclaimed, blushing, and pulled her hand away.

Barbarat laughed aloud. "Bring the priest some tea and tell him I will see him soon. He may walk with me to the fort."

The maid, still embarrassed by his behavior, gathered up the hem of her skirt and rushed from the room, leaving the colonel, naked and thoroughly bemused, in the center of the room.

"Scamper off, my petite plum. I'll taste your nectar on

my return," he called after her. Pleased with himself, Lucien swaggered over to an end table and poured a glass of brandy to sharpen his senses and with drink in hand, sprawled naked in a well-appointed wingback chair. His body was lean and pale, and though born to good breeding, his deportment bespoke decadence. In some ways it was said he took after his father who likewise was given to a reckless lifestyle that had left his estate bankrupt and forced his son to enter the service of the king rather than face debtor's prison.

The widow rolled over on her backside, her ample belly rose and fell as she tried to return to sleep. Then she propped up on an elbow and glanced at the naked man seated near the bed. "*Quelle heure est-il?* What time is it, my lovely?"

"Time I was on my way." Lucien sipped the brandy, enjoying the bouquet and the warmth as it spread through his limbs. Roxanne LeBret had no illusions about her paramour. But she liked men she could understand. She had not always been wealthy; however, her earthy sensuality had attracted the attentions of a lonely merchant whose company carried on a lively fur trade throughout the length and breadth of Lake Champlain from the settlement of Fort Carillon to Quebec.

Shortly after her marriage, the old fur trader died; there were rumors that he had succumbed during a particularly strenuous evening of lovemaking. Barbarat didn't doubt the story for a minute. Throughout the night, the widow seemed almost insatiable and it wasn't until the early morning hours, well after midnight, that she fell asleep and allowed his spent strength a much-needed respite.

"Were you naughty to poor Nicolette? I think you were," the voice drifted from the covers. The Widow LeBret was an amply-endowed brunette, a round and luscious woman ten years his senior who might have passed for a courtesan with her rouge red cheeks and her complexion hidden beneath a layer of white powder that the evening's romp in bushy park had left smeared.

LeBret swept the covers aside to reveal herself in all her carnal glory. "Where must you go that is more important than being here with me? God has a generous heart but there is one sin he cannot forgive, if a woman calls a man to her bed and he does not accept."

"Then I must offend the Almighty, *mon petite choufleur*." Barbarat finished his wine, set the glass upon the floor next to the clawed foot of the chair, stood and padded naked about the room as he gathered his clothes. "I must trade your pleasing company for that of a multitude of savages." He began to dress while the woman slipped quietly into her bed jacket and summoned her maid to return by a pull of a bell cord by the bed.

"We have all heard talk of this Gathering." The widow walked to the window, stood in the sunlight, and looked out across the narrow stone-paved streets of the settlement. She had followed the French army out from Quebec, a commoner taken into the service of the man who had become her husband and in death, her benefactor. There were ladies in Quebec who might look down upon her but what mattered most was the strongbox hidden in the loose floorboards beneath her bed.

Lucien Barbarat did not choose to confide in the woman about his intentions when he met with Atoan and quickly dressed in his gray *justacorps*, donned the blue and gray waistcoat and white breeches. He sat on the side of the bed and pulled on his calf-length black boots. His ceremonial sword and pistol were the last of his apparel.

"*Père Jean* waits below. I prefer to meet with the priest in private."

"The priest . . . here?" the widow blurted out. "Now? Well as you say, my love. I must surrender you to the regiment. But when you return from the heathen, I claim you for my own."

"And I live for the day, Madame," he replied and bowing, doffed his plumed hat.

Father Jean Isaac was lost in his thoughts. His long black robes absorbed the heat of the morning sun where he stood in the walled garden that separated the front of the widow's house from the street. He doubted his chances of convincing Colonel Barbarat to amend his ways. The man was a libertine. He was consumed by worldly pleasures and desires at the risk of eternal condemnation. But he had not come to the widow's to preach salvation to the commander of Fort Carillon. Today, Father Jean hoped there might be a way of preventing the colonel from destroying a people along with his jaded lust for wealth and glory.

"You did not take any tea?" asked Barbarat, emerging from the house to find the priest admiring the blossoms Widow LeBret's servants had been carefully tending since the first shoots sprouted from the earth. Many of the buds were wildflowers cultivated to grace the courtyard with a palette of colors.

Father Jean gave a start, glanced up at the officer. To the eyes of the officer, the black robe seemed even more gaunt, as if somehow he alone bore responsibility for these terrible times. And perhaps he did. The foolish hymn-keeper was certainly not helping the French cause with his sermons and proselytizing.

"I was told at the fort I would find you here, *Mon Colonel*."

"I should imagine you would be at your church, *Père Jean*."

"My flock will wait for me."

"Ah, yes, your obedient savages."

"They have been baptized and have been welcomed into the body of Christ. Are you not comforted by the fact they are saved?"

"Because of your influence, they refuse to fight. No, priest, I am not comforted." Barbarat waved a hand toward the gate that opened out onto the street of the settlement. "I must return to the fort. We march this day. So be quick. What do you want of me, *Père Jean*?"

"I wish to accompany you to the Gathering Place," said the black robe.

Lucien Barbarat halted in his tracks and glanced sharply at the Jesuit. "*Quelle folie est ceci?* Do you take me for a fool? You are the last man I would bring with me to the Abenaki."

"Many have already been baptized."

"*Oui,*" said the colonel. "In name only. But they fight alongside my troops. We have need of them. The last thing I need is for you to preach to them of peace."

"I *serve* the prince of peace," the priest pointedly replied. "*Mon Colonel*, I answer to a higher authority. This is our great challenge." Father Jean Isaac sighed, clasped his hands before him. The black robe's fingers were gnarled and ugly-looking, like twisted roots. He had spent what seemed a lifetime bringing Christianity to the Iroquois and Abenaki and had suffered terribly at the hands of the very people he had come to save. And still he remained. Barbarat would have been happy to pack the troublemaker off to Rome.

"It is a terrible wrong, to use these people as you do," the priest exclaimed, "to fight for us, to die for us, because of a war that is none of their making."

"I will not have you undermine my alliances," the officer snapped. He walked away from the priest, opened the gate, stepped out into the street where a detachment of marines and his personal guard, awaited him, standing at attention.

Barbarat reached beneath his coat and produced a glass brandy flask he had pilfered from the widow's pantry. He tossed it to the soldiers who cheered the officer and proceeded to pass the dark brown flask among themselves. Barbarat grinned. The colonel knew who he needed to please. And it wasn't the Jesuit.

He returned to the entrance and glanced at the priest

standing on the other side of the wrought-iron gate. The church bells had begun to sound yet again. No doubt his flock was becoming overanxious. Barbarat touched his ear, pursed his lips a moment as if listening intently to the bells while his men prepared to escort him to the fort.

"I hear your calling, *Père Jean*. Never fear. Your time will come, when this war is won, and I no longer need these heathens. Then you can worry about saving their souls." He touched the brim of his plumed hat and then drew close to the gate and added in the soft, stern tone of voice one might reserve for a child, "Right now I must worry about saving New France."

34

The wind moaned. The spirits spoke. The man on the bluff overlooking the golden lake waited while the sun dipped toward the western shore. He kept a solitary vigil, reverent, listening to his gods, to the voices of those who had gone before him and came to him now in his hour of need. No trees grew on the crest. It was as if they feared coming too close to the edge of the cliff. The jagged half-submerged rocks a hundred feet below looked singularly uninviting.

Atoan knew a wise man must be wary in the presence of the Old Ones. Tricksters walked among them and played with the destinies of men, raised them to glory, brought them to ruin. A man must be careful. And he was. To be certain that his brothers among the Seneca and Huron would not mistake his intentions, Atoan painted the left side of his face white, signifying peace. The Grand Sachem was regally dressed in a fine hunting shirt adorned with porcupine quills and silver medallions, likewise his buckskin leggings and moccasins were intricately decorated with glass trade beads. He wore a leather cap topped with raven feathers and had draped a bright yellow blanket over his shoulder. Atoan carried no weapon. In the camp in the valley below, a rifle and war club would always be close at hand. But he did not anticipate trouble. The valley in the shadow of the Pass Through Rock was a place of peace, where tribes might hold council with one another no matter how fierce the enmity between them.

Wisdom sits here. *I will need it*, he thought. To the east the sky was a deep and burnished blue dome. To the west, where the sun died behind the hills, the horizon looked like polished copper. Atoan, between light and darkness, began to sing a song from long ago.

"When Grandfather Thunder walks upon the mountain,
He shall strike the earth with his club.
Then we shall dance. Then we shall sing in his honor.
Then we shall join with our brothers
And paint ourselves for war."

But who was his brother? Lost Arrow of the Seneca? Claws In The Water of the Huron? Or the Frenchman, Colonel Lucien Barbarat? Ha! The Frenchman was just another long knife, like the *Anglais*. But he had his uses. Atoan could foresee a day, after the *Anglais* were driven out, when at the head of a mighty confederacy of Seneca and Huron and armed by soldiers like Barbarat, the Grand Sachem would demand the French withdraw from their settlements or perish. This land belonged to only one people.

My people, Atoan said in a whisper, lost in his thoughts.

The drums started. The sound seemed to roll up the hillside toward the cliff, it curled around the trees like a slithering snake, its primal cadence stirred his soul. Atoan sensed movement off to the side and spied a familiar figure on the trail.

Kasak arrived and called out to his father. The young warrior was breathing hard, having run up the path to the hilltop to summon the Grand Sachem to the camp. "Father . . ."

"I hear the drums."

"The council waits."

Atoan held up his hand. "Do you hear them?"

Kasak listened to the voices in the hills, keening on the wind. "What do the Old Ones say?"

"When you can understand them for yourself, then you will be ready to lead the People of the White Pine." Atoan turned his back on the cliff and started toward the path. He froze for a second as his blood ran cold; felt a shiver along his spine, as if a ghost had suddenly reached through his chest to clutch at his heart. For a fleeting instant he thought the voices whispered a warning. He looked over his shoulder at his son. "Did you send lookouts to the hills to warn us if necessary?"

"I did as you told me. Our men stand guard on the far hill where they might watch the approach to the Gathering Place. They will signal if there is trouble."

Atoan nodded. "Good. I hope they remain on their guard."

"Lobal is with them," Kasak confidently replied. "He has the eyes of a hawk."

Lobal gasped as a forearm encircled his throat and dragged him back among the pines. He dropped his rifle, clawed at the air, realized he should have fired a warning shot, clawed at the arm, tried to twist free. Fear added strength to his efforts, frantic, like a fox in a trap, struggling to live, wanting to see another dawn. Then he spied a glimmer of cold steel seconds before the knife was plunged into his side. His body violently arched. Pain blinded him as well-honed steel pierced his vitals once, twice, a third time. Lobal shuddered and went slack.

Stark lowered the man to the ground and dragged him into the underbrush. He wiped the blade on the dead man's chest. He looked up at the stars, and wondered where a man's soul might take root. This was grisly work and he took no joy in it. He might have even felt remorse, until he noticed the scalp locks dangling from the dead man's hunting shirt. Some of them might have come from Fort William Henry. Then his eyes hardened.

"How does it feel, you son of a bitch?" he whispered into the man's face, frozen in death's grimace. The branches overhead stirred with the breeze and clattered against one another like dried bones.

Elsewhere along the ridge, the Abenaki sentries suffered a similar fate. The Rangers in their dark green buckskins materialized out of the night shadows to fell the warriors guarding the entrance to the valley. The Abenaki had not expected anyone to approach from over the ridge, not at night and soundlessly; their focus had been on the eastern trail. When the last of the sentries had been dispatched, the Rangers filtered through the trees and reunited along a ragged line in the forest, well back from the collection of bark-covered wigwams and campfires that illuminated the valley floor.

Choosing a granite shelf for their vantage point, John Stark and Robert Rogers used their spyglasses to study the collection of warriors and marines assembled in the center of the camp. The gathering was ringed by several ceremonial fires which helped immensely. Stark made a quiet approximation of the force arrayed against them. It appeared the Rangers were outnumbered two to one. But they had surprise on their side. And Stark figured they would whittle down the odds within the first few minutes. If not . . . he did not want to consider the consequences.

Atoan's features suddenly filled the spyglass. He seemed to be staring straight at Stark who lowered the spyglass and gasped, then realized it had to have been an illusion. The Grand Sachem could not possibly have seen him in the night-shrouded forest. But he had a palpable connection to the war chief. The man had warned about the next time the two met. Stark slowly exhaled and resumed his scrutiny. He recognized the Seneca presence and mentioned it to Rogers who nodded in agreement.

"Looks like the Huron have come to hear what Atoan has to say. That is the Grand Sachem, in the cap and yellow blanket?"

"Yes." Stark nodded.

"He doesn't look like all that much," Rogers scoffed.

"He is," Stark said. He turned and motioned for Benoit Turcotte to scramble over to the outcropping. Stark passed him the spyglass. "Do you see Lucien Barbarat?"

"*Non,*" the *voyageur* said, adjusting the eyepiece. "Wait. Yes, now I see him. The man in the plumed hat. That is Colonel Lucien Barbarat."

Stark took the glass from the Frenchman and studied the scene below, taking time to memorize the face of the Butcher of Fort William Henry. He lowered the glass then with Rogers, made his way back to where the Rangers waited. The unearthly keening that emanated from the earth made for an uneasy wait. The Englishman, Strode, seemed especially unnerved. Sweat beaded his leathery features, glistened along his hairline and in his bushy sideburns.

"You wishing you stayed with the Regiment, Tom?"

"I won't deny it," said the sergeant. He wasn't alone though. All of the raiders looked anxious to depart this valley as soon as possible. "These are cursed hills."

"How's it look below, Johnny?" asked Moses Shoemaker, he had to clear his throat to speak. The old long hunter brushed back his shoulder-length silver hair and repositioned his Scottish bonnet to hold it in place.

"Abenaki, Huron, the Seneca have come for a parley, and Colonel Barbarat and his marines . . . it looks just like we expected."

"I warrant your topknot will look just fine dangling from some red devil's belt," Locksley Barlow chuckled.

Moses glared at his youthful tormenter. "I'd have sliced you for cheese long ago, but you're such a *pretty* lad." The men within earshot began to snicker. Their repartee served to ease the tension. Stark grinned. This bunch was a salty lot. He could think of no better men to lead into battle. He glanced over at Sam Oday. The scarred man crouched in the shadows, cradling his blunderbuss, tight-lipped, but in control now. Amazingly, the eerie voice of the wind streaming through hidden cracks in the earth left him unfazed. The smoke from enemy fires drifting up the slope and the sounds from the enemy camp, the occasional drumming and chanting, all seemed to steady his nerves.

"How do you want to play this, Johnny?" Rogers said. The smaller man, though tentatively in command, had his own idea.

"We need to be close enough to make the first volley count."

"Right," said Rogers. "But we'll need a diversion, something to focus that crowd while we move in."

"A diversion?" Stark agreed. "I can handle that."

"Son," said Moses. "I don't like the sound of that. Molly said if I let anything happen to you I'll answer to her."

"She said it to all of us, one time or another," Rogers added with a smile.

"Just bring the men down. And on my signal, let 'em have it," said Stark. He waved to the men, and crouching low, trotted off through the trees. Barlow started forward as if to follow the big man. Moses caught him by the arm.

"But . . ."

"There'll be plenty of time to die. Don't hurry it."

"But Major Rogers, what's the signal?" the question floated from the column.

Robert Rogers checked his rifle, motioned for the men to do the same. "Knowing John Stark, I have a feeling it will be impossible to miss."

35

Lucien Barbarat didn't like this at all. First there was the night itself and these hills, one moment wailing, then silent, then, murmuring, or sobbing. And if his surroundings weren't enough to cause him consternation, he had Atoan to deal with. And the Seneca and Huron.

The officer studied the firelit features of his allies: Lost Arrow of the Seneca, cautious and revealing little of his thoughts, or Claws In The Water, the ferocious-looking Huron war chief whose eyes glittered with a feral light whenever Barbarat caught him staring at the Frenchman. What was afoot here? Atoan was up to something. But what?

The four men held council with one another in the center of the camp, surrounded by the contingent of Abenaki, Seneca, Huron, and marines. The Frenchmen looked especially uncomfortable and kept their muskets close at hand, twenty-four veterans drawing some comfort from each other and mistrustful of these mercurial-natured savages.

Atoan had welcomed them all. And after they had passed the pipe of peace, the Grand Sachem spoke. "My heart is glad to see that my French brother has come to smoke the pipe with us, to hold council here in the place of our ancestors."

"It is a good thing," Barbarat replied, his voice steady. He was determined to refrain from showing any sign of weakness. If the Grand Sachem thought to intimidate him, the officer was not about to let him succeed. "The great chief Montcalm will be happy to know that his children, the Seneca and the Huron have come to council with us."

"They have come on my word," Atoan said.

"The Grand Sachem will speak for us," Lost Arrow said. His features were not painted. Like his counterpart among the Huron, Claws In The Water, the Seneca wore a trade shirt and buckskin leggings, he had placed his weapons of war, tomahawk, war club, and knife, upon a striped woolen blanket folded on the ground at his feet.

Barbarat nodded. He glanced aside at Kasak who sat just behind his father and was watching the proceedings with nervous excitement. "I have come to listen to the words of my friend, the Grand Sachem of The People of the White Pine."

And after Atoan had his say, the French officer resolved to lure Kasak off by himself. The Grand Sachem might be a cunning fox, but his son was another matter. Hand him another trinket like the French dirk he so proudly carried and the young brave would open up like a piece of ripe fruit.

It was another gauntlet. Another encampment, a man alone, outnumbered, soon surrounded and all he had to do was stay alive. John Stark took the measure of his enemies, saw the hopelessness of the situation he was about to enter and said, "On my oath, there shall be a reckoning here or Molly Stark will sleep this night a widow."

The long hunter emerged from the shadows, crossed an open expanse and headed into the encampment. The wigwams to either side were dark and empty. Smoke drifted up from the campfires. Stark gripped his rifle in his left hand, balanced it in the crook of his left arm. His left hand held a brass powder flask with its measuring spout broken off, leaving an open hole in the top.

The three tribes and the French had congregated in the center of the camp. So far so good, he congratulated himself. He was still alive. Of course the test was still to come. He looked toward the hillside and tried to imagine the Rangers starting down the slope. The longer he distracted

the host in the camp the closer in Rogers could bring the column.

Stark quickened his pace and entered the outer fringes of the firelight. Cradling his rifle, tall and broad, his allegiance clear to one and all by the green-dyed buckskins and Scottish bonnet he favored, Big John Stark ambled past the first cluster of braves with the assurance of one who belonged among them, despite his Ranger garb.

The young Abenaki guards had been trying to hear what was being said at the council. When they heard the man approach, the guards glanced over their shoulders, gave a start as they noticed the intruder for the first time. Jaws dropped open, the guards became like statues rooted in place as the towering individual sauntered past. No one quite knew what to make of this? Stark ignored them as if they didn't exist. He waited for an outcry from them and when it did not sound, he allowed himself a brief sigh of relief and continued.

The Abenaki behind him closed ranks, but they made no other move against him. His arrival shocked them into inaction. Ahead, other copper-skinned warriors turned, stared in mute amazement, uncertain of how to react, then parted to permit him to pass. The marines too, although several muskets were raised as if to block his passage, none stepped forward to block his passage. The Frenchmen muttered amongst themselves, uncertain of their orders and loathe to begin an action that might be misinterpreted by these savages.

Stark neither looked to right or left but kept his gaze locked on the inner circle, where the war chiefs held council, where the French officer, Lucien Barbarat sat, no doubt plotting other betrayals, other massacres. Seeing the colonel so close at hand steeled the Ranger's resolve. Nothing and no one was about to keep him from confronting the Butcher of Fort William Henry.

Perhaps it was the valley itself, hallowed ground, the great Gathering Place that stayed the hands of Atoan's people, or maybe it was the voices in the wind, or the deep-

rooted respect for a bold enemy that held the throng at bay. Was it the flickering flames that danced like death in his fierce eyes or his shifting shadow that seemed to prowl behind him, stalking, like some . . . beast?

Kiwaskwek!

Lucien Barbarat stood before the war chiefs. It was his turn to speak. But he waited, gathering his thoughts, knowing he must choose his words wisely. Atoan had just finished explaining to the officer why the Grand Sachem had invited Lost Arrow and Claws In The Water to this council. The Huron and Seneca had agreed, in principle, to join with the French and crush the *Anglais* at Fort Edward. But like the Abenaki, they demanded Barbarat supply them with muskets, rifles, powder, and shot. If this did not happen, Atoan explained, the Abenaki might rethink their own alliance with the French.

Such a veiled threat galled the officer. And it alerted his innate sense of caution. Insuring that his Abenaki allies had a limited supply of weapons was one thing. Arming the three major tribes of New France was another matter entirely. But if Atoan thought for a minute he could outfox Lucien Barbarat, the heathen was in for a surprise.

He decided to agree, to buy time and lead the assault with the same promise he had used a year ago at Fort William Henry. Barbarat folded his hands behind him and paced imperiously to and fro as he spoke.

"I welcome the Seneca and the Huron and shall call them brothers as I do the Abenaki. And I agree wholeheartedly that our new allies should receive all that you request." Barbarat flashed a winning smile, his face beamed with honesty. "But it will take time to dispatch orders to Quebec and more time to gather the shipments of powder, shot, and rifles." He drew his sword and drew an irregular square to represent Fort Edward alongside a wavy line for the Hudson River. Then he drew a couple of peaks for mountains and another rectangle. "We must march on Fort

Edward before the moon is full," he said indicating the first square. "If we wait much longer, the *Anglais* will be reinforced. General Amherst prepares an army to march across the mountains." He drew a line of march in the dirt from the rectangle to Fort Edward.

"But if the Seneca and Huron will join with us now, then not only will you receive all that I have promised, but all that Fort Edward holds will also be yours. The guns, the women and children for slaves, even if they march out under a white flag, I will hand them over to you." Barbarat thrust his sword into the center of Fort Edward for emphasis. The hilt swayed in the air, the brass hilt gleaming. "What say you?" He looked up at Atoan and the other war chiefs who at first seemed to be staring at the colonel. Then he realized they were staring past him, at someone else entirely. The French officer became aware of an almost unearthly stillness. Even the voices in the hills had ceased. He slowly turned. And stood face-to-face with John Stark.

"Atoan!" asked Barbarat. His voice rang out. "What man is this who walks through your braves unheeded and stands before my own troops and no one lifts a hand against him . . . this man who defies us all?" The Frenchman was a lot of things. But he wasn't afraid. Why should he be? The intruder, however *formidable*, was ringed by marines and red-skinned warriors. No. One gesture from Lucien Barbarat and this churl would breathe his last. *"Qui êtes-vous?"*

Atoan met the Ranger's stare. He could scarcely believe his eyes. What had brought him here? Perhaps the trail had been set for him long ago, for them both. And Atoan knew fear then, not for his life so much as that of his people, his son. He spied Kasak as the brash young warrior reached for the dirk in his belt. The Grand Sachem stepped in front of his son. "It is the beast," he told the Frenchman. Atoan grudgingly tore his gaze from the Ranger and checked the shrouded hills. The stillness, why now? And what were his sentries doing as the long hunter approached? And why did the Old Ones no longer speak?

He looked again at the man with the crooked nose and the flashing eyes, this man in Ranger garb. He was big, he was ugly, he had dignity, and he wasn't about to die. "It is Stark."

Barbarat's eyes widened with recognition at the name. "At last we meet."

"At last," the Ranger replied.

"And I am . . ."

"I know who you are."

"Indeed," said Barbarat. "Then you are either a brave man or quite mad. Which is it, Monsieur?" The colonel retrieved his sword and turned once more, with the flames of the council fire between them. Dried wood crackled, sent a column of sparks coruscating upward from the fiery bed. The officer glanced about, swung the sword up and pointed the blade at the intruder. "And where did you come from, *Jean le fou*."

"I bring you a message from Fort William Henry."

Colonel Lucien Barbarat frowned, pursed his lips. From the ruins? The Ranger was indeed mad. "What message?"

"This," said Stark. And shot the colonel between the eyes.

36

"Let them have it . . . !"

Everything happened at once. The long rifle made a deafening sound that shattered the tableau of red men and white. Barbarat flew backwards, trailing an arc of blood from his shattered skull. The officer was dead before his shoulders hit the ground. Stark tossed the brass powder flask into the campfire and dove to his left, hurling himself like a human battering ram into the startled warriors. In that same instant, the French marines closest to the center of the firelight, seeing their colonel murdered before their eyes, opened fire in Stark's direction.

The fusillade missed its mark but killed several of the Hurons as they tried to intercept the Ranger. The powder flask exploded like a thunderclap, its bright flash and choking cloud of smoke further obscured the scene. The Hurons in turn opened up on the marines and killed several of them where they stood.

Atoan dove for his war club and tried to end the melee. Kasak yelped and fell forward. A bullet from a French musket pierced his groin. Rifle fire erupted from the shadows, a great and terrible volley that dropped several of the Seneca and Abenaki warriors on the fringe of the council fire. Atoan instantly grasped what was happening. Stark had tricked them. He shouted for his warriors to turn and meet this new threat as the Rangers came charging out of the shadows, horns blaring, shouting war cries, firing as they came.

The marines, thinking they were under attack from all sides, poured fire into their allies. Atoan leaped among them, his massive war club smashing skulls and shattering bone. He had seen his son fall at their hands and he was merciless in his outrage. He ground them under, shattered their formation, then when they fled before him he shouted for his warriors to head for the hillside to the rear. They would make their stand on the Pass Through Rock.

It was a hellish sight. There was panic and gunfire, flashing tomahawks, the thud of slugs puncturing flesh, of blades slicing flesh, the crack of war clubs shattering skulls. The night air was awash with screams and moans, pleas, curses and animalistic howls. The Rangers struck like a raging torrent. The warriors before them tried to stem the onslaught. But to no avail.

Stark threw off the bodies pinning him to the ground, clutched a marine by the throat who tried to club him, the Frenchman succumbing to that iron grip. Stark used him as a shield as rifles were pointed in his direction. Lead slugs thwacked into the dying man. Two warriors charged forward. Stark hurled his human shield in their faces, knocked the men off balance. Stark sprang forward, his own tomahawk hacking left and right felling his attackers like stalks of wheat. Another group of marines spied that broad expanse of shoulders and chest and charged forward, snapped up their muskets. Stark turned and faced this makeshift firing squad, stared down half a dozen gun barrels. He lunged for them, determined to sell his life as dearly as possible.

A terrible roar sounded behind the marines, shattering their ranks. Men fell to the ground, writhing in agony, blood seeping from a terrible assortment of wounds left by the spray of lead shot from Sam Oday's blunderbuss. Those who survived Oday's attack had to answer to Stark. They did not last long. Oday grinned and began to reload.

"Well met, Sam Oday," Stark said.

"Saving my own skin," he replied. "I'll not be the one to answer to Molly should you lose your topknot this night."

Robert Rogers arrived, with part of the column. The warriors were breaking for the hillsides. Rogers snapped off a shot and sent a man tumbling over before he could reach the line of trees. He reloaded as he approached. "Some signal!"

"Figured you wouldn't miss it," Stark shouted back, taking up his own rifle once more. "C'mon."

Benoit Turcotte stared down at the ruined features and the lifeless remains of what had once been Colonel Lucien Barbarat. The *voyageur* knelt by the officer, peered into those unseeing eyes.

"Now who will you hang, *mon Colonel*?" Turcotte asked. Leaning forward, he spit in the dead man's face.

Behind the *voyageur*, a mortally-wounded marine managed to prop himself up with one arm and with the other, trembling, raise his musket, take unsteady aim. Turcotte never heard the shot that killed him.

The surviving Seneca and Huron, with the remaining few marines who they eventually cut to pieces before disappearing into the forest, scattered from the valley, eager to quit these cursed hills. The Rangers were green devils and no doubt outnumbered them all, judging by the ferocity of their assault. It was better to flee and live to fight another day.

So Lost Arrow and Claws In The Water, the latter, gut shot and dying, abandoned the Abenaki to their fate. The two tribes departed together. For many hours the Huron and Seneca would keep to the same trail until they reached a place where it forked. Then the survivors were forced to make a decision. Despite Atoan's dreams of a confederacy,

the two tribes split and chose to make their own way along
the Great War Path.

Atoan, carrying his wounded son upon his shoulders, led a
fighting retreat up the forested slope of the Pass Through
Rock. His warriors darted from tree to bush and back to
tree, firing as they went. The Grand Sachem hoped to thin
the ranks of the *Anglais* before his own warriors reached
the barren summit and were forced to fight with the cliff at
their backs. Had he been contesting British regulars his plan
might have succeeded. But these were Rangers and they
fought from tree to tree, from rock to rock. It was as Atoan
had always warned, the Rangers fought like the Abenaki
themselves. Some of them died on that slope to be sure,
but his own men also fell. And he had none to spare.

Gunfire blossomed orange in the night. Rifle and pistol
fire reverberated up slope and down. Men cried in alarm,
cried for their loved ones, sang their death chants, or simply
grunted, groaned, and expired alone with their deaths.

Stark sighted on a patch of underbrush, squeezed off a
round, was rewarded with a yelp of pain and the glimpse
of a warrior staggering from cover. Tom Strode, the sergeant, fired his own rifle and the wounded man sank to his
knees.

"Major Ransom would have had us marching in ranks
with our bayonets fixed, if the lads of the Regiment were
here," he said, reloading.

Stark nodded. "And lost many a brave soul, I warrant
you."

"Yes," Strode said, filing away in his mind all that he
had seen this night.

The moonbeams filtered through the branches overhead, draped the slope in silver while acrid black clouds of
powder smoke drifted through the fractured light. Stark
crept forward. There was a violent exchange of gunfire off
to his right.

The skirmish lasted but a few brief but intense seconds.

He veered toward the sound and as the echoes faded, drew abreast of Locksley Barlow and a few other Rangers clustered around the base of a white pine. Moses Shoemaker sat with his back to the trunk, legs splayed out before him, blood seeping from his chest.

"No," Stark whispered. "You Old Jehu, what have you gone and done?"

"Got myself killed, can't you see," Moses snapped. He stared down at the wound. He heard a kind of whistle every time he breathed and pink froth formed around the ragged punctures in his hunting shirt.

"You had to take the lead," Locksley said, his voice tight as he choked back tears. "It should have been me." He glanced up at Stark "I never saw them, but he did. And shoved me down. Knelt on my back while he fired away. Bloody old fool."

"Don't sass me, lad. I can still take your measure." Moses grinned.

Stark checked the path ahead. Three Abenakis were sprawled in death in the baleful moonlight. Locksley and the others had avenged the old Indian fighter.

Moses looked past the men gathered by him, clutched a handful of soil, yellow pine nettles, a few blades of grass, and raised it to his lips.

"I died here," he said. Moses Shoemaker held out his hand to show the others what he had learned. "That makes it mine." His head sank to one side and he no longer saw his hand or the earth in his grasp.

37

Atoan, carrying his son draped across his shoulders, reached the cleared summit and turned to await the arrival of his warriors. He lowered Kasak to the ground. The young man would have a hard time fighting on one leg. The wisest course was for him to hide in the underbrush by the forest's edge.

"Kasak," he said. "You cannot fight if you cannot stand. We must return to the trees and find a place for you to wait for the *Anglais* to leave."

Atoan stared at his own beaded hunting shirt. The porcupine quills were matted with blood. And Kasak was not answering him, not even protesting his father's council. The Grand Sachem lowered the youth to the ground. Kasak made no sound and his arm dropped listlessly to his side.

Atoan stared unbelievingly at his son. He had no way of knowing the French musket ball that had passed through young man's groin, severed an artery. Kasak had bled to death while his father carried him out of harm's way. The war chief took the French dirk from his son's clenched fist, stood and stared at the knife, his gaze hardening as he fixed blame on the French blade and all it represented. He angrily hurled the weapon toward the trees with all his strength.

The Grand Sachem of the Abenaki walked to the edge of the cliff and stood, with his war club resting on his shoulder, soaked with Kasak's blood, and waited for the People of the White Pine to join him. At long last, he saw his warriors materialize out of the woods and started to call out but his cry died in his throat. It was John Stark flanked by Robert Rogers, Locksley Barlow, Tom Strode, Sam

Oday, and a column of ragged, battle-weary men in war-torn green buckskins. Their faces were smeared with blood and gunsmoke, some were wounded, but all of them were ready to continue the fight. They would never stop. Atoan knew that now. And in that moment he glimpsed his own fate and those of his kind.

Stark held up his hand and motioned for the Rangers to remain where they were. Rogers started to object then held back, sensing rank had no place on this bluff. Stark crossed the summit, laying aside his rifle and his pistol, keeping only the tomahawk in his hand. He kept his eyes on the Abenaki warrior and did not underestimate him for a second.

"My son is dead," said Atoan.

Stark had recognized the fallen man back where the Grand Sachem had laid his burden down. He thought of Moses Shoemaker, of Abel Page, of all the ones who had been lost.

"Many sons are dead. And daughters. Too many."

"Yes," Atoan replied. "Perhaps, just one more."

"It doesn't have to end this way," Stark said, standing as close as he dared to land's end. The waters below rippled and splashed among the jagged rocks.

"It always had to end this way," Atoan said. "It was written in our stars."

"Then let it be as when we once shared a fire, face-to-face, as men," said Stark.

The Abenaki's white war paint was streaked with sweat and blood. The irony that he wore a mask of peace was not lost on the Grand Sachem. Somehow, it even seemed fitting, as if the gods had played one last trick on him. "*Kiwaskwek . . .*" Atoan muttered.

"I am no beast," said John Stark. "I am just a man who wants to live free." He studied his adversary, wary of the man's speed, poised to meet him head on. "To live free or die."

"Then live," Atoan said. He stepped backwards off the cliff.

John Stark started forward, not quite believing his own eyes, halted, as the warrior vanished from view, plummeting through the night. Stark heard the sound of the body striking the rocks with a sickening thud. His hands began to tremble and he lost his grip on the tomahawk. A breeze stirred. And the ghostly voices of the Old Ones whose spirits were hidden in the haunted hills, began to sing their lament.

John Stark had no desire to walk to the edge of the cliff and see what lay below. He wanted to remember his enemy as he had known him. Free. He turned his back on the dead and returned to the living. The column of Rangers waited in silence, each man fixing in his memory what had happened on this night, waited for Stark to take up his rifle and pistol, to stand before them, hesitating at long last, as if uncertain. What now? He listened then, and heard beyond hearing. He took his marching orders from the wind and the rivers and the call of the wilderness.

John Stark . . . lead them home.

And so he did.

**HE LEFT HOME A BOY.
RETURNED A MAN.
AND RODE OUT AGAIN A RENEGADE ...**

TEXAS ANTHEM

❖ KERRY NEWCOMB ❖

AT THE BONNET RANCH, they thought Johnny Anthem
had died on the Mexican border. But then Anthem came
home, escaped from the living hell of a Mexican prison,
and returned to find the woman he loved married to the
man who betrayed him. For Johnny Anthem, the time
had come to face his betrayer, to stand up to the powerful rancher who had raised him as his own son, and to
fight for the only love of his life.

"Kerry Newcomb is one of those writers who lets
you know from his very first lines that you're in for
a ride. And he keeps his promise . . . Newcomb
knows what he is doing, and does it enviably well."
—Cameron Judd, author of *Confederate Gold*

AVAILABLE WHEREVER BOOKS ARE SOLD FROM
ST. MARTIN'S PAPERBACKS

"An entertaining tale of high adventure
and low villains." —*Booklist*

RED RIPPER

KERRY NEWCOMB

NEW ORLEANS, SEPTEMBER 1829. Brothers William
and Samuel Wallace board a ship for Mexico with
bold visions of wealth and adventure in a new land.
But when a vicious storm lands the two on the shores
of Mexico, clinging for dear life, a brutal band of
freebooters attack the brothers, murdering Samuel in
front of William's very eyes. Now William has sworn
to avenge his brother's death. This haunting quest will
take Wallace to the mist-laden bayous of Texas,
where he will become embroiled in the fight for its
independence and earn himself the name that strikes
fear in the hearts of his enemies . . . The Red Ripper.

"A compelling mix of passion, revenge, and a
gallant people's quest for freedom."
—John J. Gobbell, bestselling
author of *The Last Lieutenant*

"[An] action-filled plot, [with] broad-brush sage-
brush scenes and the romance of the Texas
Republic." —*Publishers Weekly*

RR 12/00